PRAISE FOR ASA MARIA BRADLEY'S WORK

"When it comes to paranormal romance with explosive action scenes, Bradley has that nailed…. *Loki Ascending* is a riveting adventure tale with a thrilling climax to match."

~*Entertainment Weekly*

"Action-packed, sexy, and fun! Reminiscent of J.R. Ward—but with Vikings!"

~Ilona Andrews, *New York Times* Bestselling Author for *Viking Warrior Rebel*

"An entertaining read when you like crime stories with a touch of paranormal and shape-shifting."

~Honest Bookworm for *Flash of Fear*

"…a swoon-worthy hero who sizzles across the pages in this tale full of passion, blood, and destiny! Sexy, stubborn, and smart lovers clash in a tension-filled race to outwit science and control fate."

~Rebecca Zanetti, *New York Times* Bestselling Author for *Viking Warrior Rising*

"Bradley's story is a whirlwind of action, suspense, humor, and a ton of romance! …you'll be reading this page-turner the whole day!"

    ~Bookstr for *Loki Ascending*

"Nonstop action, satisfying romantic encounters, and intriguing world building make this a thoroughly enjoyable paranormal-romance series."

    ~Booklist for *Viking Warrior Rising*

"…blends Norse mythology and evil government experiments into an unusual paranormal…the immortal Viking premise is perfect for paranormal romance readers who are looking for something different."

    ~Publishers Weekly for *Viking Warrior Rising*

FLASH OF FEAR

ASA MARIA BRADLEY

KAERING LLC

This one is for the sexy Brit who's been my husband for twenty years. He inspires me, encourages me, calls me on my crap, and always supports me. Thanks for giving me my very own Happily Ever After. Here's to another twenty years filled with love and laughter.

From eternal pain comes eternal blood becomes eternal life.

CHAPTER 1

 ed and blue lights from two police cruisers illuminated the main farmhouse as Molly Nyland drove up the tree-lined driveway. She eased around the medical examiner's transport van and parked next to a gray Ford. The classic sedan-shape of the car, plus the multiple antennas, gave it away as another police vehicle.

She reached for her sketchpad on the passenger seat, opened the door, and slid out of her car. Cradling the pad in the crook of her arm, she paused to smooth down her skirt and snap the cuffs of her sleeves in place. A sigh escaped her lips as she gingerly picked a path through the brown fall grass to the back of the house. Her black leather boots had been stylish in the office of the graphic design firm where she worked full time. They were less practical in the field on her gig as a freelance forensic artist.

"Literally, in the field," she muttered as she avoided a pile of horse manure and walked down the side of the building. Pants and comfortable flats, or even better, rubber boots would not only be more practical but also make her blend in better with the cops. Detective Zedler had been short on the phone, his voice laced with urgency. She hadn't dared take the time to go home and change since the farm was several miles outside of Prairie Falls, and her navigation system was based on the city's official maps. On the rural roads of eastern Washington State, what was planned and what was built didn't always match.

Behind the house, police and crime scene technicians bustled under bright lights powered by generators. Their feet had trampled the dry grass such that it partially covered the cracked mud. Molly scanned the crowd and spotted Zedler at the same time he saw her. The middle-aged detective jogged toward her. His bushy gray eyebrows looked like two caterpillars facing off over kind brown eyes. The tweed jacket he always wore made him look more like a college professor than the seasoned detective he was. Since he'd been somewhat of a mentor to her ever since she moved to Prairie Falls five years ago, the teacher role fit.

"Nyland, about time you got here." He said, slightly out of breath.

Molly fell in step beside him. "What's going on?" On the phone, he'd given her the farm's address and asked her to bring the sketchpad she used when working with kids, but hung up before she had a chance to ask for details.

"We've got a body." He stopped when she froze mid-step and briefly touched her elbow. "You okay?"

Her stomach clenched, but she managed a nod. The medical examiner van should have tipped her off, but she'd worked fifteen cases with Zedler, and none of them involved a death. She rubbed her shoulder where the scars from a lightning strike back when she was twelve were already tingling. The Lichtenberg figure that covered her back, shoulder, and arm in spidery fern-like patterns had been a curse when she was younger, but in college, she'd discovered their advantage. The lightning had given weird scars, but also abilities that made her such an excellent sketch artist.

Sympathy shone in the detective's eyes as he studied her. The eyebrows straightened, the caterpillars relaxing in a temporary truce. "Welcome to your first murder scene, Nyland." He reached out and placed his hand on the small of her back, gently propelling her forward. "Do what you always do. Ask the witness questions and make a brilliant sketch of our suspect. It's not different from what you've done before. Just another crime to solve." As close as she was to the detective, he didn't know about her scars or her ability. She'd only shared that with her best friend.

Molly nodded and took a deep breath to steady herself. "Who's my witness?"

Zedler opened the farmhouse backdoor and chaperoned her across the threshold. "A terrified eight-year-old girl." His voice lowered. "She got up in the middle of the night to get a drink of water and saw a stranger in the back, holding a knife. When he noticed the girl, he rattled the door, but ran away when she screamed."

Molly instantly felt sympathy for the witness. As a little girl, she'd learned to be scared in her own house, but not because of evil outside the walls. In her case, the monsters had been living in the same house as her, calling themselves "family."

As they walked through the kitchen, Molly took in brief impressions of well-worn but gleaming clean counters and wood cabinets. An older white refrigerator hummed in the corner, the low tune of the appliance accompanying the beat of her heels against the linoleum floor. The neat welcoming home was another contrast to her own upbringing.

Her job tonight came back into focus. A murder.

She'd never drawn a murderer.

Molly swallowed, hard. "Who did he kill?"

"We don't know the victim's identity yet. Neither the girl or her mother has seen him before."

"You showed the girl the body?" Molly's voice rose an octave.

Zedler shot her a look. "Of course not. We showed her a picture of his face. A very peaceful picture without any gore."

They entered a cozy living room where a woman with long brown curly hair sat on a worn beige corduroy sofa, cradling a little girl in her lap as she stroked the child's back. A fire crackled in a large fireplace, its warm glow reflecting off the polished coffee table.

Molly's impractical boots caused her to stumble slightly when the flooring went from linoleum to carpet. Zedler grabbed her elbow and addressed the woman and child on the sofa. "Mrs. Lidgren."

The woman turned, her heart-shaped face pale. The girl peered over her shoulder. She was her mother's carbon copy, reduced in size, except for equally big brown eyes.

"Yes," the mother said, her voice thick.

"This is the forensic artist who will work with Annie."

Molly took a few steps into the room and crouched in front of the little girl. "I like your name, Annie." It earned a small smile. "My name is Molly."

The mother tightened her grip on the child. "Do we really have to do this? She's distraught." Nervous laughter escaped her lips. "As am I. My husband is away this week. To think that a stranger—" Her voice broke.

Molly glanced at the mother before looking into the girl's tear-rimmed eyes. Even with her unique talent, the first few hours after a crime were crucial. After that, witnesses started to forget details. Especially witnesses in shock. "Do you like to draw?"

The little girl nodded.

Opening her sketchpad, Molly showed her a drawing of a landscape. "So do I." She flipped the page to show a dolphin jumping over a boat, water splashing the people on the deck.

Annie scooted a little closer, bending over the paper.

The next page showed a court jester tumbling across a pasture filled with horses and cows, the animals laughing at his antics. A tentative smile turned up the corners of the little girl's mouth.

Some of the tension drained out of Mrs. Lidgren's face, and she released her daughter, keeping only an arm around Annie's back. "How about you make a drawing with Molly?" She stroked her daughter's cheek.

"Okay," Annie whispered, scooting off her mother's lap to sit fully on the couch.

Molly sat down beside her and pulled a medium graphite pencil and a kneaded eraser from the hard-plastic case she'd brought in her purse. She flipped to an empty page on the pad. "Why don't you describe who you saw, and I'll try to draw that person."

The little girl nodded.

"Let's start with some easy things. Was it a grown-up?"

Annie nodded again. Her brown eyes focused on Molly.

"Was it a man or a woman?"

The girl whimpered, quickly sliding to her mother and grabbing her hand. Molly envied their closeness. She'd been raised by a grandmother who used spanking as her favorite child-rearing tool. She'd been the last person Molly had turned to for comfort as a child. Extremely religious, home-grown-militia-fan Grammie would do somersaults in her grave if she knew her granddaughter worked for "the bacon," which satisfied Molly in a slightly twisted way.

Mrs. Lidgren caressed Annie's curls. "It's okay, Sweetie. Just tell Molly what you saw."

Annie turned toward Molly, leaning forward a little. "I saw a monster," she whispered.

A small electric current ran down Molly's left shoulder and arm. She made herself sit as still as possible. A kid's imagination could run haywire under stress. The 'monster' description could mean anything, but her Lichtenberg patterns itching conveyed that Annie was on the right track. They just needed to flush out the details. A completely incorrect description would make the scars on Molly's back react. "Okay," she positioned the pencil on the pad, "tell me what the monster looked like. Did he have a small or big head?"

"Big."

Molly continued asking questions about eyes, nose, chin, mouth, and teeth. She pulled out more pencils of various hardness from her case and filled in the drawing in multiple shades of gray and black. After each feature, she swiveled the pad toward Annie and adjusted anything the girl wanted changing. A broad face slowly grew on the page. Wide-set eyes, which Annie described as black, gazed out of the paper straight at Molly. She shivered as the scars on both her back and shoulder went haywire. That was a new sensation, one she didn't know how to interpret.

"More dark," Annie touched the paper and smudged the pupil. "His eyes were black all over."

Molly filled in the whites of the eyes with quick strokes. "Like this? Are you sure?"

The little girl nodded, and they continued building the rest of the man's features. A nose with a long straight ridge and flared nostrils hovered over thick lips stretched into a snarl, showing white cusped teeth.

Zedler sat on the couch across the coffee table and watched the procedure. Molly could feel his eyes focusing on her as she asked each question.

"What did his ears look like?"

Annie paused. Her voice had grown stronger and more confident with each detail added to the drawing, but now it was barely above a whisper again. "Like Batman."

Molly's back tingled and itched. She couldn't help but squirm on the sofa. Out of the corner of her eye, she saw Zedler leaning forward, studying her. His eyes seemed too intense, too focused on her. When he saw her noticing his gaze, he relaxed into the back of the couch.

She turned her attention back on Annie, ignoring the familiar pins and needles still fluttering on her back, down the white web of disfigurement, left shoulder, and arm. She shifted on the couch. As much as she loved what she did as a forensic artist, she hated those scars. They marked her as a freak and were also the reason Grammie had escalated from regular spanking to full-on beatings that she thought would drive the evil out of her only grandchild. The pastor of the fundamentalist church that Grammie and Molly's Great Uncle had attended, insisting that the devil had put his mark on Molly's skin.

The tingling on her back didn't indicate that Annie was lying. The little girl just couldn't find the correct words to match the picture her mind recalled. And somehow the Lichtenberg pattern picked up on the mismatch. She now knew that oddities like hers were appeared often in lightning victims, at least in those who survived. That had been of little comfort when she was a little girl, and Grammie referred to the scars as "the mark of the devil." When the beatings didn't work, she'd tried to starve the evil out of her granddaughter by locking Molly in a closet.

She felt Zedler watching her again. Frowning, she picked up the pencil. Had he picked up on her skin's reaction? She hadn't shared her abilities with him. Being one of the few women working with the police force and the only forensic artist made her an oddity enough.

"Like Batman," she replied cheerfully to Annie. "Do you mean he had pointy ears?"

The girl nodded. "They were sharp, like Batman's, but not on the top of the head, on the side, like mine." She cupped her own ears.

Molly's shoulder stopped itching. She drew human ears, pointed at the top.

Annie peered at the drawing for a few minutes when Molly turned the sketchpad around. The little girl's breath hitched. "Longer."

Molly adjusted the shape of the ears, keeping her eyes on the page while she asked another question. "What about the hair? Short? Long?"

"Like Austin Moon's."

Mrs. Lidgren intervened. "She watches reruns of *Austin & Ally* on the Disney Channel. He has shaggy half-long hair."

Molly didn't know the program but sketched the shaggy just-above-the-ears style that had been preferred by teenaged boys around Prairie Falls a few years ago. She showed Annie.

"More bangs."

Molly complied and twisted the pad around again.

Annie gasped. "That's him." She pointed to the paper, and then quickly pulled her hand back as if the figure would pop out of the page and bite her.

Mrs. Lidgren met Molly's eyes above her daughter's head, her palm stroking Annie's hair. "I don't know how much this will help you." She gestured toward the drawing on Molly's lap. "But thank you for being kind to Annie." She turned to Zedler. "If it's okay, I'll take Annie upstairs."

The detective nodded and addressed the little girl. "You have been so helpful, Annie. Thank you very much for being brave."

Mrs. Lidgren stroked her daughter's cheek. "Sweetie, how

about we go upstairs to see Teddy? He'll probably want a hug just about now."

"Okay." The little girl slid off the couch and walked out of the room. Her little feet beat at staccato as she ran up the stairs.

Her mom followed at a more sedate pace.

Zedler peered down on the page in the sketchpad. "Who is that? Some comic book character?"

Molly shrugged. "The shock of seeing a stranger, the darkness, the shadows, witnessing a violent attack, they all combine to create this picture in her mind." Annie had described exactly what she'd seen, but what had emerged on the sketchpad didn't look remotely human.

Zedler sat down on the coffee table, still staring at the picture. "Nobody looks like this. Do you think he's wearing a mask or something?"

Molly suppressed a shiver as she looked back down at the otherworldly creature whose eyes drank darkness. "Could be. This is who Annie remembers in the backyard."

Zedler sighed. "If you say so. At least we tried." He stood. "Come back outside with me. I want you to meet our new detective, a transfer. His name is Rankin."

Heat rushed through Molly. That name, surely it couldn't be the same man she knew—had known. Her mind flashbacked on calloused palms sliding up her thighs, lighting her skin on fire. She quickly suppressed the memory and slowly put away the pencils and the eraser to hide her shaking hand.

Oblivious to the turmoil going on inside her, Zedler waited impatiently. "You may know of him, he's from California."

Molly had been able to start working with Prairie Falls PD as soon as she'd moved to the city because the lieutenant for whom she'd freelanced while at Santa Clara University, had given his recommendation. For a short time, she'd been on loan to the Sacramento PD and had worked with someone named Rankin—and made a poor decision—but the universe couldn't be that cruel. There must be more than one Detective Rankin from California. Either way, she was in deep shit. Just the mention of his name had her blushing like crazy. She wished it was out of embarrassment, but the truth was that the details of that very unwise, but oh so pleasurable, decision were still vivid in her mind. "But shouldn't I drop the sketch off at the station?" If this was the same Rankin, she would not be able to deal with him right now. Not this close to doing a sketch. Working with a witness always drained her.

Zedler studied her face. "Are you okay? You look a little flushed."

"I'm fine." She fiddled with her sketch pad.

He shrugged. "Drop the sketch off later. I want you to meet Rankin. You two will be working together." He gestured for her to walk out ahead of him.

As she crossed the kitchen this time, her heels against the floor echoed *trou-ble, trou-ble, trou-ble*.

A LIGHT RAIN had started to fall, and Detective Desmond Rankin wished he'd brought more suitable clothes than just his favorite leather jacket. Through the drizzle, he saw the shadowy shapes of Zedler and a woman exit the farmhouse. Good thing they'd set up the tarp tent over the crime scene before the weather turned. The white plastic would protect any ground evidence.

The senior detective and, judging from her oversized drawing pad, the sketch artist, trudged across the field. Zedler's shoulders slumped, and he looked more rumpled than usual. The little girl witness must not have been much help.

As they got closer, Des sucked in a breath. He'd recognize that wavy red hair and the gentle sway of her hips anywhere. His hands clenched at the memory of caressing those curves. He thrust them into the pockets of his jacket to stop them from reaching out. The last time he saw Molly Nyland, she'd been up against a wall with him buried deep inside her.

Correction.

The last time he saw Nyland, she'd scrambled into her jeans before bolting out the door, mumbling something about "a mistake" and "being on the rebound."

Raindrops glistened in Zedler's hair and bushy eyebrows as he approached Des. "Any news?"

Des zipped up his jacket against the night chill and glanced toward the corner of the clearing where the techs were still working under a hastily constructed white tarp tent. The medical examiner had just removed the body. "Nothing good." He flicked a quick glance at Nyland, she refused to meet his eyes.

Great. This wouldn't be awkward at all.

She looked good. A little pale, which made her adorable freckles stand out more starkly. The designer duds she wore —so different from the jeans and long-sleeved t-shirts she'd always worn when they worked together—hugged a lush body in all the right places. The past five years had obviously treated her well.

Back when he'd known her, she was in her last year of college and making some money on the side through forensic sketching. She'd done some work for the Santa Clara PD, and their lieutenant recommended her to Des' department in Sacramento when they couldn't catch a break in a string of violent home invasions and robberies. Nyland's sketch of a potential suspect had been released to the media, and within two days, they'd arrested the perp.

Zedler sighed, interrupting Des' recollection. "That would be too much to hope for." He lightly touched Nyland's elbow. "This is Molly Nyland, our forensic artist. She's the best, we're lucky to have her work with us."

"We've met." Des' words came out harsher than he intended. He cleared his throat. "We worked a case together in Sacramento." He held out his hand. "Good to see you again, Nyland." Silently he congratulated himself on how normal he acted. As if she hadn't been on his mind ever since she bolted out of his apartment. As if he hadn't tried to find her through social media when she left Santa Clara. He'd refused to use the police databases to search for her. That reeked of too much desperation. Even he had a little bit of pride left to salvage. Not much after Mitchell's death, but Des held on hard to the few crumbs that were still there.

She finally had to look at him, but her gaze quickly darted away. At least she shook his hand, but then dropped it like it burned. "Good to see you too."

Des ignored Zedler's puzzled look. Fuck, he didn't even know what had happened between Nyland and himself, never mind trying to explain it to someone else. He'd been in trouble as soon as he'd seen her walk into the Sacramento PD headquarters, those five years ago. The only thing that had kept him from claiming her right away was that sleeping with coworkers was never a good idea, plus everything about her had said "relationship girl." And Des didn't do long-term.

But the night they caught that perp, all his noble intentions had gone to shit. He could blame it on the celebratory tequila shots, but the truth was he could no longer resist the chemistry that sizzled between them. She must have noticed those spark as well because she'd been watching him too. Her gray eyes hesitant, but enticing, daring him to make a move. So he did, and then the joke had been on Des when "relationship girl" hadn't wanted anything to do with him after he'd made her come against the wall of the entrance hall in his apartment. He was slightly ashamed over how eager he had been. He'd reached for her as soon as the door closed behind them. Hadn't even taken the time to get her all the way into the bedroom. Shit, the encounter had been so quick, he didn't even get her shirt off.

And yet, he still couldn't get that brief hook-up out of his mind. However, much had happened since then. He was a very different man, a different cop, now. The death of a partner would do that, and considering she couldn't even look him in the eye this many years after, he should stay well clear of Nyland. He shot her another brief glance before concentrating back on work, a true and tested escape when things got complicated.

"We still haven't been able to ID the victim. No wallet, or anything else in his pockets. We've expanded the search parameter, but so far all we've found is grass and mud, and more mud," he said to Zedler.

"Any tracks?" the older detective asked.

"Tons of them, from animals. Goats apparently graze back here all the time, and this is where the farmer trains his dogs to herd." Des wished he had something to share. As the new transfer on the squad, he needed to prove himself. Clearing a murder—the first PFPD had experienced in more than a decade—would go a long way toward earning respect from his new colleagues. He was hoping it would be enough to have them ignore the ugly gossip that would sooner or later catch up with him from Sacramento. When your partner died under mysterious circumstances, the boys and girls in blue became uncomfortable with you. Des knew that from first-hand experience.

Had Nyland heard the rumors? The thought bothered him more than it should.

He forced his mind away from her. She would be a distraction he couldn't afford. He'd come to Prairie Falls for a fresh start, but also to shake down the vague connection between Mitchell and this place. He hadn't expected to find a department full of hardworking and honest policemen and women, but he did, and he liked them. And he wanted them to like him.

Plus, this particular case had already gotten under his skin. He wanted to nail the sick-shit who'd gone after a scared little kid after killing someone in her back yard. Des was good at catching bad guys, and this one seemed particularly sadistic. The adult male victim had been hung by his feet and drained. They'd found enough splatter to know he'd been alive before hung in the tree at the farm, but most of the blood had been removed. This murderer was one sick fucker. "Was the little girl at least able to provide a description of who she saw?"

Zedler looked at Nyland, but she seemed to find her boots extremely interesting and wouldn't look up. The detective cleared his throat. "The kid did good, but she's only eight. In her mind, she saw a monster, so that's what she described."

Des nodded. Young witnesses were hit or miss, especially when they were scared or shocked. "What next?"

"You know the drill. Keep canvassing the area. Pick up every little thing you find. Bag it, tag it, and send it to the lab for analysis."

"That's all?" Des couldn't help but ask.

The other detective briefly squeezed Des' shoulder. "That, and hope for the autopsy to give us clues. Oh, and it would be good if dental records gave us an ID of the poor guy." He sighed again. "I've got to go talk to the techs." He turned to

Nyland. "You'll be okay?"

She nodded.

Zedler gave Des a questioning look before taking off.

Des shrugged in response even though he wasn't sure what the question had been.

He stood quietly next to Nyland as they watched Zedler follow the yellow tape along the cordoned area until he reached the end where the crime scene technicians were picking up nearly microscopic fragments from the ground. Probably none of them useful.

The silence stretched on. As the rain drizzled down, Des considered offering her his jacket, but some perverse passive-aggressive side of him refused the gesture. After hastily climbing off his dick and bolting out the door, she hadn't bothered to return any of his calls or texts.

"So you left Santa Clara," he finally threw out without taking his eyes off Zedler.

In his peripheral vision, he saw her turn to him with a puzzled look on her face. "I got offered a job at a design firm here in Prairie Falls right after graduation."

If her forensic sketches were any indication of her design skills, she'd probably had loads of job offers. "And how do you like it?"

"The job or the town?" She shivered in the rain.

He faced her. "Both, I guess."

Strands of hair lay plastered against her cheeks. Des's hands unclenched in his pockets as he wanted to wipe the rain from her face. He shoved them deeper into his jacket and then cursed under his breath and pulled them out. Des unzipped his coat and shrugged out of it before sweeping it around her shoulders, refusing to dwell on how her wearing his jacket satisfied something deep inside him.

She pulled the coat tighter. "The job is competitive but interesting, and I've learned tons. I work with cutting edge design methods and software, and the firm uses innovative marketing strategies. It was a good place to start, and now a great place to work."

"And the town?" he prodded.

She cocked her head. "You're here now. What do you think?"

He had almost forgotten how she could go from shy to sassy in seconds. He bowed his head to hide the smile playing in the corner of his mouth. "I've only been here a few weeks. Other than fast-food joints and the police station, I haven't seen much of it."

She grinned. "Still maintaining a healthy diet of grease and milkshakes?"

"You know me, body by burgers." He patted his thankfully-still-flat stomach. Now that he'd passed thirty, he actually had to pay attention to what he ate. And spend more time in the gym. But there was no way he'd let Nyland know that little metabolic fact.

She chuckled weakly. "It's a nice town. With three hundred thousand people, it's large enough to have some culture—we have a vibrant theatre community and a symphony—but still small enough to almost have everyone being connected to everyone else, somehow."

Des knew the size of the population but hadn't bothered learning about the cultural amenities. He'd just been happy to transfer out of Sacramento after Mitchell's murder. The town that his partner had jotted down in a notebook having positions open was a happy coincidence. Besides, as long as there was a movie place, he had all the culture he needed. "You don't miss California? The weather?" Eastern Washington winters could be brutal, he'd heard.

A shadow chased across Nyland's face, and she quickly glanced down. "No, I'm good with having four seasons again." She looked up at him, her features neutral again. "Plus, my best friend from college lives here."

He wanted to ask more about where she grew up and who her best friend was, but he didn't know where to start. They'd never discussed anything but work. And never really been alone together except for that one night when she came home with him.

And stayed only long enough to get her rocks off.

Nyland interrupted his thoughts. "I should get back into town and drop the sketch off at the station." She pulled off his jacket while balancing her sketchpad in one hand. "Thanks for lending me this."

"Keep it. I can get it from you later."

She shook her head, holding out his coat. "Thanks, but I'll be okay until I get to the heater in the car."

He pulled on his jacket and zipped up the front as he watched her leave. The hem of her skirt swung back and forth, flirting with the top of her tall boots, utterly inappropriate for a farm and mud.

The cold rain came down harder. Maybe Des should follow and make sure she got to the car safely. He flipped up his jacket collar to stop icy drops from snaking their way inside his shirt and down his back. The jacket smelled like a combination of vanilla and citrus, a fragrance that was uniquely hers. He took a step after Nyland.

"Rankin, get back here," Zedler shouted from behind. "We may have something."

Des sighed and jogged across the field.

"What did you find?" he asked as he reached Zedler, who held a plastic evidence bag up to the light.

"Check this out." The older detective showed the bag toward Des. "What do you make of this?"

A strip of metal glittered in the high-powered crime scene lights. "Is that gold?" Des turned the item over in his hand. "It looks like a hand-held sickle." Twelve inches long and about half an inch wide, the grip of the curved blade would fit comfortably in his palm.

Zedler nodded and traced a finger on top of the curved blade through the transparent plastic. "Gold or some alloy of it. What about these symbols?"

The gold—if it was gold—was stamped with Russian letters or something belonging on a fraternity sign. "Cyrillic or Greek?"

"Don't know," Zedler said. "The techs say it's a possible match to the wounds on the victim's neck."

"Shit. Is this some kind of weird ritual killing? Drain the body of blood using a weirdo knife?"

Zedler shrugged. "Your guess is as good as mine. We'll get an expert on it, but let's go see if this is the weapon Annie saw in the monster's hand." He walked toward the house.

Des trailed after, still studying the weird blade and letters. Something nagged at him in the back of his mind, but whatever it was slid just beyond his focus. It would come to him eventually.

olly squirmed in the design firm's conference room chair and avoided looking at her client. Anger did not flatter Raymond Wymer's appearance. With a cauliflower nose and pudgy cheeks, he would never be described as attractive. Scrunched up in a fury, his face was even less pleasant. Spittle glistened in the corner of his mouth as he complained about the graphics Molly had created for his company's bubble gum campaign.

"They're supposed to do teenager stuff, not sitting around a bonfire." His stubby finger poked one of the foam boards she had arranged on easels along the wall of the firm's largest conference room. As one of Berker Studio's most significant accounts, Marvelous Melon warranted not only the big space but also the fancy pastry on the table.

Molly eyed the sweet treats. She'd picked them out herself at the Scandinavian bakery and imagined almond paste melting on her tongue. She'd always been a stress eater, and right now, Molly was filled with all kinds of anxiety. Rankin was in Prairie Falls, and she was going to have to work with him. She would like to blame their hookup on tequila and a bad break-up, but the truth was that she'd wanted Rankin from the very beginning. Never before—or since—had she felt that kind of instant attraction.

However, chewing on flaky—and oh so deliciously sweet and buttery—baked goods during a client's hissy fit might border on disrespectful. Wymer definitely didn't need anything else to complain about. Molly silently cursed her boss' delayed plane. Anthony Berker, the owner of the design company, had a gift for smooth-talking. Molly was the artist, the talent, she shouldn't be in here alone. And after last night, she was not at her best and most certainly not equipped to handle Wymer's anger. She hated confrontation, and today she just couldn't deal with it.

She'd laid awake most of the night, bothered by the murder and also worried about Rankin. Her body refused to forget how his caresses had heated her blood. Clark—her only serious boyfriend—had dumped her right before the case in Sacramento. Everyone knew rebound sex was a bad idea. But Clark's vile parting words about her body size and the scars on her skin had still echoed loudly in her ears. And his caresses had never made her skin as feverish as Rankin's touch.

And now the detective was here in Prairie Falls. There were new lines around his lips and in his eyes that hadn't been there five years ago. She'd wanted to ask him what had put it there, but chickened out. Even with that new edge, he was still handsome. Still tempting. What the hell was she supposed to do now?

Wymer's fist hitting the table brought Molly back with startling speed. "I want wholesome fun while enjoying our product. Not some hippie get-together."

She shifted in her chair again. Trying to find a comfortable position in this uncomfortable situation proved useless. Through the glass walls of the room, she could see her coworkers following the exchange. They couldn't hear, but Wymer gestured wildly, pacing back and forth as he ranted about her work.

Molly took a deep breath. "Mr. Wymer, the specifications—"

"Don't interrupt me." Wymer turned around, taking a menacing step toward her.

Molly glanced at her coworkers but doubted any of them would come to her aid. Quite a few of them coveted Molly's position as design lead on one of the firm's hottest accounts. Fred Mueller shot her a look through the glass, a sly grin on his lips. He'd had it in for her since she started. Preceding her hire by two years, he insisted accounts should be handed out based on seniority.

She glared back at Fred and then did the mature thing of flipping him the bird while keeping her middle finger out of Wymer's field of view.

Luck may have helped her receive an offer from Berker Studios straight out of college, but she'd been promoted on her own merit. She was an excellent graphic designer, and her work spoke for its self. She'd be damned if she'd allow someone like Mueller to play politics to advance his position within the company. Molly snapped the cuffs of her turquoise silk dress in place. She raised her voice. "Mr. Wymer, the specifications said 'hip people in their early twenties, enjoying trendy places and fun activities'—." Molly took a breath to continue, but Raymond interrupted her again.

"I wanted young people doing young stuff." Spittle flew in her direction.

Her cheeks grew hot, and she clenched her jaw. Molly pointed to the posters to make Wymer aim in a different direction. "This is 'young people doing young stuff," she said. "Young people these days are going to concerts, gaming with friends, dancing at a party, hanging out around fire on the beach, and attending poetry slams."

"That's not what I told you I wanted." Her client's corpulent body shook with fury. "Why aren't they roller skating? Why aren't they hanging out at the mall? At that drive-in burger place, the one with milkshakes? I want young Americans doing American things." Wymer finally ran out of breath.

"You wanted me to target teenagers," Molly pointed out. "I don't think they roller skate anymore." She swallowed her anger and forced her voice back to business-like cheerful. "Maybe I could do a roller derby? Or a skateboard park?"

"Listen to me." With his index finger, Raymond stabbed the air close to Molly's face. "I told Anthony what I wanted. Unless he delivers, I'll take my business elsewhere."

The finger in her face broke Molly's hold on her temper.

"Mr. Wymer, I have followed the guidelines your company emailed me. I can't help that you're stuck in the fifties." Maybe that last part was a little mean, but the man did almost spit on her boots—her new and expensive boots. She'd bought them to replace the black ones she'd ruined earlier in the week at the crime scene on the farm. She suppressed a shiver.

A murder in Prairie Falls was still unthinkable. Guilt assaulted her when she realized this was the first time she'd seriously thought about the killing and little Annie. She should have been worrying about the violent crime instead of focusing on the detective working the case.

She stood and faced her irate client. "I've fulfilled my contracted obligation and can't help that you're out of touch with your target audience."

Fascinated, Molly watched as fury mottled the client's face an even darker red than before. He looked like a squishy plum, which oddly was an improvement.

"I will have your job for that," Wymer bellowed, opening the door of the glass-encased room.

Her colleagues scattered down the hallway, pretending to be busy while making sure they didn't miss the heated exchange.

"You're done," Wymer hollered. "Anthony better call me, or I'm pulling my account." He stomped down the hallway. "I'll make sure he fires you," he threw over his shoulder.

Molly sighed and glared at the people still milling around in the hallway. They ambled away, but not before Mueller sent her another gleeful grin. He was such a dick.

She groaned. She'd have to call Anthony about the botched meeting. Hopefully, she'd reach him before any of the spectators told him their version of the meeting. Pressing her palms to her cheeks cooled them down. Once she felt in control, Molly began gathering the designs and stacking the easels in the corner.

"Wow, Molly, that seemed really intense." Samantha, the office manager, glided through the door.

Molly sighed inwardly at the sight of the blonde, five-foot-ten former model. There was no justice in the world. She patted down her unruly hair and avoided looking at Samantha's glossy long mane. "Hi, Samantha," she mumbled.

After haphazardly picking up an easel and dumping it in the wrong corner, Samantha leaned one hip gracefully against the conference table. She smoothed down her white blouse over a gray pencil skirt. The blonde always looked like she'd stepped out of the pages of a fashion magazine. It was impossible not to feel envious of her perfect figure and her perfect clothes. Despite looking like every man's ideal woman, Samantha was okay for the most part. "What did you say to him to make him so angry?" She picked at an invisible speck on her skirt.

Self-consciously, Molly smoothed down her own dress.

That morning she'd thought its empire waist flattered her bust while minimizing the flare of her hips. But next to Samantha, she felt frumpy.

"I didn't say anything that wasn't true." She stacked the posters with a little more force than necessary. "He has out-of-touch ideas about the campaign designs that I refuse to follow." Molly looked around to see if anyone else heard her explanation, but her previous audience had disappeared into their cubes and offices. They were probably posting all over social media about the Wymer explosion.

"I tried to keep an eye on you in case things became too intense," Samantha smiled. "Since Anthony is out of the office, I figured you needed someone to have your back."

Molly hadn't seen her in the hallway but didn't doubt Samantha had spied from somewhere. The office manager knew everything that went on in the company. "Thank you."

The other woman waved her hand. "Don't worry about it. You're a talented designer. I know Anthony would have supported you if he'd been here."

Samantha had claimed Anthony on her first day, and thinking of him had probably triggered the hair toss unconsciously. It was an open secret—Samantha had made sure of it—that they were sleeping together. What the office manager didn't know was that bets had been placed on how long Anthony would stay in her bed. He was a young widower. His wife had died in a tragic accident only a few years into their marriage. Maybe that's why he now switched girlfriends more often than he bought new Italian loafers, which was at least three times per year. Samantha had lasted longer than Anthony's previous girlfriends, but his frequent business trips to Los Angeles fueled rumors around the office. The gossip alluded to dates with a soap opera actress.

"I'm going to call him right now," Molly said.

"That's good because Marvelous Melon gum is important

to him. He worked hard to land the account." Samantha's amber eyes widened with sincerity. "But he wouldn't have allowed Wymer to go on like he did."

"I wish he could have been here for the meeting instead of mingling in la-la land," Molly said. "He would have handled all of this much better than I did today."

Samantha's cocked her head, sympathy in her amber eyes. "He lands late tonight. I'll set up a meeting with both of you and Raymond Wymer for tomorrow or the day after."

"Tomorrow's Saturday," Molly sighed.

Samantha stood, smoothing down her skirt. "You may have to meet over the weekend to do damage control before Monday." She smiled apologetically.

"Let's hope not." Molly gathered her posters under one arm and headed out the door.

Back in her own office, Molly deposited the designs in a corner and reached for the phone. Anthony's voicemail picked up on the first ring. Maybe he was still on the plane, or perhaps he hadn't left the actress's bed yet.

She described the meeting with Wymer as "disappointing" and asked Anthony to call her back. He'd get the lurid details of Raymond's temper tantrum from the gawkers and Samantha. That weasel Fred had probably already called him.

As Molly sorted the papers on her desk, she indulged in some wishful thinking. Maybe Wymer would calm down and see reason by the time Anthony got back into town.

She snorted and shook her head. Yeah, and soon a magic frog would appear on her doorstep. He'd ask for a kiss and turn into a handsome, wealthy philanthropist who had waited all his life for a temperamental short girl on the wrong side of a size six.

Rankin liked your curves, a little voice whispered in the back of her mind.

Molly ignored her hormones and tried to concentrate on another design campaign that needed to be finished before she officially started her weekend.

What were Rankin's weekend plans?

Shit. She couldn't be distracted by the detective right now. What had happened between them was ancient history. So what if he gave her the most fantastic orgasm ever? She knew better than to get involved with a cop. Her reputation had been shredded after Detective Clark O'Hare dumped her, and then bad-mouthed her to the entire department.

She opened her graphic files with a harder click than necessary and tried to focus on the screen.

* * *

A FEW HOURS LATER, Molly rushed from her parked car toward Sinful Soul, a new, and the only, jazz club in Prairie Falls. Running late to her best friend Nina's twenty-seventh birthday celebration, she tried to catch her breath as she joined the queue in front of the club. She smoothed down the skirt of her dress and then her wavy hair. Molly couldn't actually afford the designer labels she often wore to the office, but there were advantages to being best friends with the owner of a trendy boutique. She checked the gift bag to make sure it wasn't harmed during her dashing from the car and then fidgeted while waiting in line.

"Molly." A hand touched her shoulder.

She turned around to find her best friend grinning at her. "I thought you were inside already."

Nina held up her phone. "I left this in the car and came back outside to get it." She flicked her eyes to Molly's outfit. "I told you that dress would be perfect for you."

Molly hugged the willowy brunette and admired her olive

linen skirt, topped with a gauzy lime-colored top. "You don't look so bad yourself. Happy Birthday."

Before Nina could answer, it was time to show their IDs to the bouncer. At well over six feet and clad entirely in black leather—a sleeveless vest and tight pants highlighting impressive quads—he towered over her like some ancient warrior from one of those video games Nina was so fond of. Long straight black hair hung halfway down his back, contrasting beautifully with his bronzed skin.

His bottle-green eyes barely glanced over Molly's license before handing it back, but they did a double-take when they landed on Nina's.

"Sorry, ladies, we're full tonight." He flattened his hand against the door as if guarding it.

A frown marred Nina's pretty features. "No, you're not. I've already been inside."

The bouncer frowned. "I didn't let you in."

Nina tapped her foot, a sure sign of her temper rising. "No, you didn't. It was a different door guard. A polite one who knew his job." She turned her hand to show a stamp of double S's on the inside of her wrist.

Sighing, he held the door open without a word, his piercing eyes glaring at Nina as they went inside.

Molly handed her entrance ticket to the woman inside. Not as tall as the bouncer, she was still close to six feet. The heels of her black lace-up boots contributed at least three inches of the height. Spiky short bleached hair contrasted with her black leather outfit, a bustier over tight leather pants. Maybe leather was the staff uniform, which seemed a little odd for a jazz club.

"What was that about?" Molly asked as they walked into a circular room filled with tables covered in white linen.

"I have no idea. That bouncer was a dick when I came

here for a work function last weekend. Then he accused me of having a fake ID."

"Too bad his attitude sucks because physically he's everything you like."

Nina opened her mouth as if to say something, but then just shook her head. "Carol's keeping seats for us." She walked toward a table on the other side.

Walking gingerly through the packed room, Molly tried to not upset the glasses on the tables or purses hanging on the back of chairs. The bouncer hadn't lied about the place being close to full.

Carol smiled and stood when they approached the table. "I was beginning to worry that something had happened to you."

"Just had to argue with the bouncer. They switched, and now it's the same guy as last weekend." Nina said.

"I think he has the hots for you," Carol winked. She was the same height as Nina, five-foot-eight, but with bleached-blonde hair and a much more voluptuous figure. The plus-sized model looked stunning in a brown velvet dress.

To Molly's surprise, Nina blushed. "Does not."

Carol grinned. "Okay, but admit it. You think he's hot."

Nina sat down in one of the chairs. "Let's talk about something other than the moron at the door." She turned to Molly. "How come you're late? "Was the boss giving you a hard time about consulting for the cops?"

Anthony had protested a couple of times when Molly left to work a case in the middle of a workday. Once she'd made it clear that she always caught up on any missed work on her own time, he'd mostly let it go. Every now and then, he'd give her a little scathing comment, which she ignored. "No, this time it was something else," Molly answered. "He called me right as I was leaving. He's concerned about a client meeting that went bad."

Nina sat down and pulled Molly into the chair beside her. "Are you okay?"

"Yeah. Anthony mostly apologized for how a client treated me, but also explained how important this account is." Her boss treated his designers fairly but still kept his primary focus on assuring a quarterly profit.

"I don't mean just about your day-job. I got your text about working on the murder."

Nina had traveled the last couple of days, and except for a few quick calls and texts, Molly hadn't had a chance to talk to her. "I didn't see the body or anything, but the witness was pretty shaken up." Thinking about how scared little Annie had been put her day-job problems in perspective. "I'm okay, though."

She briefly thought about telling Nina about Rankin, but the conversation was better suited for when it was just the two of them. She had never told her best friend about hooking up with Rankin. She didn't know why, but there was something about that encounter that was just hard to talk about, even with her best friend. It was too intense, too raw.

Carol shook her head. "I can't believe there's been a murder in Prairie Falls." Her eyebrows rose. "Is it true it was a ritualistic murder? I heard the body was drained of all blood."

Molly frowned. "Where did you hear that?" She's left messages for Zedler during the week, but he hadn't called back. She figured he'd been busy, but maybe she should call him again, although she didn't know that there was anything else she could help with.

"It was in the paper," Nina answered. "An unknown source from the police said there wasn't enough blood at the crime scene to account for how drained the body was, and that they think a cult may be involved."

"I don't know anything about that." Molly pushed the gift

bag she'd brought toward Nina. "Are you going to open this?" Discussing her work with the police always made her uncomfortable. She never wanted to be the cause of an "unnamed source" quote. As a freelancer, she couldn't risk it.

"I can take a hint." Nina pulled the tissue paper out of the gift bag. "I know you don't like talking about your freelance gig, it's just that murder is big news in this town." She peeked inside the bag. "Oh, this is gorgeous," she said, pulling out a hand-painted silk scarf. Iridescent greens and blues reflected the club's lights as Nina caressed the fabric.

Carol leaned forward and touched the scarf as well. "Where did you find this?"

"At an artist collaboration website." Molly silently congratulated herself for getting the gift right. Nina loved clothes and accessories, but had a particular taste and was hard to shop for.

Carol grabbed the scarf and tested the strength of the silk. "This is perfect for tying someone up in bed." She winked.

Nina giggled. "Like who?"

"Oh, I don't know. Maybe Molly could call her good-looking boss."

Molly snorted. "Not going to happen. I don't go out with people I work with." Except for Rankin. But that wasn't really a date. She flashbacked again on calloused palms sliding up her thighs, lighting her skin on fire. Even through the tequila-induced hazy memory, she recalled how good those hands had felt on her body. How hot their union had been. How full she'd felt when he slid into her. Heat flushed her cheeks. "Besides, Anthony wouldn't be interested in me. He dates women who look like Samantha. What would he want with me?"

Nina exchanged a glance with Carol, and they both rolled their eyes.

"What's with the look thing? What did I say?" Molly asked.

Nina draped the scarf around her neck. "Honey, first of all, you're gorgeous. And second, you're the only woman in that office your boss hasn't slept with."

"I'm pretty sure Mrs. Broadcreek in Human Resources hasn't slept with him. She's sixty and very happily married," Molly countered.

Carol laughed. "Okay, the only woman under fifty who hasn't slept with him—yet." She wiggled her eyebrows. "I don't know how you can be immune to his charms, I find him very attractive."

"When did you meet Molly's boss?" Nina asked.

"We met at a photoshoot."

Molly shook her head. "I'm not going to bed with my boss. Worst career move ever." She was happy to leave Anthony in Samantha's capable hands.

"Or the best," Carol counted. In addition to her modeling, Carol worked as a writer for a sports clothing catalog. She'd dated most of her male colleagues.

Nina slapped Carol on the arm. "You should know. But even I would like to check out the moves that Molly's boss might make, career or otherwise."

Molly groaned but secretly loved the banter. And with these two, the talk usually turned naughty at some point.

A server interrupted the laughter. "Can I get you something to drink?" His blond hair was tied back in a short ponytail. Startling deep blue eyes and a strong jaw in a sinfully handsome face distracted Molly. Her eyes traveled lower, across his sculpted shoulders and what his vest exposed of a well-defined chest. Leather *was* the staff uniform.

Nina gave her nudge under the table. "Ah, do you have a house red wine?" Molly finally said.

The other two women tried unsuccessfully to keep their giggles contained.

A slight smile played at the corners of the waiter's mouth. "We have a bold Shiraz from Yakima Valley. Would you like to try a glass?"

"Yes, thank you," Molly managed. "And a glass of water, please."

"Coming right up." He executed a short bow and strode away from the table. He'd gotten about ten steps before Molly's companions giggled.

"That's not the only thing she likes 'coming right up,'" Carol cackled.

The waiters' steps didn't falter as he continued to the bar. Hopefully, he hadn't heard her.

"You guys," Molly hissed. "Behave. You can't say things like that. It's disrespectful. You'd never allow a guy to speak that way to a woman."

"Oh, and you ogling the staff as if they were shaking their booties for money was way respectful," Nina said, which caused a new round of laughter from Carol.

"It was just that his eyes were such an amazing color," Molly explained. "Have you ever seen eyes that deep blue? It was like looking into the ocean."

Rankin's hazel eyes were like looking into a forest lake hidden deep within the trees. They changed colors from almost brown to light green depending on his moods.

"Uh, huh," Carol said oblivious to Molly's distraction, "and his chiseled face or awesome bod didn't have anything to do with your speech center short-circuiting?"

Nina pretended to come to Molly's rescue. "Give the girl a break. You know she doesn't date."

"Thanks," Molly said, sticking out her tongue.

"And she's been trying hard to not fall for hot Tony's charms at the office. Those built up hormones had to be released at some point," Nina continued, winking at Molly's grimace. "Maybe she'll like to test out the scarf on the waiter later tonight."

Molly swatted at her friend, but Nina leaned out of reach, joining in Carol's giggle—more like cackling at this point. Before she had a chance to ask how much the other two women had drunk already, the overhead lights dimmed, and a single spotlight clicked on, illuminating a lone microphone stand on the stage. The opening bars of "My Baby Just Cares for Me" spilled through hidden speakers, and as if conjured by magic, a stunning redhead appeared in the light circle. Molly gasped and turned to her companions, but they were staring at the woman.

The singer took a deep breath before adding deep throaty lyrics to the music. Her pale white skin glowed in the spotlight. Auburn wavy hair flowed down to just above her waist. A long, red satin evening gown with a sweetheart neckline hugged her curves.

Almost as if she noticed Molly's scrutiny, the woman's gaze swung toward her, and she could swear the singer frowned at her. Surely there was no way the woman on stage could see her in the dimly lit club.

Molly's silenced phone vibrated on the table. She checked the display.

Detective Zedler.

Sliding out of her chair, she walked hunched over to a side aisle and made her way to the ladies' room where she answered the call.

"Yeah, Nyland, we need you here ASAP."

"What's going on?"

Some muffled cursing traveled down the line. "Another murder."

"What?" The crime rate in their city was the same as in other places the same size, but...another murder?

"I hear music? Have you been drinking? Can you drive?"

"I just got here. I haven't drunk any alcohol." Molly dug in her purse for a pen. "What's happened, and where do you need me?"

"I can't discuss this over the phone, get down to the station and find Rankin." He hung up, but she didn't blame him for the curtness. He must be under a ton of pressure.

Molly stepped out of the restroom and collided with the blond waiter's chest.

"Are you okay, miss?" Concern shone in his eyes, but there was also a flicker of something else. Curiosity? Confusion? It disappeared before she could pinpoint it.

"Yeah, sorry about the phone," Molly said, once she found her voice. "I'm on call and had to take it." Technically, the contract she had with the police didn't stipulate that she always be available. But on an earlier case, Zedler had asked her to keep the cell phone handy during regular waking hours—whatever that meant to a police detective.

The man smiled. "But you haven't tasted the Shiraz," he said. "Let me escort you back to the table." He took Molly's elbow and led her, firmly, toward Nina and Carol.

She had to pull hard to snap her arm out of the server's grip but then saw the glass of red wine on the table. Maybe that was why he acted so weird. He thought she was skipping out on the bill.

"How much do I owe you for the drink?" She whispered.

"What?" he said in a normal speaking voice.

Molly glanced around, but everyone's eyes were on the stage. She turned back to the waiter.

He frowned down at her.

"The wine." She pointed to the glass. "How much?"

He glanced at the table and then shook his head. "It's complementary."

"Oh, okay. Thanks." Molly's smile felt brittle. Why was he

acting so weird? She couldn't be the first customer who had gone to the bathroom during the show. Or didn't finish her drink.

Molly touched Nina's shoulder, but she didn't react. After a harder shake, her friend finally turned around. Nina's eyes were glazed over, and she blinked several times before focusing on Molly.

"Zedler called, I have to leave."

"Okay," Nina said slowly, turning to face the stage again.

Molly had expected more of a protest but wasn't going to argue. She stepped around the waiter, searching for a clear path back to the entrance. A glance over her shoulder showed the waiter staring after her, looking puzzled.

Molly pushed the doors open. The bouncer jumped when she stepped through. "Have a good night," she said, breezing past him.

"Where are you going?" He reached for her but then stopped.

"Work called," Molly said with a bright false smile. Apparently, this place took it personally if you didn't stay for the show. "But please tell the singer she's fantastic."

At first, the bouncer took a step as if to follow her, but the cell on his side rang.

Molly walked off as fast as her boots allowed. She looked back.

The bouncer was still watching.

CHAPTER 3

*D*es rushed through the Prairie Falls PD lobby on his way from the kitchen to his office. He sipped the lukewarm coffee in his hand, his fourth this evening, but who was counting. The desk sergeant was losing the battle against her ringing phones, and he threw her an encouraging smile as he walked by and up the stairs.

He breezed into his office without looking and then doubled over as an elbow made contact just below his ribs. Catching a fleeting impression of startled gray eyes, he sucked in his breath when brown liquid splashed all over his white shirt.

The impact propelled Nyland forward. As she pivoted out of control, her bag and sketchpad flew up into the air. She pitched her hands forward, probably to keep her head from smacking the desk, and toppled a pile of manila folders. They tumbled to the floor, and Nyland landed ungraciously on top of them.

"Shit." Des reached over her head for some napkins on the desk. He blotted furiously at the brown stain rapidly spreading over his torso and glared at the woman sprawled on top of the files he'd spent most of the afternoon sorting into some semblance of order.

She blinked repeatedly but didn't appear to be hurt. Des would find her cute if she wasn't the cause of the disarrayed papers and his stained shirt. Hell, he was totally lying to himself. He always found her attractive. "Give a guy a warning, will you?" He continued blotting at the coffee stain. Good thing he kept extra shirts in the office.

Nyland pushed herself off the floor. The folders slipped away under her hands, becoming even more jumbled.

"Shit," she said as her skirt rode up while she floundered.

Des enjoyed the view for a moment before remembering how much work it was going to take to get those files back into order. He sighed and muttered, "Are you okay?" as he helped her to her feet.

Nyland's cheeks flushed red. "Fine, thanks."

He looked down at his shirt to hide a smile. "You need to work on your entrance." He threw the napkin on the desk. The brown stain now covered half his chest.

"I was already here when you entered," she snipped and squatted down to retrieve her sketchpad and bag. She stood, snapping her cuffs in place, and smoothing down the skirt of her dress. Its bright blue color made her gray eyes even more startling.

The effect was disarming.

He glanced down and adjusted his tie, trying to cover the stain. It was futile. He was going to have to get a new shirt from the stash in his desk.

"Work on your dismount then." He couldn't entirely hide the smile from his voice. He cleared his throat. "Step outside. I need to change this shirt."

"Ehr, what?"

"Wait outside for me while I change." He tugged the shirt

out of his slacks and popped the buttons open. Nyland stared mesmerized. She must have hit her head.

Or maybe not.

He studied her closer. Could it be she wasn't as immune to the chemistry between them as she pretended? "Do you want to watch me strip?" Des quirked an eyebrow.

Her cheeks blushed crimson before she stepped outside the office, slamming the door behind her. The papers on the floor rustled.

He chuckled as he reached for a new shirt. So Nyland had a temper to match that lustrous red hair.

A few minutes later, wearing a blue shirt creased from the cellophane package, Des strode down the hallway at a quick pace. Nyland scrambled to follow. "Here's the situation," he said over his shoulder, struggling to get the same tie he'd worn before into a slipknot. "We've got another dead body. This one was found with multiple stab wounds in River Park, but little blood and no murder weapon." Preliminary findings showed wounds similar to those of the first victim, most likely done with the same weird scythe, but Nyland didn't need to know that.

She quickened her step.

He slowed his pace a little so she could keep up with him. "What we do have," Des continued, "is a witness who saw someone running from the area only a few minutes before the body was discovered. I need you to get a sketch from her."

"No problem," Nyland said. "Do you know who the victim is yet?"

Des pulled a small notebook out of his back pocket. "He had a wallet on him. The name is Raymond Wymer." He heard a little gasp, so he slowed down further. It took a few paces before he noticed she wasn't following. He turned.

She stared at him with a deer-in-headlights look. What was going on now? He walked back toward her, slowly

Nyland swayed on her feet.

He grabbed her arm. "Steady."

He couldn't remember if she'd hit her head when she fell. Shit, she may have a concussion. He checked her pupils. They appeared normal, but without a light, he couldn't check if they expanded and contracted like they should.

She clutched at his sleeve, opening and closing her mouth as if she had trouble getting air into her lungs. "Raymond Wymer? From the candy company?" She gasped.

"Did you know him?" Des kept his tone leveled.

She nodded, swaying in a larger arc.

He gripped her arm more tightly, lowering his voice an octave and put authority into it. "How did you know him, Nyland?"

"He was a client of the design firm I work for."

Des raked a hand through his hair. "Fuck." Prairie Falls didn't have an abundance of forensic artists. Or detectives, for that matter. He stared at his shoes and made a fast decision. "Well, it can't be helped. We don't have anybody else available. I need to get the sketch while the witness remembers the details. Are you're up for it?"

She nodded, but still looked pale. Des better keep an eye on her during the interview and watch for any signs of concussion.

He kept his hand just under her elbow as they continued down the hallway. As they approached the door of the interview room, Rankin shot Molly a quick glance. Chances were, her working the case would come back and bite him on the ass. But if it led to them capturing the killer, it was a risk he was willing to take.

* * *

MOLLY STUDIED the lady in her seventies sitting across from her. Mildred Bunsig had been walking her terrier mix in the park when a man came running toward her.

"He scared both Blitz and me when he came out of nowhere, barreling down the path." She patted her elaborate coiffure and smiled at Detective Rankin.

Sitting in a corner of the stuffy interview room, he grinned back

Molly had asked him to observe from behind the one-way mirror, but he'd insisted on being with her. His exact words had been, "No fucking way am I leaving you alone with a witness when there's a risk of a fucking conflict of interest."

She was stuck with him and his limited vocabulary.

During the case in Sacramento, Rankin had never observed her actually working. He'd only asked her about the finished sketches. His nearness now was distracting. She was nervous and couldn't tell her own fidgeting from the signals her scars were sending. Only Nina knew about Molly's freaky ability, and she wanted to keep it that way. If anyone in the PFPD found out about what it was that made her sketches so precise, she'd be out on her butt before she could say "lightning." Cases that involved help from psychics and other clairvoyance professionals had been thrown out of court more than once.

And she loved her job with the police, it made her feel worthy like she contributed to something good.

She turned to anger to mask her anxiety over Rankin being in the room and glared at him.

Not only was he a distraction to Molly, but the witness also couldn't take her eyes off him.

Rankin grinned broader as Ms. Bunsig fawned over him. Men.

A few crow's feet fanned out from the edges that hadn't

been there when they worked together in California, but his eyes still turned a brilliant light green when he smiled.

One perfect eyebrow arched as the detective noticed her scrutiny.

Molly quickly studied her sketchpad and cleared her throat to get Mildred's attention.

The older woman turned and looked at Molly from across the dingy metal folding table at which they were both seated. "Yes, dear?"

"Ms. Bunsig, if you could answer a few questions about what the man looked like, then I will make a drawing from which the police can work."

"Well, why don't I just describe him to you?"

"I've found it works better if I ask about particular details. People remember more when they concentrate on one area of the face at a time."

"Go ahead then." Ms. Bunsig leaned back in her chair, smoothing down the beige jacket she wore over a matching skirt. She adjusted the pink scarf at her neck. Blitz doing his business was apparently an occasion that required business attire.

"Tell me about the general shape of his head," Molly said. "Was it oval, square, round, heart-shaped?"

Ms. Bunsig closed her eyes for a moment. "It was round, with a slightly pointed chin," she finally said. "His ears stuck out a little. I remember because my nephew had problems with protruding ears when he was younger. My sister used to tape them to the side of his head." She opened her eyes. "Such a dear boy that Henry, too bad he embezzled all that money. Those ears are not going to earn him any dates in prison."

Detective Rankin made a noise that sounded suspiciously like swallowed laughter, and his chair scraped against the floor.

Molly frowned at him before concentrating on the pad in front of her. She had learned to tune out any details of the conversation that weren't relevant to her sketch. With a graphite pencil in hand and a sheet of paper to trace it on, her focus narrowed, and the surroundings blurred.

"What about his forehead? Was it pronounced, or narrow?"

"He was bald. I'd forgotten that until you just now asked me." Ms. Bunsig fidgeted with her scarf. "He had a very shiny forehead, and it reached clear across his scalp."

Molly made the necessary adjustments on the pad and asked Ms. Bunsig about the shape of his eyes.

"They were almond-shaped," she answered. "I think the man was Asian-looking, perhaps Chinese."

The scars on Molly's arm tingled. She shifted in the chair and glanced at Detective Rankin under her lashes while she rubbed her shoulder.

He frowned, but kept quiet and turned his attention back on the witness.

Molly did the same. "Tell me more about his eyes. Were his eyelids low across the eyeball, or could you see the color of his eyes?"

Mildred closed her eyes again. "They were brown. I must have seen the irises."

Molly altered the sketch. The shape and size of the eyes of people from Asia were quite diverse, and almond-shaped was not the right way to describe them. Caucasian and black people had eyes that shape too. She knew better than getting into a conversation with a witness about the non-offensive way of describing facial features, though. Instead, she added mono-lidded eyes with an epicanthal fold, a common trait among people of Chinese, Japanese, and Korean descent. Those were the countries people usually thought of when they used the term "Asian," no matter how geographically and politically incorrect that might be. She continued asking about other facial features. The skin on her back reacted while they worked on cheekbones and the shape of the man's mouth. Again, she asked detailed questions about those parts before moving on to the next feature.

The detective stayed quiet in his corner, but Molly felt his gaze tracing chills along her spine. She shook them off as inconspicuously as she could and kept working on the sketch.

When she showed Mildred the final result, the woman nodded. "Yes, that's him. That's the man I saw in the park. I remembered more details than I thought."

Detective Rankin rose. "You've been very helpful, Ms. Bunsig." He pulled out her chair as she stood. "I'll walk you out, and we'll find you a ride home."

"How nice of you," she simpered, patting his sleeve.

Molly snorted.

Rankin shot her a warning glare.

"Goodbye, dear," Ms. Bunsig said to Molly, sailing out the door the detective held open.

Molly picked up her supplies and followed, but Rankin blocked the doorway. "You stay," he said. "We need to talk." It wasn't a request.

She let out a big sigh as she settled back down in the chair. Maybe the detective just wanted to talk about her connection to Wymer, but she didn't think so. He'd been watching her too closely during the interview. She should have known he'd pick up on her ability. It had happened before with other detectives, which was why she didn't like or want to be observed. Only Zedler didn't seem to care.

Like the others, Rankin would ask why Molly had asked additional questions about certain features. She produced quick and accurate forensic drawings. More accurate than most artists, which had some defense lawyers suspicious already, but so far she'd managed to elude anyone investigating her success streak.

She'd stumbled into the field of forensic sketching while in college in California when she took a few forensic art classes as electives for her design degree. That's when she'd discovered the weird tingling of the scars. They almost always reacted when she worked as a sketch artist, but rarely, if ever, when other people told untruths. It was a good thing Grammie never found out about Molly's ability. The old woman had considered just the scars on Molly's skin the mark of the devil. If she'd found out the rest, she probably would have killed her granddaughter in her efforts to beat the evil out of her.

The Santa Clara lieutenant Molly had worked with never questioned her sketches, probably because they had helped his high closing rate of cases. Most of the other detectives she had worked with did, though, including her ex-boyfriend.

She rehearsed the excuses she had used on Clark. The witness's body language changed when they were uncertain about the details, the pitch of their voice altered, or they hesitated on certain words.

She wasn't looking forward to being interrogated by Rankin. He'd scrutinized the sketch session. There was a possibility he wouldn't believe she picked up on witness behavior he didn't notice. Or worse, he'd want to talk about the night she went home with him.

She snorted.

He probably didn't even remember what had happened. It was more likely that he wanted to interrogate Molly about Wymer. She should take herself off of the case, there was an evident conflict of interest, but she had a personal stake in the game now. Wymer had been an unpleasant person, but he didn't deserve to die.

Hopefully, the person Ms. Bunsig saw had something to do with the crime. If not, maybe he or she would lead them to someone else who had experienced Raymond Wymer's hot temper. Someone with more of a motive to kill him than Molly. She was not looking forward to having to tell Rankin about the argument she'd had with Wymer.

The interrogation room door opened, and she jumped up from the chair. She preferred to be standing when confronted by the detective.

Detective Zedler strolled through the door. As usual, his gray polyester suit looked as if he'd slept in it. The drab garment did nothing to cheer up the rest of his rumpled appearance. His salt-and-pepper hair stood up on one side and was plastered to the skull on the other. Sallow bags drooped under his eyes, but they were the kindest eyes Molly had ever seen on a man.

They could convey genuine sympathy for victims of crime, but she'd also seen him use their warm friendliness to pull confessions out of seasoned thieves. Today, his cater-pillar eyebrows were at peace. The memory if his intense gaze during Annie's sketch session flashed through her mind. She dismissed it as a trick of the light from the fireplace.

"What are you still doing here, Nyland?" he asked. "Shouldn't you be out doing whatever you were doing before I called you?" He put an arm over her shoulder and escorted her toward the door.

"Rankin wants to discuss the sketch."

"I'll tell Rankin that you had better things to do." Zedler smiled. "Can't let a dress like that go to waste on a Friday evening."

Molly smoothed down her skirt and fiddled with the sleeves. "If you say so."

Of all the cops she'd worked with, Zedler was the most accepting. He never asked about how Molly knew when to press for details. She sometimes wondered about his lack of questions but had long ago decided not to question the good things in life. There weren't that many.

"Are you sure about this?" Molly asked as they walked down the hallway. "Rankin insisted I stay."

"Don't mind him," her companion answered. "He's not on his best behavior today."

A rude snort escaped Molly's throat.

Zedler smiled and shrugged. "He's new and thinks he has something to prove. Don't let him get to you." He patted her shoulder and opened the door to the outside. "How do you know him, anyway?"

"I was on loan to his department from Santa Clara PD. We didn't really have much contact." She blushed furiously and looked down to hide it.

The detective studied her. "What do you know about his reputation? Will he be a good addition to our PD?"

Molly shrugged. "I don't really know, but he was respected and got along well with everyone in Sacramento."

Zedler nodded. "Good enough."

She took the first step down and then turned back to face Zedler. "I still can't believe I'm working on murder cases."

The older detective reached out and held her wrist. "We'll get the bastard who did this." He looked at her, his eyes soft. "Molly, if you feel…overwhelmed or just need to talk to someone, you know you can come to me, right?"

"Of course."

He didn't let go of her arm. Instead, he studied her for a long time. "There are things I can't tell you. Things that aren't mine to tell, I mean. But I…," he shook his head. "I just want you to know that I'm here for you. You're very special to me, and I will always look out for you."

"Okay." She wasn't sure why Zedler had turned so severe

all of a sudden. This wasn't like him. "Am I in trouble because of knowing Wymer? Should I excuse myself from the case?"

"No, no." The detective shook his head and smiled. "You're fine. We'll get that straightened out. Go home and get some rest."

Molly nodded good-bye and headed down the rest of the stairs, as Zedler went back into the building. Hopefully, they'd get the perp. Soon, she thought as she fished her car keys out of her purse. When details about the second murder hit the media, people would be panicked and scared.

She beeped the locks open.

Someone shouted her name. Rankin.

Pretending not to hear him, she quickly slid into the driver's seat. For the second time that evening, Molly left a frowning man behind her. She glanced in the rearview mirror. Even without sound, she could tell Rankin used his favorite word, repeating it over and over.

DES WATCHED Nyland drive down the street. Her brake lights flared briefly as she slowed down for a curve and then sped out of view. He knew she'd heard him because she'd hesitated as she got into the car. Maybe he'd been a little hard on her, but that was no reason to take off like her underwear had caught on fire.

She'd done a superb sketch, but he had a million questions. Like how she knew Ms. Bunsig needed help describing the eyes, cheekbones, and mouth of the man. He'd watched as Nyland paused for a few brief moments before rubbing her shoulder and then start to ask very detailed questions. He'd worked with other sketch artists, and none of them had honed in on specifics the way Nyland had. She'd had an uncanny instinct about precisely what to ask. Almost as if she already knew who she was sketching.

Hopefully, she didn't play much poker. That shoulder rub was a clear tell. Nyland was hiding something, and he was going to find out what it was. His career depended on it. It wouldn't take long before the rumors from Sacramento caught up with him. The boys in blue always ferreted out information about their colleagues. Even classified files didn't keep their secrets for long. When they found out how his partner had died, there would be a lot of talk and suspicion. Des forced the images of Mitchell's mauled body out of his mind.

Right now, he needed all the information he could get on Molly Nyland and her involvement with the murder victim. Zedler should have some answers.

With one last "fuck" thrown after the vanished car, Des walked back into the building. He'd get another cup of coffee before he went in search of the older detective. Maybe he'd even manage to keep his shirt clean now that Nyland had left the building.

CHAPTER 4

*M*olly scanned the small coffee shop for her boss Anthony. That morning there'd been a message on her cell phone asking to meet at eight. Unfortunately, she hadn't woken until seven-thirty, and the neighborhood café Anthony picked was straight across town from her condo. She'd allowed herself ten minutes to shower and brush her teeth before heading out. She'd slept poorly, dreaming about being chased through the park by someone she couldn't see, and now she felt drained and sluggish.

The place was already filling up. People balanced mismatched china cups and delicious-looking pastries on the small tables dotted around the room. She picked a path that avoided most of the backpacks, laptops, and stretched-out legs as she searched for her boss.

A crisply pleated pant leg and a well-polished shoe stuck out under a raised newspaper. Molly recognized the shoes as a pair Samantha had pointed out. Apparently, they were bought in Rome during a trip Samantha and Anthony had taken together.

As Molly smoothed down her unruly, and still wet, hair,

the newspaper lowered. Anthony's tanned face appeared. His black wavy hair looked recently cut and matched the color of his shirt, pants, and shoes.

"There you are." He flashed impossibly straight and white teeth. With his polished handsomeness, he could be the star in the TV advertising campaigns Berker Studios launched for their clients.

"Here I am," Molly agreed. Sweat trickled down her back as she sat down in the rickety chair across from him. On the car ride over, she'd rehearsed what she was going to say about the bubblegum account—and the dead client—but there just wasn't a way to put a positive spin on either.

Anthony grabbed her hand. "I'm so sorry to hear about your unpleasant ordeal."

Molly leaned back, pulling her sweaty palm out of his. Was he talking about the meeting or the murder? The news media could have already mentioned the killing. Would they have released the victim's name?

"Yes, it was very trying," Molly hedged. Even if Anthony knew about Wymer's death, how would he know about her working on the case?

"I know Raymond can be a bastard sometimes," he flashed another smile, "but he is a good client. Maybe a little stuck in the past." He put his hand over hers.

Oh no, he didn't know yet. Molly tried to pull her hand back, but Anthony held it in his.

"I want you to know that I looked over the designs, and you've done a wonderful job."

Molly swallowed. "I have to tell you something—"

Anthony let go of her hand. "Not until I get you something to drink and eat." He stood. "What would you like?"

She asked for chai and a chocolate croissant. As her boss strode over to the counter, she mentally rehearsed how to break the horrifying news.

Anthony stood tall and confident, as always, by the pastry display. She couldn't tell his facial expression, but she bet he was smiling—charmingly so. The teenaged girl behind the counter twirled a strand of hair as she giggled. He enchanted women, no matter their age.

When that enigmatic smile beamed on Molly, she felt flattered but knew it wasn't sincere. Her boss had that smile on this face whenever he spoke to a woman. Anthony appreciated all women equally. The wattage of his smile never varied, which is why it always struck her as fake.

She glanced around the café to distract herself from what she would soon have to tell her boss. Surreptitiously, she pulled the sticky fabric of her shirt from her skin.

Through the window, she saw a long-haired man quickly turning away. The glossy black hair reminded her of the bouncer from the night before. She should call Nina and get the details of the rest of the birthday celebrations. Or at least send a quick text.

She retrieved her phone from her purse and tapped out a message.

"Sorry to interrupt." Anthony slid into his seat. A friendly smile revealed those blinding teeth, but there was an edge to his words. He put the plate and cup in front of her with extra and unnecessary force.

Molly threw the phone in her purse and grabbed the cup. As she wiped up the spilled liquid with a napkin, she frowned. "I was just texting a friend. I had to leave her birthday party early last night."

Anthony avoided her gaze, changing his tone back to one of concern. "Oh, did you feel unwell?"

Her nerves were already all over the place because of Wymer's death. She couldn't deal with the unpredictable mood swings of her boss on top of everything else. She had to tell him. She took a breath—

"Darling, there you are," Samantha swept through the café, tossing her hair, the long tresses landing perfectly down her back.

Several male patrons followed her progress to Molly and Anthony's table. Samantha wore a tailor-made short charcoal dress. If it had been a size bigger, her outfit would have been conservative. Instead, the effect was that of a sexy librarian fantasy.

"What are you doing here, Sam? I told you I would call you later today." Anthony's smile was blinding, but his tone curt.

"I'm on my way to Nordies down the street for an early-bird VIP event and thought I'd stop by to give you a kiss. I haven't seen you for days." She pouted prettily, cocking a hip on the table.

Molly steadied her cup once again. "Nice effect, but do you mind the coffee?" she muttered under her breath.

"What was that, Molly?" Ice glittered in Samantha's eyes.

Oops, she hadn't meant for that to come out loud. "Sorry, Sam." She grabbed her abandoned cell phone and held it up. "Phone trouble."

Samantha gracefully slithered into one of the empty chairs, ignoring Anthony's frown. "I hate when my phone doesn't work." She leaned toward Anthony, offering him a generous peek at her cleavage.

The guy at the next table over took advantage of the view, until Anthony aimed a steely glance his way.

Now she had to tell both Sam and Anthony about Wymer's passing. Molly took a gulp of her chai.

"We're in a business meeting here," Anthony said. "I'll call you later."

Samantha crossed her legs and shot Anthony a challenging look. "I'm part of the company."

Anger clouded his face, and his jaw clenched, but then he sighed and shook his head.

Before she got caught in the weird undercurrents between her boss and his lover, Molly better announce her news. "Look," she interjected before Anthony said anything about Samantha's participation in the meeting. "There, something I really need to say."

Two pairs of eyes turned her way.

She fidgeted. "Raymond Wymer is dead."

A peal of laughter escaped from Samantha. "No, Honey. The account is dead unless Anthony manages to charm us back into Wymer's good graces." She shot Anthony a look, her laughter dying when he didn't join in.

Anthony stared at Molly. "What do you mean?"

"You probably should keep quiet about this until the identity of the victim is announced, but there was a murder in River Park last night."

Samantha leaned forward. "Whatever are you talking about? And how do you know? There was nothing on the news last night."

Molly shook her head. "I was called do a sketch for the police last night."

Anthony exchanged a strange look with Samantha. "You had to sketch the body?" he asked.

"No, I had to sketch the suspect. Or at least what a witness described as a suspect."

"How terrible for you." Anthony leaned forward and caressed Molly's hand. "Was the witness able to identify the murderer?"

Molly shook her head. "I can't share any more details. I'm already telling you more than I should."

Anthony nodded. "Yes, of course, thank you for the information."

"I don't know what to say." Samantha broke off a piece of

Molly's croissant. "How can he be dead? We saw him in the office yesterday."

"It was a shock for me too." Molly slid her plate closer to Samantha.

"The guy was a jerk, but he didn't deserve to die." Anthony's fingers tapped the table. "I know this sounds crass, but we have to think about how his death affects us businesswise."

Samantha's cheeks turned a pretty pink. "Maybe Wymer didn't have a chance to report what he thought of the new Marvelous Melon designs. He'll simply be replaced, and we'll keep the account and the art as is."

"That's cold even for you," Anthony said.

Samantha frowned, but then shrugged. "I'm just practical. I'm sad for Wymer's family if he had one—the guy was awful —but we're not emotionally invested."

Molly agreed about the awful part, but nevertheless, life had been lost. Two lives if she counted the first victim. But then, Samantha was just honest. If she'd been a man, nobody would have had any problems with how ruthless and cold she could appear. A man with Samantha's ambitions and drive would be admired for those qualities.

Anthony leaned closer to the table and lowered his voice. "Both of you were probably among the last people to see Wymer alive. The police are going to want to talk to you."

Samantha gasped. "Molly, are you going to be in trouble because of the fight? Would you be considered a suspect?"

Molly laughed, but the sound came out much louder and shriller than she intended. Other patrons turned their way. "Why would I want him dead?"

Anthony looked around the coffee shop. "I don't think we should discuss this now. Let's reconvene first thing Monday morning. If you hear anything else, let us know." He squeezed Molly's shoulder. "Don't worry. People argue all the time without killing each other, the police know that."

Molly nodded and stuffed her cell phone back in her purse. She'd only had a sip of her chai and briefly considered taking the pastry with her. Her stomach convulsed at the thought. Instead, she headed out the door, blinking back the moisture gathering in her eyes. Could she really be considered a murder suspect?

Blinded by the sunshine, she dug out her sunglasses and perched them on her nose. She still felt a prickle in her eyes and set a brisk pace toward her car before anybody caught her crying in public. She knew the police would question her about the fight, but who would kill someone over a work dispute? Of course, in every Masterpiece Mystery episode, if the murder wasn't about love, it was about money.

Footsteps echoed behind her. "Molly, wait." Anthony caught up with her. "Are you alright?" He grabbed her elbow gently.

She quickly blinked away any remaining moisture in her eyes. "I'm fine. Just a little worked up about Wymer's death."

"I can understand that. If you need to take a few days off…."

"Don't worry, I'll be fine." She continued walking and smiled, maybe more like grimaced, over her shoulder. "I'll see you on Monday morning." She turned around, catching a glimpse of a man dressed in a leather vest walking into a store. It was definitely the bouncer from the club.

* * *

LATER THAT AFTERNOON, finally back home, Molly unloaded two bags of groceries from the back of her car. Usually, she'd treat herself to eating out or do take-out on weekends, but today she wanted to curl up on her sofa with a good book or a movie. After already being low on energy from a night filled with restless dreams, the meeting with Samantha and Anthony had drained the rest of her reserves.

The heavy groceries pulled her down as she trudged up the stairs to her condo. She'd loaded up on junk food and chocolate, despite her squirrely stomach. Eventually, the stress would require comfort eating, best to be prepared. She'd also picked up a bottle of vodka. She never drank alone, but she hoped Nina would come over, so they could have a proper pity party. She should really feel sorry for Wymer, not plan her own selfish consolation, but it was hard to feel sorry for someone she'd never liked. Hopefully, his family was doing okay. She'd never bothered to find out if he had any, which made her feel even worse.

As she rounded the corner, she stopped abruptly. A man waited outside her door. His light blue T-shirt stretched over broad shoulders and was tucked into faded blue jeans that hung off narrow hips before skimming down muscular thighs.

Detective Rankin, even hotter in casual clothes than his work suit.

Even from a distance, she felt the invisible strings that always pulled her toward him.

Nothing good could come out of getting involved with Rankin. She knew better, Clark had taught her a harsh lesson. Mixing work and lust resulted in heartache. Especially when she couldn't risk exposing her secret of how the scars really worked. Plus, if Rankin ever saw her without her shirt on, he'd run away anyway.

She sighed and continued walking. If the detective considered her a suspect, he'd hopefully let her put away the groceries before he arrested her.

Rankin pushed off the wall, watching her approach with austere eyes. Yesterday they'd been light green when he'd smiled at Ms. Bunsig. So far, while working this case, they'd been nothing but dark whenever they scrutinized Molly.

She put down the bags and wiped her bangs out of her eyes. "What can I do for you, Detective?"

"I have some questions, Nyland."

With shaking hands, she dug around in her purse for the keys. Avoiding his eyes, she leaned forward to insert them into the lock. The heat of his body surrounded her as she struggled to unlock the door. Rankin stepped closer, crowding her even more. The hairs on her arm stood. Her stomach swirled, and her heartbeat sped up. She'd hoped that geographical distance and time passing would have cooled her hormones' response to the detective. Apparently not.

The same crazy sizzle that traveled through her body each time she was near him when they worked together before had her nerve endings at full attention now. She didn't respond this way to other men. Silently in her mind, Molly counted the reasons for why she shouldn't react this way to Rankin. He was surly, antagonistic, condescending, and…and very male. The sandalwood scent of his aftershave combined with his body heat made her knees buckle.

His hand closed over hers, and she jumped from the crackle of electricity between their fingers. Did he feel this too?

"Here, let me help you." He loomed over her.

"I've got it." Her head connected with his jaw as she jerked back.

"Fuck." Rankin massaged his chin.

Molly rubbed her own sore spot. Correction, the man was surly, antagonistic, condescending, *and* foul-mouthed. She snuck another glance at him through lowered lashes. And still very hot. "I told you I had it."

He glared. "I was trying to help. It looked like you were having some trouble."

Molly turned the key. "If I wanted your help, I'd ask for it." The traitorous door swung open without trouble this time.

"I'll keep that in mind," Rankin said and then blatantly ignored her words by picking up the two grocery bags before he strode into the apartment ahead of her.

Molly opened her mouth to point out she hadn't asked for help with the bags. She closed her lips. No need to aggravate the man further. She still had to answer his questions.

In her apartment.

With just the two of them around.

She closed the door behind her and then walked through the short entryway and into her living room. Rankin was already in the small kitchen, which was separated from the where she was by a granite-covered island. He'd placed the bags on counter.

Molly brushed by him and reached for the bags. "Let me put these groceries away."

Rankin took a quick step away from her. The man learned fast.

She hid her smile by opening the refrigerator to put away the milk. "Can I get you something to drink?" she asked. "Soda, water, beer?"

"What kind of beer?" He tried to peer into the fridge, but the space between the door and the island was too small.

She moved various bottles and jars around. *When had she accumulated all these condiments?* "I got Sierra Nevada, Moose Drool, or Corona Light."

"Corona Light?" He sounded like she'd asked him to drink toxic waste.

Molly straightened. "Yeah, most of my beers are left-overs from friends coming over. I have no say in what ends up in there." She looked over her shoulder and raised her eyebrows.

"I'll have a Moose Drool."

Molly retrieved a bottle of the Montana-brewed brown ale and got a bottle opener from one of the drawers. She quickly handed him the opened beer. Rankin grabbed her wrist before she could pull back.

His thumb caressed the sensitive skin just below her palm. "I make you nervous." It was not a question.

Heat flushed her neck and up into her cheeks. "Why do you say that?" She pulled on her wrist.

Rankin released her but instead took a step closer. "You're skittish."

She felt his hot breath in her hair, the warmth traveling all the way down her body in delicious tingles. "Why don't you have a seat while I put away the rest of the groceries?" She tilted her head toward the sofa in the living room to show where she wanted him.

Away from her.

About as far away as the small living space would allow two people to be in her apartment.

Close by, he was too much of a temptation.

Rankin chuckled and then drank deeply from the bottle.

Molly watched him swallow through lowered lashes. He made even the muscles of his throat working look sexy. "Please have a seat. I'll join you in a minute."

Rankin completely ignored her request. Instead, he walked over to her desk, which was set up right next to the kitchen in the nook that was really designed for a small dining table. He studied her bulletin board, a big jumble of pictures, sticky notes, and receipts.

Molly loved her home office area. The desk was the most expensive piece of furniture she owned, and she polished the solid dark cherry wood every month. Many of her design campaigns had been created when inspiration struck in the middle of the night. She'd get out of bed and work in her pajamas, sitting in her ergonomic chair at the gleaming desk. Two over-sized monitors stood side-by-side, with a state-of-the-art electronic drawing tablet next to them.

She waited for Rankin to make a comment about her technology fetish. Clark had always made fun of her, calling her a techno-geek. Rankin silently moved further into the living room, browsing her bookcases and studying her framed photographs. She waited for a comment, but he only continued his investigation of her knick-knacks and books. Her stomach churned. What conclusions did he make about her from his observations? What kind of judgments?

She shook her head. And why did it matter to her what he thought of her?

Molly hurried to put away the last of the food, filled up a glass with ice water, and joined Rankin, who was now gazing out the window. Her third-floor apartment had a view of the grassy lawn in the courtyard between the condo buildings. A large tree grew just next to the window, and a few of its leafy branches stretched across the pane, creating privacy.

"So, what can I tell you that you don't already know?" Molly asked and sat down in one of the two armchairs that flanked the sofa. No way was she going to take the risk of sitting next to him. Her traitorous body could not be trusted in the vicinity of this man.

Rankin studied the glass of water in her hand and then made a point of glancing at the bottle of vodka Molly had sat on the kitchen counter.

"Hitting the hard stuff early today?"

She frowned at him. "You're not a very good detective if you can't tell that bottle is still unopened."

"Relax." He grinned. "I'm just teasing." Rankin's smile lit his eyes from within and erased half a decade from his face.

Molly couldn't help but smile back. Her stomach fluttered when his eyes turned light green. The light from the window played off the highlights in his dark blond hair. She wanted to reach up and brush back the strands that teased his forehead. She remembered why he'd come to see her and quit grinning like a fool. She cleared her throat.

Rankin studied her, the smile slowly fading from his face. He used the same intensity he'd previously applied to her bulletin board and photographs. The man had changed back into a police detective.

He put the beer down on the coffee table, using a coaster. The bottle was still full. "Let's go back to when you were sketching Mildred Bunsig's description of the man running in the park," he said.

Molly sighed and leaned further back into the chair. The cold of the glass she held sucked the warmth out of her hands. Now she wished she *had* cracked the bottle of vodka open.

CHAPTER 5

*D*es watched Nyland. Worry clouded her eyes, furrowing her brow. With her oval face and small upturned nose sprinkled with a band of freckles, most people would consider her just cute. To him, she had always been beautiful. He'd thought so even before he'd traced those freckles with his fingertips and then his lips.

Did she know how much she gave away, with both her body language and facial expressions? When she'd first seen him in the hallway, her shoulders slumped, and she'd dragged her feet the last few yards. Dressed in cropped jeans, a plain white long-sleeved T-shirt, and wearing very little make-up, she'd looked years younger than she was. He decided he liked her better in casual clothes.

He mentally shook himself. He needed to get in the game, to concentrate on work. The thought came too late. Those freckles and already bespelled him. He shifted in his seat to adjust the tightness of his jeans.

Rankin already knew the woman sitting across from him on the couch couldn't murder someone in cold blood, change clothes, and then go out dancing with friends. Not only did she not have it in her, but more importantly, there wasn't enough time for her to do it. They'd already had a preliminary time of death by the time she came to the station the night before. Zedler had said he got a hold of Nyland at some music joint. So, why did she not want to talk to him? What was she hiding? This was more than just wanting to avoid him because of their past.

"Is there something wrong with my sketch?" She didn't look at him.

He kept quiet. Most people were uncomfortable with silence and would eventually talk. Sometimes they'd slip up and say too much. He glanced around the apartment again. Abstract paintings in bold colors contrasted against plain white walls. Spine after spine of books shared space on pine shelves with framed photos of what he assumed were friends because they seemed to all be the same age as Nyland. There were no pictures of older family members, and the overall impression was one of open space and light. No clutter, he liked that.

She's spent some dough on the home office. He wouldn't mind duplicating her well-polished setup at his own place. The two large monitors and a state-of-the-art printer showed her as a tech-geek, or maybe she needed the equipment for her work at the design firm.

A small hallway led off the living room to two doors. The open one showed a half bath. He assumed the other led into a bedroom. Was Nyland's sleeping area as neat and clean as the rest of her apartment, or did she leave her bed unmade? His pants grew tight again, and he turned his attention—his professional attention—back to the woman across the table.

She fidgeted with her glass but didn't seem inclined to talk any time soon. He could wait a little longer. Last night, Zedler had warned Des to go easy on her. When asked how she knew exactly what questions to ask to get the witness to remember details, Zedler said, "It's no different than a cop knowing facts the evidence doesn't yet show. Call it a gut feeling, forensic instinct, whatever. She just knows when to ask more."

Des' "forensic instinct" said that Nyland knew something about this murder. She may not run around killing people with cult sickles, but she'd been jumpy as hell out in the hallway before she clocked him. He fingered the still sore jaw. He'd probably have a bruise tomorrow. Wouldn't that entertain the guys at the station? Knocked out by a feisty redhead.

She finally met his gaze with those captivating gray eyes. Her hand played with a modest silver necklace. Her v-necked shirt revealed a stream of freckles that started by her collarbone and then trailed down towards the cleft in the middle. How far did they go? In Sacramento, he hadn't had a chance to trace them past her neckline before she stopped him by grabbing his ass, insisting he'd concentrated on other parts of her body. After that, the details got a little hazy. All he remembered was a delicious slick heat embracing his dick.

Des switched position, again, hiding his hard-on. "I was impressed by how well you coached Mildred Bunsig." Fuck, she'd gotten him to talk first. He rubbed his face. Why was he always at a disadvantage with Nyland? She rattled him off his game each time.

"I just got lucky and was able to tease out the details." Nyland shrugged. The shirt neckline slipped, revealing more of the trail of freckles by her collarbone. He caught a quick glimpse of white tendrils gracing her skin, but she pulled on the cloth, hiding her shoulder but revealing more of her cleavage.

He wanted to see more of those white tendrils. Were they some kind of tattoos? "Zedler thinks it's more than luck. He says you're the most skilled he's ever worked with."

A blush crept up her neck, and a small smile played in the corner of her mouth. Des waited for her to speak, but she just played with the necklace again.

He avoided looking at where her hand trifled with the trinket just above the swell of her breasts. Too tempting. He tried a different opening. "How do you decide when to let the witnesses talk and when to ask questions?"

"I guess I just know."

"Could you elaborate?" This crazy attraction didn't make sense. Before he met her, he'd always gone for women who never expected emotional attachment. Why had she distracted him so in California? Why did she still?

She put her glass on the low table between them. "Something in their voice or body language tips me off when they grasp for details."

Just like your voice and body language tells me there's something you're hiding. "And how do you know Raymond Wymer?" he studied her carefully.

Nyland frowned and once again twitched her shoulder before fiddling with the sleeves of her shirt. She sighed and slumped like she'd done in the hallway. "I might as well come clean." She leaned forward, elbows on knees, hands clasped in front.

He averted his eyes so he wouldn't be that creep that looked down her cleavage. He really wanted to, though. *Get it together, Des.*

"Rankin? You okay?"

Shit, she'd been talking while he'd been distracted.

By a pair of boobs. Was he thirteen again?

He ran a hand down his face. Lack of sleep had made him loopy. For the last couple of nights, he hadn't slept more than a few hours. He kept having the bad dream, making himself wake up right before the dreadful moment. Tonight he'd pop some Ambien and catch up on sleep.

Des focused on their conversation again, not looking at anything below her face. "I'm fine." He cleared his throat when the words came out a little rough. "You wanted to tell me something?"

Her eyes darkened, a worry wrinkle displayed between them. "I told you that Raymond Wymer was a client at the company where I work."

"Berker Studios."

She startled. Did she think he wouldn't check her out? Zedler thought her a star with a sketchpad, but Des always covered his bases. At least he did now. There would be no repeats of the disaster that had led to Mitchell's death.

"That's right." She leaned back in the chair. "Wymer was our client. I worked on the designs that would launch a new bubble gum." She paused, squaring her shoulders, looking Des straight in the eyes. "Wymer and I had a big argument yesterday afternoon."

Interesting. "What did you argue about?"

"He didn't like the designs I'd created. He wanted them to be more…old fashioned, I guess you could say." She glanced out the window.

"Do you often argue with clients?" He kept his voice neutral, relief spreading through his veins. A disagreement was her secret? From what Wymer's secretary had told him that morning, the man couldn't have a conversation without getting into an argument.

"No, never. I usually don't lead meetings. Anthony, my boss, is in charge of client relations."

"Why wasn't he meeting with Wymer yesterday?"

"His flight from LA got delayed." Her shoulders sagged. Des waited it out and was rewarded after just a minute or two. "Wymer threatened to have me fired. That's how much he hated the designs."

"Does Berker Studios often fire their employees when a client is unhappy?"

"No, Anthony is very supportive of his staff." She stood and walked across the room to put her glass in the sink, glancing at the vodka.

Was she expecting company? A stab of irritation hit when he imagined her having a guy over for drinks. Des shook his head. He seriously needed some sleep.

She must have been talking while he contemplated her love life because he only caught the tail-end of her words.

"—and then he got in my face after he almost spat on my boot, and I couldn't take it anymore."

"Wait, he spat on you?"

"Not really. Wymer is…was a spitter when he talked. He didn't mean to. But the boots were new." Nyland tilted her head, her eyes imploring him to understand.

He dutifully copied down "spit" and "new boots" in his notepad. "So you were insulted when he spat on your boots and called you names."

"Not insulted. Irritated." She leaned against the counter. "I created the designs according to the specs Wymer gave us."

"How irritated were you?"

"A lot." She hugged herself. "It wasn't my fault that he was unhappy. And it wasn't my fault that Anthony wasn't there to deal with him."

"And this was the last time you saw Raymond Wymer?"

"Yes."

"Were you irritated enough to be angry?"

She frowned. "What do you mean?"

"Maybe you were angry enough to lure him out in the dark park later and kill him."

"No." She took a step toward him. "Wait, what did you just say?" She took another step. "He was killed in the evening?"

67

"That's what the ME tells us."

"But then I'm not a suspect." Her voice rose, and she waved her hands. "I was at the office until late and then with Nina at the jazz club."

He struggled to keep a grin off his face. "Why would we suspect you?"

"You're interrogating me as if I'm a suspect." She glared at him.

"We're just having a conversation." He shrugged, glancing away to hide the glee in his eyes. "Since we'll work together, I need to know more about your drawing techniques." Did she seriously think he'd let her work the case if he thought her a suspect?

"I think I've told you all you need to know about my sketch methods, so if there's nothing else…."

Uh-oh, she'd gone from upset to furious. And fast.

She shook her head. "I can't believe you let me think I was a suspect."

"I didn't let you believe anything. I never mentioned any suspects." Okay, so maybe he'd let her hang there for a little while, but he'd never *said* anything.

"But you implied it."

"When?" To imply you had to speak. He hadn't uttered a word about suspects. "It's not my fault you didn't tell me exactly how you knew Wymer or what had happened. Don't take out your guilt on me."

She crossed her arms and glared at him. Her arms pushed her chest higher. He stood and walked over to her side of the room. Keeping a safe distance, just in case she was about to injury another of his body parts. "Look, I'm sorry if you misunderstood."

"Fine." She still glared, but her posture relaxed a smidgen. Hopefully, he could coax her into an even more relaxed position. He took a step closer and waited, but she said nothing more. Just glared at him, but a little less venomously than before.

Closing the distance between them, he ignored her indigent gasp and pushed a wayward curl behind her ear before tracing her jawline. "I still think about us."

She shifted her stance, trying to lean away from him, but the counter trapped her. "Liar, I bet you haven't thought about me at all until you saw me a few days ago."

He leaned closer, letting his breath caress the delicate curve of her ear. "I'm not the one who bolted out the door that night. I would have preferred our...," he smiled when he felt her shiver, "liaison to continue for a lot longer that night. Preferably in my bed, with a lot fewer clothes."

She whimpered and placed her palms against his chest. Where she touched him, heat seared his skin through his jacket and shirt. This was a terrible idea, but that spark between them was impossible to ignore. She drove him fucking crazy.

He claimed her lips with his. Gently at first, but when she sighed and relaxed against him, fisting his shirt and pulling him closer, he delved deeper. His tongue claimed her mouth, and he groaned as she met him thrust for thrust.

Des untucked her shirt and caressed the smooth skin of her stomach before moving upward.

Nyland froze. Her hands let go of his shirt, and her palms pushed against his chest. "Stop," she whispered and cleared her throat. "Please stop."

He took a step back. "Why? We weren't doing anything we haven't done before?" His pulse raced.

She threw him a withering glare. "That's no reason to do something stupid."

She was right, of course. Becoming involved with her was a mistake. A big career mistake.

But now that he'd tasted her again, he knew he wouldn't

—couldn't—stay away from her. He would leave for now so he could cool down and think of a strategy. A proper approach for how to start operation Seduce Nyland. This thing between them, this sizzle, was far from over. "I'll see you around. Just in case we need to double-check your alibi, give me the names of the people you went to the club with."

Her incensed stare heated up a notch, but she gave him a couple of names. He wrote them down, sure he'd never need them. After a few pleasantries, from his side only, he let himself out. He'd barely gotten all of himself through the opening before she closed the door with more force than necessary.

Still smiling, he unlocked his car. Nyland rattled was a magnificent sight, and it gave him hope that she wasn't as unaffected as she pretended to be. As he got in, he heard the rat-ta-ta of a Harley engine. Des watched with envy as a dude with long dark hair and black leathers parked a vintage Heritage Softail in the space beside him.

At one time, Des had ridden a Sportster but sold it to a buddy when the long hours of the job kept him from riding. The long-haired guy noticed him staring. Des lifted his hand in greeting, and the two of them exchanged a nod before Des drove away. He threw one wistful look at the bike in the rearview mirror before he pulled out of Nyland's parking lot. The owner strode toward the apartment building. If he was one of her neighbors, Des would have a chance to take a closer look at the bike next time.

He sighed. He'd be better off staying away from Nyland, but that one kiss had made that impossible.

* * *

MOLLY HEARD a knock on the door as she was pouring mango juice over ice and a generous splash of vodka. Screw not drinking alone. After Rankin's visit, she not only needed something to take the edge off, she more than deserved it.

What did that obnoxious man want now?

She opened the door, ready to tell him a few choice words, but they died on her lips.

The bouncer from the club stared back at her. His chiseled face looked carved in stone, impossibly smooth and angled planes.

"C...can I help you?"

The man towered over her. "Will you invite me in?" His accent was hard to place. Not exactly foreign, but definitely not local. Canadian? Maybe French-Canadian?

She shook herself loose from his hypnotic stare. "What do you want?" She peered down the hallway. Just her luck. An intimidating stranger knocks on her door and not a neighbor in sight. Not even nosy Mrs. Coolridge was out today.

"How rude of me." He flashed a gorgeous smile, but his eyes still scrutinizing her as if trying to read her mind. "You remember me from Sinful Soul." It wasn't a question.

"I do." Technically better looking than Desmond Rankin, she should be attracted to this guy, but instead, she felt nothing but admiration for how handsome he was. He was like a piece of art made too perfect.

"We were sorry you had to leave early. We want to make it up to you."

Who are "we?" She rechecked the hallway, there was no one else there. Since when did bouncers do house calls? "Okay," she hedged.

"How about we talk inside?"

Persistent. Molly tightened her grip on the door. "You know, now is not a good time. I've got a ton of projects to work on, and I'm expecting an important phone call." It wasn't exactly a lie. She was waiting for Nina to call her. Usually, her friend got right back to her. Must have been one heck of a drinking session last night if Nina was still sleeping it off.

The stranger—who still hadn't said his name—stared at her. The charming smile flashed again. "I should have introduced myself. My name is Tasunke, but people call me Dakota."

Whoa, weirdness alert. "Dakota is not in anything close to your name." She licked her lips.

A genuine smile played across his features, briefly. "Tasunke is a Dakotan word."

"What does it mean?"

"Horse."

Nina and Carol would have immediately looked lower to see if he lived up to his name. She forced her gaze to remain on his face. "So, Dakota, what can I do for you?"

"Since you will not invite me in, I'll just give you these." He handed over two postcards with the red Sinful Soul logo blazed against a black background.

Molly turned them over. The back had VIP written in big red letters.

"We'd like to invite you and a friend to come back next weekend for a show and a meal. Our treat."

"Listen, this isn't necessary. I'm sorry I had to leave early, but I was on call—"

Dakota interrupted. "Please accept this gift. Our establishment is new, and it's important that all of our guests enjoy their visit." He smiled again.

Molly couldn't help but respond. "Okay, well, thanks then." She pulled on the door to close it.

Dakota smacked his hand on the top, forcing it to remain open. "Please, Ms. Nyland. Make sure you come again. We have a great VIP party lined up for next weekend."

"I'll do my best." Molly pulled a little on the door. The

resistance rock solid. "I really have to go now." Her smile felt fake and brittle now.

As if he noticed her discomfort, he quickly let go of the door. "I'll see you next weekend then." He bowed and backed away.

"Bye." She quickly swung the door closed and latched the safety chain.

A chill ran through her, leaving her left shoulder and arm achingly cold. Maybe there had been a draft in the hallway. She rubbed her arms and went in search of a sweater.

It wasn't until she opened her closet that she wondered how he'd known her name. Had Nina told him? Her sweater trailing behind her, she went back into the living room in search of her mobile phone. Better grab the drink as well. This had been one weird Saturday, and the day was only half over.

She really needed to talk to her best friend so they could talk this over. Why wasn't Nina calling her back?

CHAPTER 6

A loud pounding startled Molly awake on the couch. The ice in the three-quarter full glass of vodka and juice clanked as she sat up. Late afternoon sunlight filtered through the leaves of the tree outside her window.

The racket at the door continued, and she rushed across the living room, patting down her hair and wiping moisture from the corners of her mouth. She checked the peephole and then hurriedly swung the door open when she recognized Nina.

Her best friend stepped inside and embraced Molly in a bear hug. "What took you so long? I've been knocking for ages."

"Sorry. Was asleep." She mumbled into Nina's shoulder.

Her friend held Molly at arm's length. "Wow, you must have been working late. Did it have anything to do with the new murder?"

Wymer's death must be all over the news. Two murders would have the reporters buzzing with excitement. Sometimes the local affiliations had to be creative to fill the broadcasting hours. Regular daily coverage reported mostly on new public ordinances and minor nuisances like cracked sidewalks. Luckily the college sports teams were reasonably successful. Half the news hour contained athletes running around on various fields.

Molly nodded. "I still can't believe our town is dealing with two murders so close together."

"I know." Nina walked across the room and sat down in one of the armchairs. "I hate violence of all types, but taking someone's life seems especially gruesome."

Molly smiled at her friend's indignation and sat down on the couch across from her. She grew serious again. "It gets worse, I actually knew the latest victim."

Nina's eyes widened. She came and sat next to Molly. "Honey, you better start from the beginning."

Molly described the fight she'd had with Raymond Wyder and how she made Rankin spill coffee all over himself.

"I'm sorry," Nina said between snorts, "but that is one hell of a first impression."

The corner of Molly's mouth tugged upward. "That's not exactly what I was hoping for." She pushed down the guilt of misleading Nina. It hadn't been her first impression, but she wasn't ready to talk about Sacramento yet. It had been a hellish time after her breakup with Clark. She hadn't been herself for a while after he dumped her.

"Oh, come on. You said the guy was hot. He's sure to remember you now." Her friend wiped tears.

"I'm pretty sure he'll remember me even without the spilled coffee." She swallowed and forced the memory of Rankin's branding kiss out of her mind. "I told him about the fight I had with Wymer."

Nina's face turned serious. "Surely they don't suspect you of murder?"

"Rankin acted like he did, but he wasn't." Heat rushed into

Molly's cheeks when she thought of Rankin's visit. The detective saw too much. Touched too much.

Her friend held up a finger. "Wait a minute. You talked to the detective today?"

Molly gazed out the window. "He was outside the apartment when I got back from meeting Anthony. Said he had some questions about my sketch technique."

"Dang, you've lived a lifetime while I slept." Nina twirled her finger in a circle. "Rewind. How did the meeting with Anthony go?"

"Both Anthony and Samantha are in shock, but they're trying to concentrate on how this will affect the design studio.

"That seems cold."

"They have to think about the financial aspect of this."

Nina snorted. "More like Samantha's looking after Anthony's business, and therefore her own."

Molly shrugged. Nina never liked Samantha, but couldn't say why other than that she gave off a "bad vibe." For the most part, Molly was okay with Samantha. She was a little bit too much...well, too much everything. Too cheerful, too friendly, but it seemed strange to hold that against a person.

"But get to the interesting part." Nina playfully slapped Molly's knee. "Tell me more about this detective. Is he hot? Is he single?"

Another blush heated Molly's neck and face. She should come clean about Rankin's and her history.

A knowing smile played across Nina's lips. "Oh, he *is* hot."

"Stop it. Rankin's good-looking, but extremely obnoxious. I don't know if he's single, but that doesn't matter. The only reason he'd even pretend to be interested is because he's suspicious."

"What do you mean suspicious? Suspicious of what?"

"Suspicious of me."

"But you said he didn't think you were a suspect." Nina frowned.

"At first, I thought he wanted to talk to me because of the blow-up with Wymer, but he asked a lot about my sketching." She rubbed her left shoulder.

"Oh, Honey. Why are you so hung up on not telling people about your gift?"

"You know why." Nina was the only person in Prairie Falls who knew about Molly's curse. Of course, her best friend called it a gift, but then Nina also believed there was goodness in everyone. Molly knew better. Her grandmother and her great-uncle had taught twelve-year-old Molly enough about fanaticism and pain. She pulled at her T-shirt sleeve. "And it's not a gift."

"How can you say that," her friend cried out. "You help people. Thanks to you, loads of criminals have been caught and are now behind bars."

"And I am proud of that, but sometimes I think that if I could trade out my *whatever*, I'd rather just be normal." Or at least whole.

"Honey, you are normal." Nina cradled Molly's hand between her palms. "You just have an unusual ability, and you are generous enough to share it."

The words made Molly feel better, but this was an old argument. Nina grew up with a grandmother and aunts who had the "sight" in various degrees. Predicting the future and interpreting dreams counted as normal. She thought Molly's scars and ability were terrific things. Molly didn't have the heart to tell her how alienated it sometimes made her feel or how cruel people could be when they found out. And how ugly she felt because of the marred skin. "I know you think I should explain about this…this way of knowing when to ask more questions. But it's not that easy."

"Why isn't it?"

"You know why. People treat me differently when they find out."

Nina walked to the fridge and grabbed a bottle of water. "You're not exactly giving people a chance. It's not like you share the information voluntarily. If I hadn't seen your scars in college, I don't think you'd ever have told me."

Molly shifted positions. "I did tell someone once."

Nina sat back down on the couch. "Are we talking about Clark? Because that asshole was an exception to the rule."

True, Molly's ex had been a jerk, but he'd also been her first serious relationship. Insecure and inexperienced, she didn't stand a chance when Clark showered her with attention. She'd fallen hard and still had the bruises. "It wasn't all his fault that we broke up."

"Excuse me." Nina's eyebrows shot up. "You can't seriously take responsibility for the breakup. *He* ruined your relationship."

"We were both young." Molly shrugged.

"Oh no, you don't." Nina shook her head vehemently. "You do not get to make any excuses for him. He was twenty-five—"

"Twenty-seven," Molly interjected.

"Even older. You were in your early twenties. You were young and naive, Clark was not."

"I did act very immature. I almost stalked him at one point." Not a proud moment.

Nina swatted away Molly's words. "Who hasn't driven by a boyfriend's house or walked miles out of their way, hoping to bump into him."

Molly smiled. Guys flocked to Nina. She'd have to beat a few of them off with her designer handbag before she could stalk someone else.

Her friend wasn't done. "That doesn't count. The guy

totally used you for his own gain. You had every right to find him and confront him."

Molly sighed. It had not been her one of her best moments. She hadn't gotten any answers, only more ugly words from her ex. "Let's change the subject."

"We will, Honey, but first I want to say this. I totally understand that you are protecting yourself, but at some point, you need to let someone in again."

"I have let you in. You know almost everything about me."

"Not a friend." Nina executed a massive eye roll. "A boyfriend. A man. A lover. Hell, even a one-night stand would be a good start." Her eyes widened. "That's not a bad idea. You should start with just sex and progress to emotional involvement."

"If I get naked with someone and they see the scars, I still don't have to tell them about all that came with them." Molly threw a pillow at her friend. "Enough about my sex-life."

Nina grinned. "You mean enough about your *lack* of sex life."

Molly searched for something else to throw, but only hard objects were within reach.

Nina smoothed the fabric of the pillow, now in her lap. "Seriously, though. Do you think it would be a big deal to tell Detective Rankin about your ability? Especially if it would help solve two murders?"

Molly shivered. Even though she hadn't seen the bodies, the thought of two deaths so close together upset her. "I told him I was very good at reading body language?"

"And did he believe you?"

Molly sighed again. "I'm pretty sure that he didn't."

"Why do you say that?"

Rankin had nettled her while he was in her apartment. He took up too much space. "I can't exactly describe it, but he has this irritating way about him. Like he doesn't believe anything you say." And the man noticed too damn much. Like how her body reacted to him whenever he was near.

"I guess that would make him a good cop."

"Sure, but he kept on changing tactics. One minute he was super charming, and then the next, he was condescending." *And then he kissed you. And you liked it.* Molly waved her hand in the air. "It's annoying and frustrating, and he's always been like that."

"Please, you think all men who flirt with you are irritating or condescending. It's your defense mechanism." Nina sat up straighter. "Wait a minute, what do you mean 'he's always been that way?' You know him?"

Molly gazed out the window to avoid her friend's sparkling eyes. "We kind of met while I worked a case in Sacramento. We didn't spend much time together." Her face filled with heat.

"But," Nina prompted.

"But there was this one night after we found the perp. and everyone celebrated in the bar."

Nina grabbed her hand and squeezed it. "Honey, you better get to the juicy part of this story quick, or I'm going to combust."

Molly flashed her a guilty look. "I'm sorry I never told you about this. It was right after Clark dumped me, and I was embarrassed about being such a cliché rebound story."

"You had sex with Rankin." Nina stood up, still holding on to Molly's hand.

Molly dragged her back down on the couch. "Well, kind of. It was quick, and I ran away right after."

"Exactly how quick? Did he make you come?" Nina reached for Molly's drink and took a big gulp. "I can't believe you never told me."

"I'm sorry."

Nina dismissed her apology with a wave of her hand. "Never mind that. Answer the question. How was the sex? Quick doesn't have to mean bad."

Molly thought about how much to tell her friend. How could she described the heat that had filled her veins that night, that had made her senses explode? One quick bang against the wall with Rankin had satisfied her more than any lingering sex she'd have with Clark. She finally faced Nina. "It was pretty amazing."

Her friend grinned. "Okay, that almost makes me not mad at you for keeping hot sex a secret from me—well, I'm a little mad—but this so explains why he's flirting with you now."

Molly shook her head. "He wasn't flirting with me." She blushed. Rankin had stared at her cleavage. Maybe he saw the scars? But he'd still kissed her. One amazing hot sexy kiss. If she hadn't come to her senses when he started to take her shirt off, they might have done a lot more.

"Sure he wasn't," Nina said sarcastically. "Did you ever see him again? I mean before now?"

"He called and texted a few times, but I was busy with finals and looking for a job."

Nina shook her head as if she was disappointed. "Let's get back to the topic of why you're so scared to tell anyone about your scars and your intuition."

"I just don't want people to treat me differently."

"What about telling Zedler the whole truth? He'd probably understand."

"I've thought about it, but—"

"But what? What do you have to lose?"

Molly snorted. "Oh, nothing big. My dignity. My reputation. My job with the police department. You know cases that involve clairvoyance in any way are hard to prosecute."

"You're exaggerating. Zedler obviously likes you. He wouldn't stop working with you because you told him."

Molly thought about the weird looks she'd gotten in Santa Clara once she'd broken up with Clark. She was pretty sure he'd told the rest of the department she was a freak. Eventually, the looks had progressed to whispers behind her back, and then snarky comments to her face. She'd been relieved to move out of town. Out of state.

"I don't want to risk it," she told her friend. "Can we please change the subject?"

Nina chewed her lips but then sighed. "Fine, what do you want to talk about?"

"What did you guys do after I left last night? You must have been drinking quite a bit if you had to sleep half the day."

Nina stared at Molly for a few seconds. "You weren't at the club."

"Yes, I was. You and Carol gave me a hard time about Anthony and then about the blond waiter."

Nina shook her head. "I got a text that said you were sorry to leave me hanging."

Molly laughed nervously. Was her friend messing with her? "That was after I left. Zedler called me right as the singer in the fantastic red dress got on stage. I told you I had to leave and then texted you later that night."

Nina took a sip of water. "Wow, we must have drunk more than I thought. I don't remember you being there at all."

Molly frowned. Her friend could party, but she'd never known her to not remember an evening. Usually, Nina was the one that filled in the gaps that others experienced. "How did you think you got my present then?"

"What present?"

Molly tried a smile. "You are just messing with me. I gave you a scarf." She kept her tone light, but her voice sounded brittle.

Nina's brown eyes were solemn. "I'm serious, I don't remember. Are you sure *you're* not messing with me?"

"There's something seriously wrong with that club." Molly described the weird reactions of the waiter and the bouncer when she had tried to leave. And then she told Nina about the bouncer's visit.

"You're so suspicious." Nina patted Molly's hand. "I'm sure I just left the present there since I'd forgotten you came. I'll call them."

There was more to this than alcohol overindulgence. Molly gestured toward Nina's purse. "Call them right now."

Nina rolled her eyes, but looked up the number on her cell phone browser and dialed. After a few seconds someone picked up, and her friend explained about the birthday celebration and the forgotten present.

After she'd finished the conversation, Nina turned to Molly. "Just like I thought. My present is there, I can pick it up any time tomorrow. And they're giving me complimentary VIP passes for any show I want."

Molly sighed. More VIP passes. There was no way she'd be able to convince her friend not to go. Nina loved live music, and she loved going out. And, she loved being a VIP.

And there was no way she'd let her friend go by herself. There was something strange about that bouncer and waiter and something very off about Sinful Soul.

DES CONSIDERED BANGING his head against his utilitarian gun-metal gray work desk. Instead of the coveted Ambien and bed, he'd gone into the station. There was too much riding on this case. The town was in an uproar. Consequently, the higher-ups were more involved than they should be. Des sighed. He hated having the brass looking over his shoulder, second-guessing every decision. He needed to close this one quickly. His reputation and future depended on it. He'd spent hours going over what they had on the case so far, which was pretty much nothing at all.

The crime scene technicians had picked up everything they'd collected from the site where they'd found Wymer's body and worked overtime to process it all. Every cigarette butt, dropped receipt, wad of chewing gum, and used condom had been cataloged and examined. Nothing indicated that Wymer had been engaged in a sexual act just before his death, so the condoms were pretty much a dead end.

He'd requested DNA testing on the chewing gums closest to the body, but Des wasn't holding his breath for any groundbreaking results. The budget was already stretched thin with the overtime everyone logged. DNA testing would not be approved.

He eyed the desk again. A throbbing pain on the outside of his thick skull might make him forget the pulsing headache building inside. He reached for another folder. Maybe if he went over the statements from Wymer's colleagues and family one more time, he'd get a lead.

Fuck, he'd settle for just knowing what to do next.

Other than releasing Nyland's sketch to the media, there wasn't much to go on. Des resisted that option. Sorting through numerous phone calls from the helpful public—and from the not-so-helpful wackadoos—would tie up hours better used chasing down leads. He sighed again. If there were any leads to chase, that was.

Zedler burst through Des' door. Grinning, he waved a memory stick around. "Cheer up, Rankin. We might just have something." As always, the detective looked like he'd slept in his clothes. His hair stood at crazy angles, but the smile on his face was less tired than usual.

A twinge of hope rose in Des' chest. "What is on there?" He nodded toward the stick.

"I went back and talked to the old broad with the dog."

Des kept the comment that Mildred Bunsig probably wasn't that many decades older than Zedler to himself. "And?"

"I took her through her walk with the doggie step-by-step and asked for sights and sounds that she remembered." Zedler paused.

Des wanted to shake the older detective. "And?" He said a little louder this time.

"And...she remembers hearing a motorcycle."

Des sighed, disappointed. "So what. Prairie Falls are filled with those."

Zedler made a big deal out of taking off his rumpled coat and hanging it on the back of the visitor chair. "Yes, but how many of them are Harley-Davidsons." He sat down.

Des snorted. "You're telling me Mildred Bunsig knows the difference between a Yamaha crotch rocket and a chopper?" He shook his head and immediately regretted the motion. The intensity of his headache increased.

Zedler leaned back with a triumphant grin, oblivious to how much more he rumbled his tweed jacket. Des waited a little longer and then gave up when the older detective just gazed back at him, a manic grin on his face.

"Tell me." Fuck, that was the second time he lost the silent game today.

"Her nephew had one before he was convicted. Not only does she know the different sound it makes, but she could also tell it was close to the engine size he used to drive. Apparently, he took his aunt on rides."

Des stared. "Henry drove a Harley?"

Zedler shrugged. "Good thing his mother taped those

ears back when he was a kid. The helmet might not have fit otherwise."

It was Des' turn to grin. "She told you that story." He rubbed the stubble on his chin. He really needed to shave. "Why didn't she tell me about the motorcycle?"

Zedler flicked an invisible speck of dust off his pants. "I guess you're not as charming as I am."

Des widened his smile. "Yeah, that's why. Ms. Bunsig has the hots for you."

"Hey, this ol' man's still got it." Zedler pretended to be offended. "She told me Blitz has never been as friendly to a stranger as he was to me."

"So, it's the dog you charmed, not the owner."

Zedler coughed. "At least she told me, and not you, about the cycle. Maybe you were too busy flirting with Nyland." Mischief glittered in the detective's eyes, but there was also something serious in his gaze. A warning.

Des cleared his throat. He'd already picked up on Zedler's fatherly behavior toward Nyland. "So, there was a motorcycle somewhere in the park that night. How does that help us?"

Zedler pointed to the memory stick. "We have security footage of a Harley-Davidson leaving the parking lot behind the old YMCA."

Des straightened, his earlier exhaustion forgotten. "That lot is closed because of the demolition. Why would someone park there at night?"

"Because they didn't want to be seen?"

Des didn't want to get his hopes up. "Could just be a drug deal or a hook-up."

"Sure," Zedler agreed. "Or it could be someone connected to the murder. Either way, we should talk to this guy. Maybe he saw or heard something."

Des gestured toward the files spread on the desk. "It's

more than I got going here." He reached for the memory stick. "Show me then."

As Zedler scooted his chair around, Des popped the stick into a USB port. Grainy black-and-white footage played. The contours blurry, but if he squinted, he could make out trees and parked cars on a dimly lit street. In the frame's lower corner, a timer ticked by next to the white letters of a date stamp. As the seconds rolled by, a motorcycle zoomed across the screen briefly and then disappeared.

"Wait," Des said and dragged the media player's bar to the left and then clicked frame-by-frame. The Harley jerked across the screen. He zoomed in on the image.

"It's hard to tell the gender," Zedler said. "Odds are it's a guy, even with that long hair. Hard to control that size bike unless the rider has some muscle. The quality is too low to read a license plate, but we could put the image out to the media."

Des stared at the screen. The driver wasn't wearing a helmet. The resolution was horrible, but there was no mistaking the black hair flying behind the rider as the bike picked up speed.

He leaned closer. "What the fuck?"

"What is it? What do you see?" Zedler leaned in.

A few hours earlier, Des had seen that same Heritage Softail in Nyland's parking lot. The guy had even worn the same leathers as on the screen.

Idiot.

He had nodded at the guy, and the rider had looked straight back at Des.

Fuck. This was too much of a coincidence.

And he did not believe in coincidences.

CHAPTER 7

 olly sunk into the chair in her tiny office and slipped off her heels. She usually loved the suede pumps, but today they pinched. Her feet were probably swollen because of the hot air they'd been exposed to during the morning design meeting. There had been a lot of testosterone-driven posturing.

She'd spent most of Sunday working on new ideas for the Marvelous Melon account. In a few days, Berker Studios would present their final designs to the bubble gum company's new marketing manager. At the meeting, she'd presented three different campaign options. As the lead designer, she'd technically been in charge of the meeting, but the rest of the design team contributed input on her work. Anthony and the rest of the management team called these gatherings "creative critiques" and thought constructive feedback from peers would keep every designer at their top game.

Molly didn't mind the meetings. She liked bouncing ideas off other creative people. Their feedback improved her work, and watching others' designs inspired her. This morning had been a nightmare, though. Fred Mueller, the biggest asshole in the office and Molly's nemesis, had obviously spent his Sunday dreaming up ways to sabotage Molly's position as lead designer. Openly scornful when she'd presented her ideas, he'd dropped snarky comments that made the other designers snicker.

She massaged her aching feet and leaned back further in the chair, closing her eyes for a minute. Fred resented her position, but he'd never before been so hostile. What worried her more than Fred gunning for her job, was how little she actually cared. Fighting with someone who ended up dead a few hours later put things in perspective. Keeping her top dog position meant worrying about always staying ahead of the competition—the other designers. Raymond Wymer had constantly obsessed about his rivals, and he ended up dead in a park, leaving no clues as to who had killed him. Momentarily feeling guilty for not caring more about Wymer than she should, she rubbed her temples to chase away the morbid thoughts.

Time to shake off the defeatist attitude.

Time to show Fred she was the better designer.

She got off the chair and hung up her jacket on an antique coat rack in the corner. For a fall day, it was unusually hot, making the air in the office muggy.

Molly cracked the window open, rolled up the sleeves of her blouse, and sat back down to work on the designs. Most of the feedback from that morning had been spiteful, she didn't even bother to write down what Fred had said. But a few useful nuggets had trickled through.

Molly had some self-confidence issues, after a childhood like hers who wouldn't, but she did not lack for confidence in her design skills. Her scars didn't guide her the way they did during a forensic sketch, but she instinctively knew when a piece went in the right direction or when she'd taken a wrong turn. Anthony hadn't been able to attend the morning meeting but left instructions for them to discuss the designs and then finalize their ideas by the afternoon. Molly would show him, and the rest of the team, that she was still a force to be reckoned with.

Two hours later, Molly abandoned the drawing software and drew freehand with charcoal on her sketchpad. The ideas flew through her mind like fireflies on cocaine, and she created quicker by hand. Shades of grey and black revealed designs of teens fighting with vampires and shape-shifters, blowing Marvelous Melon bubbles and using them as shields or weapons. She wiped her bangs back with the back of the hand, holding the charcoal and then rubbed her itching nose.

Although still basic and crude, the drawings perfectly captured the theme and tone she wanted. She cocked her head and studied the designs.

These would work great as graphic novel panels.

Molly ripped off the top sheet and started with a fresh one. She was on her fourth idea when someone knocked on the office door.

"Yes," she shouted without bothering to look up. She needed to capture this last thread of inspiration before it flew out the window.

Someone closed the door behind them.

Several sweeps with the coal later, a few smudges with her fingertips, and she was done. A satisfied grin played across her lips as she raised her eyes to see whoever had entered the office.

Rankin stood on the other side of her desk, a cocky lopsided grin playing across his lips.

Great, just what she needed. A lousy meeting to start the morning. A fast-approaching deadline. And an obnoxious detective to round it all off. Obnoxiously sexy.

"What do you want?' The words spilled gruffer than she'd intended.

The arrogant man kept grinning. "Well, hello to you too."

Molly sighed. "I'm swamped. What can I do for you, Detective?" Even if his words were innocuous, his tone put her on the defensive. Wasn't it enough that he looked like the goddess' gift to women, did he have to act like he knew it?

The detective dragged the spare chair to the desk and sat down, making a big show of straightening his jacket.

Molly looked for the outline of his shoulder holster. Was he carrying? Would he let her borrow the gun to shoot Fred? She shook her head to get rid of the silly thought, but a giggle escaped.

Rankin cocked an eyebrow. "What's so amusing?'

She waved her hand. "Nothing, I'm just thinking of my next career move."

"What are you working on?" He leaned forward and peered at the papers scattered on her desk.

Molly quickly stacked them together. She didn't know why, but she didn't want anybody to see them just yet. Especially not Rankin. She didn't want him judging her work by looking at preliminary sketches.

"They're only half-finished," she said as she pushed the stack to the corner of the desk furthest from the detective.

Quicker than a waxed pencil on glossy paper, he snatched two of the drawings from the pile. "These are great," he said with what sounded like genuine admiration.

"Uh, thanks." Heat climbed Molly's neck and cheeks. What was wrong with her? Every time she came near this guy, she acted like she had a high school crush. She cleared her throat. "So, you are here because—" She left the end of the sentence trailing, but he ignored her.

Peering down at one of the drawings, his brows furrowed.

Molly peeked over the edge of the paper. Before she could get a clear view, the detective shook his head and shuffled the papers. He handed the stack to her.

"Right," he said, running a hand through his hair.

She tried to surreptitiously reorder them to peek at the one he'd studied so intently. Was it the one with the kids fighting the werewolves? She wasn't sure.

Rankin pulled out a notebook. "I have some more questions for you."

"Of course you do." Molly couldn't keep the sarcasm out of her voice.

The detective raised an eyebrow again but didn't comment. "I need you to look at some pictures."

"Why? I didn't see anything related to the murder." Did he doubt she'd been at the club during the time of the murder? Chills snaked down Molly's spine. Nina didn't remember that Molly had been in the club. She couldn't verify her alibi.

"It's not about seeing anything at the scene. It's about the identity of a person of interest."

"Why are you asking me about a suspect?" Her cheeks flushed as Rankin studied her face carefully, and she had trouble meeting his gaze.

"I didn't say 'suspect.' Stop putting words in my mouth." His tone was clipped.

"Come on. When the police say 'person of interest,' everyone knows that means a suspect," Molly countered.

The detective glared. "Could you just look at this picture and tell me if you know the guy?"

She peered at the grainy black-and-white photo he placed on the desk. The resolution was horrible, probably from some kind of security system. "If you still have the digital version, I might be able to clean it up," Molly mumbled as she squinted at the picture. She glanced up.

Rankin's eyes stared at her with bright green eyes.

She jerked back at the intensity in his gaze.

"Just look at the picture and tell me if you recognize anybody," he said through gritted teeth.

Confused, Molly studied the image again. She could make out parked cars and what looked like someone riding a motorcycle. She tilted her head and leaned in. Wait a minute. That leather vest, that long black hair, those defined biceps. "I'm not sure," she hedged, putting her right index finger on the picture. "This could be the bouncer at the club I went to with my friends on Friday night."

"Are you sure?" Rankin fixed her with his gaze.

Molly frowned. "I just told you I wasn't sure. Besides," she pointed at the date and time stamp in the lower corner, "how could it be him if he was working at the club that night?"

"Are you sure he was at the club the entire time you were there?"

"No, but he guarded the door when I entered, and I saw him again when I left."

"And how long were you in the club?"

"For about forty-five minutes."

"How sure are you about the time?"

His patronizing tone grated her nerves. "Let see," she pretended counting off on her fingers. "I got in line. I showed my driver's license. I met my friends. We chatted for a while. I ordered a drink." She paused, remembering the comments Nina and Carol had shouted after the hot server.

Rankin immediately pounced. "You ordered the drink, then what?"

"And then the show started. And then Zedler called me."

"Did you at any time during the show this see the bouncer?"

"No, but I assume Dakota stayed by the door."

"Dakota? You know his name?" Rankin leaned forward. Scribbling in his notebook like a secretary on speed.

She frowned. "I didn't that night, but he came to my apartment."

He paused his pen. "When was this?"

"What is this about?" Molly asked. "I'm kind of working on this case too, you know."

Rankin cocked that arrogant eyebrow again and just studied her.

Irritating specimen of a male. Irritatingly *hot* male specimen.

Maybe she wasn't officially working the case. "Well, I'm involved," she said out loud.

His brow shot up higher.

She realized how "involved" could be interpreted and blushed. "You know what I mean. I'm helping," she clarified, opening up her arms for emphasis.

Rankin gazed back down at his pad and continued writing. "Just answer the questions, please."

He treated her like a suspect, okay, maybe more like a witness, but she deserved the respect of a colleague. "What was the question?' She snipped.

"When did this Dakota come to your apartment?"

"He stopped by on Saturday, just after you had left." She might have imagined it, but Rankin's shoulders seemed to relax marginally.

"What did he want?" His tone kept its curtness.

Molly explained about the VIP passes and the invitation to the special show.

"How long did he stay at your apartment?" His eyes bore into hers, and the damned flush crept up her cheeks again.

"He didn't stay at all. I didn't let him in." She pressed her palms to her cheeks, wishing she could open the window wider. The air in her office was too hot.

Rankin leaned back in the chair, crossing one ankle over the opposite knee. "Why not? You know him well enough to know his name. Why not invite him in?" Anger laced his voice.

"I've met him twice, three times if you count coming and going on Friday night. He's the one who insisted telling me his name."

"What's his last name?"

"I have no idea." She crossed her arms. "Dakota is his nickname, by the way. His real name is Tasunke, I think. It means 'horse' in the Dakotan language."

Rankin's eyes flashed. "So, you chatted for quite some time, but you wouldn't let him in the apartment."

Seriously? She was starting to really hate his tone, patronizing, and disbelieving. "I'm done answering questions." She leaned back in her chair, staring defiantly.

"Tell me what's going on, or leave."

Her death stare didn't rattle him. "Just one more question Ms. Nyland. Have you ever met Dakota...Tasunke before?"

She glared at him a bit longer. Still no effect. "The first time I ever saw him was on Friday night when I showed him my ID to get into Sinful Soul."

Rankin studied her for a while and then nodded. He slipped the pad and pen into the inner pocket of his jacket. "Thanks for your cooperation, Ms. Nyland."

Why the formality, all of a sudden? When had she been relegated to the civilian side of this murder case? On Saturday, he'd referred to her by her last name only, the way cops usually addressed each other. The way he'd always spoken to her in Sacramento. She opened her mouth to tell Rankin off, but another knock on the door interrupted her. "Come in," she said.

Anthony breezed in. "Molly, we need to strategize before the next meeting." At the sight of Rankin, he stopped suddenly and flashed his client-smile. "I'm sorry to interrupt,

I didn't know you had a visitor." He held out his hand. "I'm Anthony Berker, owner of this firm and Molly's boss."

Molly rolled her eyes. Just what she needed, more testosterone in her tiny office.

* * *

DES SHOOK BERKER'S HAND. What a fucking liar. The guy knew Nyland had a visitor, alright. Berker's fake smile and insincere tone gave him away. His clothes were too expensive and his hands too soft. Des squeezed a little extra during the handshake.

The douchebag returned the pressure, the fake grin widening. "And you are?"

"Detective Rankin, Prairie Falls PD." Des squeezed harder. The guy's grill blinded him. Bleach?

And how much gel had he put in his hair? The whole tube?

Berker slipped his hand out of Des' and half-sat, half-leaned against the corner of Nyland's desk. He crossed his arms, barely creasing his uber-starched shirt. "Oh, the police. This must be about Raymond then. We are so sorry to have lost him." He shook his head and turned toward Nyland. "Molly was incredibly distraught, weren't you, Honey?"

Des flicked a quick glance at Nyland. Didn't she mind the boss using an endearment? She should.

"Sure," Nyland said. "It's always sad to lose someone."

"Of course it is." Her boss patted her arm. Why did the guy loom over her like that? He could see right down Nyland's cleavage. The neckline of her blue silky-looking blouse had too many buttons open.

Berker turned back toward Des. "I hope you find who did this horrible thing soon." His lips stretched in another fake smile. "If there is anything we can do, don't hesitate to ask." He kept his hand on Nyland's arm.

Des wanted to punch him.

Nyland frowned and surreptitiously pulled her arm out of reach. Good girl.

She turned toward Des. "Do you have any other questions for me, detective?"

The title irritated him. Molly should use his name. They worked together. He wanted—needed her to say his name. He shook his head. It wasn't his business if she was involved with her boss. The thought made him cringe, but only because Berker was such a douchebag. Nyland could do better.

He glared at Berker, and then Nyland. Both of them looked back at him expectantly.

Fuck, what was the question? Whether he had any more questions, right. "No, not at this time. Thank you, Ms. Nyland, you've been much helpful. Could you walk me to the elevator?"

"Our office manager can show you out, Detective." The Berker jerk smirked. "Although it isn't hard to find on your own."

Des stood and stretched, making sure his gun flashed briefly as he pretending working out a kink in his neck. It was a cheap shot, but this guy needed to know who would win in a pissing contest. "I need to confer with Ms. Nyland about the case." He paused and then added, "in private." He glanced over at Nyland. And caught the end of her eye roll. Des grinned.

Berker pushed away from the desk and puffed out his chest.

Nyland's boss was a few inches shorter than Des. His grin stretched wider.

"No problem." The guy glared at him. "I'll wait for you

here, Molly, and review your designs while you walk the officer out."

"Detective," Des corrected.

"My bad." The guy smirked. "Detective."

Nyland bent down under her desk and rumbled around while muttering under her breath. Finally, she stood, grabbed the stack of drawings, and handed them to her boss. She had to brush up against the jerk to get around the desk. Des gritted his teeth.

He held the door open for Nyland as she exited before him. She strode down the hall, and he followed, watching the gentle sway of her hips in a straight short skirt. It looked good on her, but he liked her better in the t-shirt and jeans she'd worn on Saturday.

She shot him an irritating look over her shoulder and almost caught him staring at her ass.

He coughed into his fist as a cover.

"What is it you wanted to talk about?" She asked.

"When do you plan to use the VIP passes?"

She stopped and faced him. "Why?"

"Just humor me." He shot her his most charming smile, wattage dialed to max.

She quirked an eyebrow. "Fine, my friend Nina and I are using them on Friday. Our friend Carol might go as well."

"How many passes do you have?"

She crossed her arms, pulling the fabric of her shirt tight against her breasts. "Again, why?"

He loosened his collar. "Just answer the question."

She sighed and rolled her eyes again. "We have four of them."

"Great, then you're bringing me as your date."

"Excuse me?" Her jaw hung open.

"You said you wanted to help this case. You have an in at the club, which I need. So we'll pretend to go on a date."

Her mouth opened and then closed. She swallowed.

"Great, I'll pick you up at eight on Friday." After a quick peck on her forehead, he headed to the elevators. Of course, he knew his way out of the building.

He pictured Berker's reaction to Nyland going out with Des and grinned again.

Punching the elevator button, he looked back down the hallway. Nyland was still standing there, but then shook herself and headed back toward her office.

The elevator dinged, and a tall blonde stepped out. Her clothes were cut very tight. In her hand, a box of pastries dangled from a string.

"Well, hello," she gave him the once-over before flashing an inviting smile. Her teeth were as blinding white as Berker's. Maybe the company had a dental group discount. Nyland's teeth weren't bleached reflectively white, though. They were the color a smile should be, and one of her front teeth was slightly crooked, it was cute.

She'd looked adorable when she in anger had grimaced at him. Especially with the charcoal smears all over her forehead and nose. He bet Nyland's hair was natural too. As opposed to this woman who obviously bleached more than just her teeth.

The woman cocked her hip, and her top slid down, revealing even more skin. "And who might you be?"

Compared to this display, Nyland's unbuttoned blouse belonged in a convent.

Des appreciated the view, even if the boobs were obviously fake. He caught the elevator door before it closed. "Just on my way out."

"Don't leave on my account," she pouted.

Des sighed quietly. Her flirting was not subtle, but she might have some information about Wymer.

"I'm not," he assured her. "I'm working the murder of your client and just had some questions for Ms. Nyland."

Her eyes grew wider and rounder. "Oh, you're a detective." She took a step closer. "You know, I worked with Wymer too. Maybe you have some questions for me" She glanced up through lowered lashes.

He played along. "I have to get back to the station, but why don't you give me your contact information, Mrs…?"

She put her hand on his arm. "It's Miss, but you can call me Samantha. I'll give you my card." She sauntered over to the reception desk and leaned over. He bet she could reach just fine without having to stretch that far. The elevator buzzed, and he removed his arm. The doors closed.

The receptionist tossed her hair as she walked back, hips wiggling and chest bouncing. The card she handed him had no last name, just "Samantha" and her phone number and email.

"I put my cell phone on the back," she said. "Call me anytime."

Des punched the elevator button. Luckily the carriage was still there. He quickly stepped in. "I'll do that," he grinned.

Samantha smiled back, but as the elevator doors closed, her friendly expression faded, and the look she gave him turned cold.

He shuddered.

The office manager's flirtations were as fake as the rest of her.

CHAPTER 8

*D*es half-filled his cup with the station's abysmal coffee and then topped off with as much cream as he could fit. He needed the caffeine after a workweek of chasing down leads that went nowhere but couldn't stomach the taste of coffee anymore. Rubbing his once-again-unshaved jaw and carrying the cup with him down the hallway, he looked forward to the upcoming evening.

He shouldn't. He needed to focus on this case, and on figuring out the connection between Prairie Falls and Mitchell. However, as much as he told himself to avoid Nyland, his body reacted just the thought of her. If only he could stop thinking about that one hook-up they'd had in Sacramento.

Shaking his head, he told himself to stop thinking about sex with Nyland and concentrate on the case. Tonight wasn't a date, it was for the job. And after the unproductive week, he'd just had, he needed the visit to actually lead to something.

Something on the case, that was.

Not something between him and Nyland.

It surprised him how much he liked seeing her face flushed each time he pissed her off. The freckles on her nose actually glowed with indignation. He wondered if that was true for the specks on the rest of her body. Not that he would find out tonight. Because they weren't going on a date. Or having sex. Or anything other than working together.

With that firmly settled in his mind, he rapped his knuckles on Zedler's door. He heard a muffled "come in" and entered an office where years of accumulated paper cups, take-out containers, and fast food wrappers competed for space with file folders and sticky notes. Des moved a stack of unopened envelopes, several broken pencils, and a bus schedule from 1992 from one of the chairs before he sat down. He knew better than to ask about the items. No doubt they were integral to some case Zedler was or had been working on. He sipped his coffee as he waited for the other detective to finish what he was doing. At the moment, he seemed to be looking for something in a shoebox.

"Dang, it was here the other day," Zedler mumbled before chucking the box on a pile of seemingly unrelated items in the corner.

"Need help finding something?'

"Nah, it's just a hunch I have. Probably won't pan out to anything."

Des doubted that very much. One of the first things his new colleagues had told him was to listen to Zedler's hunches. They often ended up breaking or making a case. Zedler's mind contained unlimited details from cases he'd worked or read about. The jumble in his office was related to those cases, filed according to some system only the older detective understood. Nobody dared to touch the troves of crap, not even the cleaning crew. They only entered to empty the garbage and occasionally wipe off the desk. If it could be found.

Zedler glanced at the spot where the shoebox had landed before turning toward Des. "So, the lieutenant still won't let you bring the motorcycle guy in for questioning?"

"She says there's too little to go on, and we might scare him away if we tip him off to having the footage."

"But you don't agree?"

Des shrugged. "It doesn't matter what I think."

"Sure it does. You're the lead detective. When the shit hits the fan, the brass will make sure your ass gets fried, not theirs."

"Well, my ass will be cooked even more if I went against orders from those higher up than me. The LT has a point, though. The guy seems pretty transient. He hasn't had a steady job or address in a while and seems to drift from town to town." Des studied Zedler over the cup as he sipped his lukewarm, slightly coffee-flavored, cream. It really was disgusting. He put the cup down on the edge of the desk.

"Alright, I get it. You're not the type to complain about things you can't do anything about. I respect that but tell me what you're doing next. This case is going nowhere fast, and we're running out of options."

Des debated whether he should include the older detective in his plans. Everything he knew about Zedler so far, and his own instinct, told him the more experienced detective wouldn't mind bending the rules a little. "Okay, so maybe I'm going to Sinful Souls tonight, as a civilian, to have a look around. And just maybe I'll find an opportunity to chat with the bouncer."

Zedler leaned back in his chair. "I thought tonight's event was VIPs only."

Des quirked an eyebrow in question.

The other detective held up his hands. "Okay, so I've snooped around the club a bit too, ever since we found out where the guy works."

"No worries, I won't tell." Des grinned. "It just so happens that a friend has some VIP passes and is kindly letting me use one of them."

Zedler studied him for a few seconds. "I don't want to tell you how to do your job. But isn't this the kind of thinking that got you in trouble in Sacramento."

"This is nothing like Sacramento." Des stood up and would have paced had there been room in the office to do so.

"Sit down. I'm not judging you. I'm just stating a fact." Zedler's tone was firm.

Des sat down and took a few breaths before answering. "Look, what happened in Sacramento is not something I want to talk about."

"Noted."

"Besides, you just told me you'd checked out the club yourself."

"Digging around in a few registers and databases is hardly the same as waltzing into the joint, starting to ask questions."

"I'm not going to call attention to myself. I just want to check the place out." Famous last words, Des thought to himself. That was pretty much what he'd told himself in Sacramento as well.

"Alright, but at least bring someone to cover your back. Don't go in alone."

"I'm bringing someone from the department." Des squirmed. He couldn't lie worth a shit. "Well, kind of."

Zedler frowned. "Who's going with you?"

"The sketch artist, Nyland." Des watched Zedler closely. He didn't want to let it show that he and Nyland knew each other from before. It was already evident that the other detective was protective of her.

Zedler's jaw tensed. "Molly is going with you?"

"More like I'm going with her. She's the one with the VIP

passes and was already going with a bunch of friends. I'm just tagging along."

The seconds ticked by while Zedler stared at Des. "Molly's one of my favorites. If she gets hurt, in any way, I'm coming after you."

"Noted."

* * *

MOLLY SANG along with the radio as she drove home on Friday afternoon. Except for the stressful Monday, it has been a good week. Marvelous Melon's new VP of marketing had loved the Urban Fantasy designs. Before they met with the client, Anthony had praised her drawings in the internal design team meeting, and she had thoroughly enjoyed the bright red shade creeping across Fred's face. She chuckled to herself in the middle of the old Kool and the Gang song blasting from the car's speaker. Celebrate good times, indeed.

As she turned into her condo's parking lot, her smile faded a little. It was time to get ready for her non-date with Detective Rankin. She was nervous. And angry about it, which made her anxious. She hadn't heard a peep from him all week. Not that he had to call her.

It wasn't like it was a real date.

But still. A phone call would have been polite, though.

At least to confirm that they were still on.

She'd even bought a new outfit. Not to impress the detective, of course. No, the dress was not for anybody but herself. Or maybe the blonde waiter.

She'd gone to Nina's boutique to pick it out, and her friend had riled her mercilessly about having a date with Rankin.

"It's not a date," Molly had insisted.

"Of course not." From behind her shoulder, Nina grinned at her in the mirror reflection as she tugged and twisted to get the gauzy mocha-colored blouse to hang as she wanted it on Molly's torso. "But I still want you to look your absolute most gorgeous sexy self on your non-date."

The top was low-cut and tight over the bust, then flared out in pleats before ending just below the hips. It was long-sleeved, of course, but with very sheer material. Molly worried her scars would show through, especially if the club would have black lights tonight.

Nina had assured her they wouldn't. When it came to fashion, Molly trusted her friend impeccably. With the top, she'd be wearing tight, but stretchy, faux suede trousers. Even Molly had to agree that the outfit suited her. Both her coloring and her figure were shown off to their best.

She pulled in to her parking spot and exited the car. As she opened the back to pull out the bag of groceries she'd picked up on the way home, she heard a low growl behind her. Slowly, she turned around.

A huge shaggy sand-colored dog sat a few feet away, watching her with eerie amber eyes. It growled again, a low craggy sound that resonated in Molly's chest.

Shit, she thought. She so did not want mauling by a giant canine to be the ending of this week or her life. "Nice doggie," she said while slowly backing away.

It sounded weak and pathetic. The animal would pick up immediately on how scared Molly was.

She'd backed away as far as she could and was now flat against the back of her car. Was it even a dog? It seemed too big. A coyote, maybe? Her mind flashed on the animal she'd seen the night she'd driven out to the farmhouse. But this couldn't be the same dog or coyote, could it?

It didn't really matter what kind of animal it was. What Molly should be concentrating on was that its teeth were big enough to rip her throat out, and she needed to prevent that from happening at all cost.

The animal seemed to sense her precarious situation. It grinned, its tongue lolling out of the mouth. Molly thought she detected a triumphant gleam as it crouched down on its front legs. Ready to attack.

She closed her eyes and wondered if any of her neighbors were home. How loud would she have to scream for someone to hear her?

The dog growled louder.

Molly couldn't open her eyes. Her whole body shook as she tried to make herself smaller by pressing against the back of the car. Maybe she could flip backward into the trunk and close it before the animal leaped for her throat. It wasn't a good plan, but it was the only one she had at the moment.

Suddenly, she heard an engine approaching. She opened her eyes and saw that the dog had heard the same sound. Its head turned toward the road, then cocked to the side as if to listen better.

A red sedan turned into the lot and parked a few spots down from Molly's space. She held her breath, waiting for what the dog would do.

The massive beast growled one more time at her and took a step toward her. When Molly flinched, it grinned big before turning around and bounding into the bushes.

In a blink, it disappeared as fast as it had appeared.

Molly let out her breath in a big whoosh. Her lungs expanded as they greedily sucked in oxygen.

What just happened, she wondered. Did that dog just psyche her out, or was it really about to attack?

She looked toward where the red car had parked. Its driver was already halfway down the parking lot toward one of the side entrances of the apartment building. He was talking on a cell phone and probably hadn't even noticed the giant dog.

Or coyote, whatever. Molly peered after the beast to see if she could tell where it had gone too, but there was no trace of it.

She grabbed her groceries and headed toward her own entrance on shaky legs. Once she was inside her own apartment, she relaxed a little but still felt shook up. Her hand trembled as she looked up and dialed the number for animal control.

"I'd like to report a feral dog or maybe coyote incident," she said as a male voice answered on the other line.

"Well, which is it?" The guy who'd introduced himself as Steve wanted to know.

"I don't know, I was just attacked by a large yellow beast in the parking lot of my apartment complex, and I'd like you to take care of the animal before it hurts someone."

"Ma'am, if you're hurt, you need to hang up and dial 911 or seek attention at the closest medical facility."

"I'm not hurt, but I could have been." Molly heard the agitation in her own voice.

"Is the dog still in the parking lot?"

"No, it ran away."

"So you want to report that you saw a dog but that it didn't attack you?"

Why did male condescension always raise her hackles? Actually, females who talked down to her bothered her too. "Listen, Steve, this dog is dangerous. Just because I didn't get hurt doesn't mean it won't attack another person."

She heard a sigh on the other end of the line. "I'll write out a report, ma'am. But there isn't much we can do if the animal is already gone from the scene. Unless you know who the owner is."

Molly said she'd never seen the animal before but gave

Steve enough information to fill out his report, then hung up. She hoped nobody got attacked by the animal. If something happened though, she'd feel better that there was a written account of her trying to prevent it.

Her legs were still shaking as she made her way to the bathroom. Hopefully, a long soak in hot soapy water would revive her. Maybe she'd even shave her legs, even if she'd be wearing long pants. And it was a non-date.

An hour later, Molly stared at her reflection and debated whether or not to apply the glittery body powder that Nina had recommended. According to her friend, a sweep of the brush over her collar bones and down the valley between her breasts would do wonders for her cleavage. Molly wasn't sure she wanted any extra sex appeal or the attention it might bring. *I've never had it. Would I know what to do with it once I did?*

It might be as intoxicating as alcohol or getting a superpower. She should probably practice in isolation before taking it out in public.

What the heck, she'd live a little dangerously tonight. Besides, Carol and Nina oozed sex appeal. They'd know what to do if she got herself into trouble.

She swept the oversized brush across her clavicles but left the cleavage unsparkled. Even with her friends as wingwomen, it was probably better to start out slow.

As she put away the various bottles and jars, her cellphone rang in the adjoining bedroom. She retrieved the phone to see Nina's name displayed on the screen.

"Are you checking up on me?"

Croaky laughter trickled down the line. "Did you use the powder like I told you to?"

"I now have the collarbones of a *Twilight* vampire."

"Good girl." Nina's voice sounded faint.

"What's going on? You don't sound very well."

"Promise me you don't think I'm bailing on you or setting you up, I know how paranoid you can be, but I have to cancel for tonight."

"Are you okay? Do you need me to come over?"

"I'm fine, or at least I will be once my body purges whatever I ate earlier today to give me food poisoning."

"I'll call Rankin right away to cancel."

"No. I won't allow it."

"Allow it? What are you going to do? Fight me like a Ninja? I have a key to your apartment, you know."

Nina giggled. "Don't make me laugh. It hurts my stomach too much. Look, please just go out and have a good time. If not for you, then do it for me."

"Do you have what you need to get better? Bland food? Fluids?"

"I'm fine. Carol is actually here. We ate at the same lunch buffet, and she's feeling a little queasy, but so far she hasn't thrown up. She can take care of me and get me supplies."

"Does that mean she's ditching me too?"

"Sorry, Honey. You're on your own with the sexy cop tonight."

"If you didn't sound so pathetic, I'd come over there and kick your asses for standing me up."

"Ouch, you're doing it again," Nina said as she laughed. "Just have a great time and call and tell me all about it tomorrow."

"Okay, get better."

Molly hung up the phone. Should she call Rankin and cancel anyway? It was already after eight pm, so it was very late notice. But, it wasn't like he needed her there anyway. He just wanted to get into the club. She could explain when he got to her apartment and just give him one of the passes. Happy with her decision, she returned to the bathroom to put away the rest of the make-up paraphernalia.

She'd just finished wiping down the sink when her door-bell rang. That darn glitter had gotten all over the bathroom. She knew it was a bad idea.

After tossing the sponge into the bathroom cabinet, she walked over to the front door. A quick check in the peephole revealed Rankin. A totally new version of the detective. He wore a black collared shirt tucked into dark pants. And the absence of his regular five-o'clock shadow revealed an attractive cleft in his chin.

Trouble.

This new version of Rankin could lead to *major* trouble.

She leaned her forehead against the door for a few seconds and took several deep breaths.

"Hello, Nyland. I can tell you're on the other side of the door," Rankin said in a sing-song voice.

Oh goodie. The new and improved detective might look like an Adonis but only had to open his mouth to ruin the image. Not that it mattered what he looked like. She wasn't going out with him. She was just handing the VIP pass over and then heading over to Nina's. Or maybe just stay home, since her friend was bound to heckle her to go to Sinful Soul.

"Hold on. I'm just getting the lock now," Molly said and opened the door.

Rankin had that obnoxious grin on his face again. Didn't he ever get tired of flashing that?

The grin drained from his face as she opened the door wider. Why was he staring at her? Was there something wrong with her outfit? She pulled on her left sleeve.

Rankin roused himself from whatever trance he'd fallen into. "Wow." He gave her a once-over. "You clean up well."

Molly sighed. And the cocky cop was back. That didn't take long. "You're early," she said.

He just smiled again and marched into her apartment. "I

thought we'd go over our cover before we leave. Besides, I didn't know you'd get all dressed up. I figured it wouldn't take you very long to get ready. You seem like the low maintenance kind."

Molly just stared at him. Was he for real? She couldn't tell whether she should be offended or take his words as a compliment. She decided on the former.

"Doesn't look like you opted for your standard outfit either." She made a show out of crossing her arms and giving him a once-over too. "If I didn't know better, I'd say those were designer duds."

Rankin actually blushed. "Yeah, well. I'm undercover." He cleared his throat. "Got anything to drink?"

"Same options as the last time you barged in here." Molly closed the door.

The undercover detective helped himself to a beer from her fridge. "Do you want anything?" He shot over his shoulder as he dug through the bottles.

"I'm good, thanks." Safer not to mix alcohol and Rankin this time around. If she drank, she might pay attention to only his looks and forget about his personality. Her body was already humming with appreciation over how the black slacks stretched over his taut ass. She cleared her throat. "Listen, we need to talk."

"Whoa, it's a little early in the relationship for those words, don't you think?" Rankin was digging through a kitchen drawer, probably looking for a bottle opener. He stopped abruptly and turned around, face flushed. "Not that we're in a relationship or anything."

Awkward.

She rubbed her shoulder. "I didn't think we were," she retorted, which seemed to relax him. He resumed digging around in the drawer. Molly sighed and got the magnetic opener from the refrigerator door. "Here you go."

"Thanks." The sound of beer fizzing permeated the kitchen.

"Nina and Carol are both sick. They can't go tonight."

Rankin studied her while taking a sip of the bottle. He swallowed. "Sorry to hear that. *You're* not planning on bailing on me, are you Nyland?"

She avoided his gaze. "It's not like you need me to come with you. I'll probably just be in your way."

He took a few steps toward her. Crowding her against the small kitchen island. "You won't be in my way," he said. "And I do need you."

She felt her brow beading up. When did the heating come on? His eyes had her spellbound. Tonight they were so dark they appeared brown.

He reached up and brushed a strand of bangs off her forehead. Extending the caress down her temple. Past her ear, tracing her jaw with his finger.

Her legs melted.

He leaned forward.

She could feel the heat of his breath on her face. Was he going to kiss her again? Her breath hitched. She closed her eyes.

He tweaked her nose.

Her eyes flew open, only to see him turning away with a smug smile. Bastard.

"Sorry, couldn't resist."

Her palm ached to slap the grin off his lips.

He took another sip of the beer. "I do need you, though. You're my cover story."

Molly shot daggers at him with her eyes, she seriously wanted to put her hands around that self-satisfied throat and squeeze until he suffocated. Let's see how smug he was then.

"I'm not going," she said and walked out of the kitchen. She needed some space between the two of them. Her traitorous body still hummed in anticipation of a kiss that could never happen. That is, could never happen again.

"Look, I'm sorry I teased you." He actually sounded contrite. "If you won't do it for me, do it for this case. Do it for Zedler."

She paused. "What do you mean? What does he have to do with this?"

"We are in desperate need of a break on this case. The lieutenant is breathing down both our necks, but won't let us bring the bouncer in for questioning. This may be the only chance we have to chat with him."

Molly frowned at the desperation she heard in Rankin's voice. "I didn't know Zedler was that involved in the investigation. I thought you were the lead."

A bitter smile appeared on his lips. "I am. But I'm also the new guy, and until I've proven my worth, the uniforms still go to Zedler rather than me."

For a short second, she allowed herself to sympathize, then she remembered the nose tweak. "I'll give you two of the passes. I'm sure someone else would be happy to go with you. You're a good-looking guy. You should be able to find a date on short notice."

"You think I'm good-looking?" That horribly smug grin was back.

"Don't let it go to your head. It's big enough already."

He walked toward her. "Look," he said, then stopped when she instinctively stepped away. "What can I do to make you come with me?"

She pretended to think for a while. "How about…" she dragged it out a bit longer. "How about you stop asking me questions about my sketching techniques and just accept that I'm good at what I do?"

"I never doubted you were good. I've seen your forensic sketches and your design work. They're all superb."

She flushed with pleasure. "Then, why the third degree about my methods?"

He studied her face for a while.

She held his gaze.

"You're hiding something from me, and it's in my nature to figure out what it is."

"Everybody's got secrets. I'm sure there are loads of things you don't want me to know about you."

A cloud quickly passed over his features. He took a swig of the bottle. "Fair enough. As long as whatever it is you don't want to tell me has no bearing on this case, I'll stop asking questions."

She opened her mouth to assure him of the insignificance of her secret, but he held his hand, stopping her words. "I decide what's relevant, though. You kept your connection with Wymer a secret."

"That's not true. I told you I knew him before I sat down with the witness."

"But you kept your fight to yourself."

"I was in shock. I told you the next day."

"Only because I came to your house asking about it."

"I would have told you, or Zedler eventually."

Electricity crackled between them as he continued glaring at her.

"Fine," Rankin finally said. "Keep the details to yourself. I'll stop asking about them. Do we have a deal?'

"Deal," Molly said and went into the bedroom to get her purse and coat. She took a moment to lean back against the wall and breathe deeply.

Should have skipped the glitter powder.

CHAPTER 9

*D*es parked his black TTS Roadster a few blocks from Sinful Soul. He got out and walked around the car to open the door for Nyland, but she'd already slipped out on her own by the time he got there. Obviously still pissed about his nose tweaking, she hadn't said a word on the ten-minute ride to the club.

He hadn't meant to tease her, but when he touched her face, and her lips parted he'd grown so hard, he forgot to breathe. The urge to taste her was so strong it scared him. The nose tweak was the only save he could think of, or he would have dragged her into the bedroom and torn her gauzy blouse to shreds.

The moment she'd opened the door, he knew he was in trouble. Her outfit wasn't as revealing as what the office assistant at Berker Studios had worn, but it showed off her full breasts to perfection. He'd been hard the instant he saw her, and things had only gotten worse from there.

The only way to discharge the attraction between them had been to piss her off. Then, he still had to count backward from a hundred twice before he could turn around and face her.

"This is a sweet ride," she said now, "but you know it isn't going to work for you when the snow comes."

He hid his smile. Of course, Nyland would find something about his car to criticize. His pride and joy. "I'll put all-weather tires on it. I'm sure it will be fine."

"It's not the traction you're going to have to worry about. It's clearance. You'll tear the undercarriage the first time you drive over a snowbank."

"I'll avoid snowbanks then. Thanks for the advice." He tucked her hand under his arm and started walking toward the club.

Nyland snorted. "Prairie Falls has a unique way of plowing streets and parking lots. They leave huge piles of snow everywhere. There is no way to avoid the banks."

"Well, when the snow comes, we'll go shopping for a more sensible winter car for me. How's that?"

She shook her head but didn't say anything.

The early fall evening temperature was still pleasant but had a crisp edge to it. A small warning of cooler temperatures to come. Des pictured car shopping with Nyland. Would she pick out a truck? They were popular in this part of the state. Or, maybe a compact SUV?

Fuck.

There would be no car shopping because anything beyond casual between them was a bad idea. How many times would he have to tell himself? Maybe taking her with him tonight had been a mistake. She was a distraction. He still needed to prove himself to the rest of the force. Sleeping with Zedler's favorite forensic sketcher was absolutely not the way to accomplish that. And there was no way that he'd be able to keep it just casual if they had sex again. The sizzle between them was too hot for that.

He was so fucked.

She wore high-heeled boots, and he shortened his steps automatically to match her gait. Her hand felt absolutely right in the crook of his arm. Her body heat filtered through the thin material of his shirt, and he had to pretend a small misstep so he could wiggle his hips for a quick crotch adjustment. Turned out, it wasn't so much his brain as his dick making the decisions when it came to Nyland.

They rounded the corner of a building, and Des let out a silent sigh of relief when he saw the entrance to the club. He let go of Nyland's hand and positioned himself slightly behind her in the queue. Why didn't he think to wear a long coat rather than his leather bomber jacket?

"So what's our cover story, detective?" She spoke so low, he had to bend down to hear her.

"The first part of our cover is for you not to call me 'detective,'" he whispered close to her ear.

She shuddered, and Des had to adjust again.

"What should I call you?"

His devious mind suggested all kinds of names, none of which he opted to share with her. "How about my name?"

"Alright, I'll call you Rankin."

"I think if we're supposed to be out on a date, you should probably call me by my first name."

She paused for a few seconds. "Fine. I'll call you Desmond."

"Let's go with Des. That's what my friends call me."

"I like Rankin better."

He punished her by leaning in close and letting his breath fall on her ear as he whispered, "You can call me Rankin again when we're not undercover." Fuck. Undercover, under the covers. He took a step back before the tremors hit her body and his. He cleared his throat. "When we're not working a case."

"What are you going to call me?" She said with a sigh and leaned back.

Before he had a chance to answer, someone else called her name.

"Ms. Nyland. I'm so happy you could join us tonight."

Des glared at the giant standing next to them. The guy from the surveillance camera was much bigger in person. He hadn't noticed the biceps the size of small tree trunks when he saw him on the bike. The dude had a chest chiseled in stone and wore nothing but leather pants and a vest, showing way too much skin.

Nyland didn't seem to mind.

She smiled sweetly at the underdressed mountain. "Mr. Tasunke. This is my friend Des."

The bouncer smiled, but it didn't reach his eyes. As he turned toward Des, they became an even colder shade of green. Tasunke held out a hand. "Nice to make your acquaintance."

Des struggled not to grimace as the dude did his best to crush every bone in Des' hand. "You too. Tasunke, was it?"

"I'm also known as Dakota." He turned back to Nyland. "Please, there is no need for you to stand in line. You have VIP access."

She looked confused. "I thought tonight's event was for VIP guests only. Don't these people have passes also?" She made a sweeping motion with her arm, encompassing the rest of the line.

The bouncer leaned down and lowered his voice. "Yes, but you are special VIP. No queuing necessary."

Molly blushed.

Des frowned, took a step closer, and put his arm around her waist. She stiffened, and he thought at first that she would shake off his arm, but she relaxed and even leaned into the embrace.

"Please, follow me," said the bouncer and strode off toward the door.

Nyland started to follow, but Des slowed her down. "Stop flirting with him," he hissed in her ear.

She glared up at him. "I'm just talking to him. What do you want me to do, ignore him?"

"No, but there's no need to encourage him. We don't know how dangerous this guy is."

"I'm not encouraging him." She stomped off.

Des grabbed her hand and pulled her back beside him. Together they followed Tasunke, or Dakota, or whatever the fuck his name was, through the door of the club.

The giant left them at the coat check, telling them to "please enjoy themselves" and to let him know if there was "anything they needed." That last part was delivered while he looked directly at Nyland. A smarmy smile on his face, he bowed to her before leaving.

Des wanted to punch him. A somewhat familiar feeling whenever he was around other guys who also happened to be talking to Nyland. Instead, ignoring the jerk, he looked around the club. White tablecloths. Silverware rolled into black cloth napkins. Cut crystal stemware. And attractive wait staff dressed exclusively in leather. He studied the bustiers on the women with some interest.

Before he had a chance to ask Nyland where she wanted to sit, another staff member approached them. Still a giant. Still way underdressed. But this one was blonde. With a ponytail.

"Ms. Nyland, may I show you to your table?"

What the fuck? Did she know every leather-wearing-Chippendale-wannabe in the joint?

His date, non-date, whatever, smiled prettily at the Viking. "Sure. But how do you know my name?"

"Dakota told me." He cupped Nyland's elbow and steered her toward the dining area.

Des stepped between them, forcing the dude to remove his hand. He placed his own hand on the small of his date's back as they followed Blondie.

Nyland leaned across Des toward the other guy. "I feel like I should know your name."

The Viking leaned down, forcing Des to retreat into the background unless he wanted to rub chests with the leather-clad meathead. "It's Eric." He smiled, flashing a mouth full of straight white teeth.

When they reached the table, Des made a show out of pulling out Nyland's chair. The waiter handed them their menus.

"Can I start you off with something to drink? Would you like a glass of our house shiraz again?" The dude smiled at Nyland.

"You remembered what I drank last Friday?" She giggled.

Des sighed and relaxed the fist his hand had automatically made.

"Of course. I always remember the drink requests of guests who make an impression."

Nyland turned toward Des. "Do you like wine?"

Rat piss. "I'll have whatever IPA you have on tap." He tried to make his smile appear natural.

Judging from the amusing look Nyland gave him, he wasn't successful.

"And I'll go for a gin and tonic tonight."

The waiter finally left the table. Des pretended to look at his menu but instead studied Nyland.

She twisted right and left, taking in her surroundings. Her neckline showed part of the trail of freckles Des liked so much.

He sighed quietly. "So, you're a bit of a celebrity here."

"I know. Creepy." She widened her eyes. "They made a big deal out me leaving early last time. The bouncer especially acted really pissed. Now they're treating me as if I'm a regular VIP. Something's not right."

"You seem to be enjoying it, though."

She reached for the breadbasket as a busboy placed it on the table. "What do you mean?"

"You're giggling and flirting."

"Again, with the flirting." She rolled her eyes. "Believe me, I find all of this weird. Something's off in this place, but I'm playing my—" She wiggled her fingers, forming air-quotes. "Undercover character."

"We're here to observe and maybe ask some questions. There's no character for you to play."

She ripped a piece of bread in two halves. "Fine. Whatever."

"Look, I'm not saying you can't talk to people. Just don't call so much attention to yourself."

She continued to massacre her roll into tiny little pieces. "You're the one that wanted me to come. If you'd rather I leave, just say so."

Des started to reply, but the waiter chose that moment to deliver their drinks.

They were both quiet as he placed the glasses on the tables.

"Have you decided on what to eat?"

Des wanted steak, and Nyland picked some kind of seafood. She wouldn't look at him while they placed their orders.

Once Blondie left again, Des reached for Nyland's hand.

She pulled it out of reach, and instead picked up her drink. She took a big sip.

"I'm sorry," he said. "I'm just a little edgy about this case."

She finally looked at him. "A little?" The words dripped with sarcasm.

"Okay, a lot. I'll try not to take it out on you, though."

She smiled. It was a tiny one, but still an improvement, and it made Des feel less like a jerk. "Excuse me. I'll be right back." She pushed out her chair and disappeared toward what he assumed was the ladies' room.

Des took a long swig of his beer and looked around the room. The other tables started to fill up, and the noise level had gone up a notch. So far, soft jazz trickled through the speakers. He wondered about the live show. Had Nyland told him who would perform? He couldn't remember.

The wait staff ran relay from the bar to the tables. The VIP folks liked to drink, it seemed. The Viking returned to their table.

"Can I get you something else to drink?" He gestured toward Des' half-finished beer.

"I'm good, thanks."

The guy hovered for a bit.

Des gave him an inquiring look.

He opened his mouth as if to say something, but then shook his head and pressed his lips together. "Your food should be out any moment now." He said before walking away.

Des watched him walk toward the alcove that Nyland had disappeared through. Before he reached the opening, the bouncer intercepted him and babbled in the Viking's ear. Whatever he was saying, the other guy didn't agree. He shook his head.

If Des hadn't been watching them as closely as he was, he probably wouldn't have noticed that they were having an argument. The signs were subtle, stiff body posture, with chests out and shoulders back. The bouncer looked right at Des, who met his gaze without blinking.

The two of them squared off long-distance for half a minute. Then the other guy bared his teeth. It looked like he was growling. What the fuck?

The bouncer spoke in the waiter's ear again without breaking eye contact with Des. Blondie shook his head, but when the bouncer grabbed his arm, he nodded once and then tore his arm free. He walked off toward the alcove. Before he disappeared through the opening, he looked over his shoulder at Des, a grim determination in his eyes.

Des searched for the bouncer but couldn't spot him. The dude must have slipped out another exit. Des stood and walked towards the alcove. Where the fuck was Molly, and why was she taking so long?

He stepped through the curtains, but before he got any further, the bouncer stepped in front of him. Where the fuck had he come from?

"Can I help you?" His massive shoulders blocked Des' view.

He still caught a glimpse of a dim hallway and a restroom sign at the end of it. "No thanks, I know where I'm going." Des tried to push past the massive man.

"The show is about to start. You should return to your seat."

"I need to use the john." Des tried to lead with his shoulder through the small space the giant left between himself and the wall. It was like pushing against a wall. A big flesh-covered wall with tattoos.

The bouncer's pocket rang. While he fished out his cell phone, Des took advantage of the distraction and slipped passed the human mountain of muscle and ink.

He reached the restroom doors and glanced over his shoulder. The giant was still talking on his phone. Des hesitated a moment, but then pulled open the ladies' room door and stepped through. There was some kind of foyer with couches and small tables before the main restroom started. Who went to the john to sit on a sofa? No wonder women took so long in here. He was about to check the stalls when Nyland came out of one of them. She stopped dead in her tracks, staring at Des.

"Is something wrong?"

Des struggled between being embarrassed over being caught and relieved that she was okay. "Just checking why you're taking so long."

"Are you freaking kidding me?" Her freckles were glowing again. "You come to get me out of the bathroom because I took too long?"

Des winced. The last couple of her words had a much higher volume than the beginning of that sentence.

"Relax, Nyland. I'm just making sure you're okay." He held up his hands. The universal sign of "I come in peace." Hopefully, it would work.

"What is your problem, Rankin? Did your mom drop you on the head as a baby?"

"Hey, no need to get nasty now. The show is about to start. I didn't want you to miss anything." He frowned. "The waiter and the bouncer were acting froggy."

Nyland made a show out of looking around the bathroom. "I don't see them in here."

"They're outside," Des muttered.

She cocked a hip against the sink as she washed her hands. "You know, I'm perfectly capable of taking care of myself. I can draw composite sketches without you looking over my shoulder. I can open the car door for myself. And believe it or not, I can even pee and wipe my own ass without having to ask for your help."

Man, those freckles would glow in the dark at this point. Reacting on instinct and needing to shut Nyland up, Des stepped closer.

"What are you doing?'

"Something I should have done earlier." He caressed the back of her neck and tilted her head towards him, turning her.

She sputtered.

Des lowered his head and put his other hand on her hip, pressing her up against the sink. Fuck, she smelled good. He could feel her body tensing up, tight as a coil, ready to spring loose.

Her hands gripped his shoulders, and she pushed against them. "Hey, I asked you what you think you're doing."

"I'm not thinking at all."

"What—"

Des pressed his mouth against hers. Soft lips muttered in protest but then yielded. When he felt her responding, he deepened the kiss. His tongue swept her mouth, tasting honey and gin.

The hands on his shoulders relaxed and moved up around his neck. He stepped closer, pressing his hardness against her.

She moaned. A sweet sound deep in her throat. The low frequency resonated through his chest, and he thought he would expire on the spot. Shit, he hadn't been this close to coming with his clothes on since Jamie Heraldfield had touched the button fly on his 501s in eighth grade.

Someone dropped something big and loud out in the hallway.

Nyland squeaked and pushed against him while twisting away. Her hip slammed against his crotch, it wasn't a direct hit, but it was enough. He moaned, but not the good kind.

Fuck, fuck, fuck.

"Oh, Rankin. I'm so sorry."

He tried to speak but could only manage another long indrawn breath.

"Are you okay? Can I do something?"

"Stop moving," he managed to say between clenched teeth.

Mercifully, she did. And wonders of wonders, she stopped talking too. Des stood there for a few minutes until he caught his breath. Then he opened his eyes.

Molly peered at him through her wavy bangs. Her lips were red and swollen, her hair tousled. She looked like she should be in bed.

His bed. He was so fucked.

"I'm so sorry," she said.

Des just nodded. He didn't trust his voice yet. His blue-balls felt like they were in a vice, and his dick wasn't speaking to him.

Nyland put her hand on his arm. "Are you sure you're okay? I'm really sorry."

"You already said that." Des looked down at her. He traced his fingers up her jaw and cheek, hooking a wayward curl behind her ear.

She blushed.

Man, she was beautiful. He wanted to say something but didn't know what words to use.

She looked up at him. Grey clouds swirled in her eyes.

He traced the outer shell of her ear, down the lobe, back down the chin, and lower on her neck. His fingers swept by her collarbone, and then down the freckled path to the valley between her breasts.

She shuddered.

He had to adjust his stance to shift his dick from busting the zipper of his pants. He flinched, it still ached, but he wanted to see where the freckles led and traced the edge of her top by her collarbone.

She stiffened.

"Shhh," he whispered and slowly eased the top off her

shoulder. He wanted to kiss the beginning of the freckled trail.

Wham. The palm of her hand cracked against his cheek. He stumbled backward.

"I'm sorry." She was shaking.

"What the fuck?" Des pressed his hand against the burning on his cheek, what the hell had just happened. Nyland packed severe strength.

"I'm ticklish." She wouldn't look at him, but he could see tears in her eyes.

She wasn't a good liar. Des watched her for twenty seconds, but she still wouldn't look at him. What the fuck had he done? He tried to trace back to see where things had gone wrong. She hadn't said anything, if she had, he would've stopped. His skin still smarted, and he couldn't quite remember the exact order of events, but he knew she hadn't said anything. "If you wanted to get me back for tweaking your nose, slamming my nuts through my throat would have been enough. No reason to knock my teeth out too."

His words had the desired effect. He saw a small smile at the corner of Nyland's mouth.

She still wouldn't look at him though, and she was still breathing fast, almost hyperventilating. Something was very wrong.

He took a step toward her, but she backed away, holding up her hands and turning her face away.

"I'll be fine. Just give me a minute."

He backed up a few steps. "Alright. Why don't you sit on this fancy couch out here in the umm room, pre-restroom, foyer, or whatever the fuck you call it. I'll wait outside in the hallway."

She nodded. "Okay," she whispered.

He exited and leaned up against the wall across from the women's restroom. What exactly had he done to freak

Nyland out? It was like he pinched a nerve? Or triggered some sort of flashback? Had she been attacked?

She'd been okay with him touching her face and the top of her breasts, but when he pushed back her blouse, she'd jumped. His hands fisted at the thought of someone hurting Molly.

Things were getting complicated. He should opt-out at this point, quit her cold turkey. But it wasn't just his dick leading him to Nyland now. Des had found a mystery to solve, which he could never resist. Especially not if the answer involved punishing someone that may have hurt Nyland.

CHAPTER 10

*O*lly turned the cold faucet on full blast and splashed water over the inside of her wrists. Her mirror image revealed enormous haunted eyes, her blouse askew, and her hair tangled.

"Fuck," she whispered.

She'd pretty much let Rankin dry-hump her against the sink. Had no problems with him sticking his hand down her bra, but when he touched her shoulder, she gave him a major bitch slap. It was apparent he didn't believe her excuse about being ticklish.

Nobody would have, but especially not an experienced detective.

She was stupid, stupid, stupid for letting him kiss her again. Her scarred skin was super sensitive to touch, but that wasn't why she'd freaked. He'd be turned off in a heartbeat if she revealed her marred shoulder and arm. The first time she'd shown Clark, he'd been sweet and said it didn't bother him. But she'd been watching his face saw the involuntary flash of disgust. They'd only ever made love in the dark.

A small voice inside her insisted Rankin would be different. The attraction between them crackled with an energy she'd never experienced with her ex. That night in Sacramento, she couldn't stop watching Rankin from across the room. He'd caught her eye and nodded toward the door. On an unspoken agreement, they'd both slipped outside, and at his apartment, he'd kissed her with a fervor she'd never experienced. Even more surprising, her body's response had been immediate and off the charts. The passion she'd seen in Rankin's eyes that night—the passion she saw in them tonight—that could never be unleashed again. She couldn't risk it.

She didn't know Rankin very well, but she did know that being rejected by him would hurt. A lot.

Molly closed her eyes against the memories of her ex flooding her mind. Her suspicions of Clark being with other women, when he insisted he'd been at work or out with "the guys" flashed across her mind. His best friend saying Clark used Molly and her talents to maintain a high case closure ratio. The final confrontation just after Clark's promotion. The horrible fight when he accused her of being too controlling. And then told her it was her fault he had to cheat. No one who'd seen her scars would be able to get it up without fantasizing about other women.

She turned off the water and blotted her face and straightened her clothes. Luckily she'd packed a comb and some lipstick in her purse. They only repaired a minor part of the damage staring back at her from the mirror, but it would have to do. Besides, it wasn't like Rankin would still be interested. Not after the behavior, he'd just experienced.

He was waiting for her just outside the door.

"You okay?" He took her hand and started walking back toward the dining room.

She nodded.

"Want to talk about it?"

She shook her head.

"You know you'll have to eventually, right? It doesn't have to be with me, but whatever it is, you should talk to someone."

Molly tried to tug her hand out of his, but he held on. "It's nothing," she said.

"It didn't look like nothing to me. I don't want to push, but I'm here if you need me. Or I can recommend someone for you to talk to."

She shook her head but didn't say anything. Obviously, he thought she needed some sort of counseling, and it was sweet of him to care, but she didn't want to deal with any of that right now. This wasn't a real date. They were working the case. As they reached the table, Rankin pulled out her chair before returning to his seat.

He looked at something behind her. "Is your boss dating the office manager?"

Molly turned and saw Anthony and Samantha at a table, their hand touching and their heads close together. She faced Rankin again. "Yeah, it's supposed to be a secret, but everyone knows about it."

Before Rankin could reply, Eric, the waiter, rushed over.

"Your food got cold, so I sent it back into the kitchen. Would you like your entrees warmed up, or should I ask the chef to prepare something fresh?"

Molly wasn't hungry anymore and considered just sending it back, but she felt terrible about ordering food and then not eating it. It seemed a waste. "I'll just have the heated plate."

"Are you sure," the blonde man asked. "Fish can turn rubbery when it's been under the heating lamp."

"Just order something else," Rankin said.

"But it's a shame to waste the food."

"Who cares? As long as we pay for it, it doesn't matter if

you eat it or not." He studied her. He looked worried, concerned.

She hated that look. It was too close to pity.

Eric seemed anxious about her as well, or at least about her food order. "It's no trouble, Ms. Nyland. I'll bring you a fresh dinner entree."

Exhaustion seeped through her body. She wanted to go home. She wanted to crawl under the covers and not come out until she had to go back to work on Monday. Maybe not even then.

Rankin leaned over the table. "Fuck, Nyland?" He said in a low voice. "I've seen you make lightning speed decisions when it comes to a pencil mark on your sketches, but ordering food has you stumped?"

This Rankin she could deal with, the rude ordering-everyone-around Rankin. She'd rather spar with him than see the pity in his eyes, and later the contempt that would eventually show up. "Fine, I'd rather not have anything. Just another drink will be fine."

Rankin grinned at her across the table. "There you go, stick to the liquid diet."

She shot him an angry look but then felt guilty. There was still a bright red mark where her palm had made contact with his cheekbone.

"I'll have a new steak and another beer, please," he said to the waiter. "And you heard the lady, she'll have another gin and tonic."

"The 'lady' can speak for herself, and she'll have a margarita. On the rocks, with salt, please."

"Fantastic." Even the waiter seemed relieved she'd finally made up her mind. He rushed off to fill their orders.

"Hitting the tequila already?" Rankin cocked an eyebrow. "Are you drowning your sorrows or just regretting our rendezvous in the bathroom?"

"You have a weird definition of rendezvous. I basically kneed you in the groin and literally slapped you. Is that the kind of kinky stuff you're into?"

"If you're going to be the one wielding the whip, sure." He wiggled his eyebrows.

She chuckled. He looked ridiculous. More slapstick than BDSM. "You're a glutton for punishment, Rankin. Aren't you sore enough already?"

He shifted his seat and pretended to wince. "You do pack quite a punch, both in your hip and your right hook."

"I'm sorry again about the slap. You took me by surprise." She couldn't quite look at him but felt the heat of his gaze on her face.

He cleared his throat as if to say something, but the lights dimmed, and music started playing.

Molly turned her chair toward the stage.

The same singer as the Friday before walked out on the stage. This time she wore an emerald green gown, which contrasted perfectly with her pale skin and auburn hair. She belted out the opening lyrics to Sinatra's "The Best is Yet to Come." As the music swelled, the light on the stage brightened to reveal a big band orchestra. Every member wore white smoking jackets with black shirts and ties underneath. Their brass instruments reflected beams of brightness into the audience as the players moved in tempo with the tunes.

Molly's mood lifted. She loved big band music.

Before her accident, her great-uncle had played his vast record collection whenever her grandmother left the house. She didn't approve of "the devil's music," but tolerated the record player in the house since her brother paid most of the mortgage.

Some of Molly's happiest memories were of her uncle dancing her across the farm's living room floor. He'd taught her the foxtrot, the rumba, and how to jive. She'd loved the musical legends, Count Basie, Louie Armstrong, and Glenn Miller. They all seemed larger than life. That had been when her childhood was filled with possibilities, and waking up every morning meant anticipating a new adventure. After the lightning strike, there'd been no more music. Her grandmother insisted it encouraged the evil forces she was convinced had entered her granddaughter through the flash of electromagnetic energy. And her great-uncle had agreed.

But she wouldn't dwell on that now. She'd concentrate on the music and how good it made her feel. She expected couples to get up and dance. When she looked around the room, though, everyone seemed content to just sit and listen. They were so absorbed in the music, most of them weren't even moving. Some of the patrons even had their eyes closed.

What was wrong with them? Molly couldn't keep her feet from tapping in beat with the music. Her shoulders swayed, and she jumped around in her seat, the rhythm too infectious to resist.

She looked over at Rankin to see if she could convince him to dance. He was staring at the singer like the rest of the audience. Instead of admiring her, his brow furrowed, as if he was in pain.

Des' head was about to explode.

The singer sounded okay, the musicians were probably okay too, but they weren't playing the same tune. Underlying the mismatched harmonics was an irritating high-pitched sound that made him want to stick a fork in his eye. The combined effect of the many-sounds assault was a vibration in his inner ear that was physically painful.

He looked over at Nyland. She hopped around on her seat, snapping her fingers, while he was trying not to vomit.

Through squinted eyes, he surveyed the rest of the audience. Most of them were blankly staring at the stage as if they were watching the second coming. A few people had slacked jaws and might start drooling any minute. They looked like they'd rise up with arms stretched out saying "brains, brains" in just a few moments.

He glanced across to the table where Nyland's boss and his date were sitting. Both of them watched the stage, but without the vacant look that the rest of the audience displayed.

He glanced over at Nyland again. Something freaky was happening, and he wanted to get out of the place before the freaky hit him. "Let's go," he shouted.

"Why," she bellowed over the music.

Of course, she had to question him. "I can't stand this. It's hurting my head."

She shot him a skeptical look. "Fine." She picked up her handbag and stood.

Des rose from the chair, and vertigo slammed into him like a sack of lead pellets. He stumbled, but Nyland rushed to his side, propping him up.

"I got you," she said, putting his arm around her shoulders.

He managed to half lean on her and half shuffle through the dining room toward the coat check. The further away from the stage they got, the better he felt. By the time they stepped through to the entry area, he was well enough to stand on his own, but just barely. He kept his arm around Nyland's shoulders.

"Thanks," he said. "I don't know what came over me. The out of sync tuning got to me somehow."

"I didn't notice anything wrong with the music."

"You were the only one that seemed to have a normal

reaction to that show. The rest of the audience looked drugged."

"I noticed, that was the way it was last Friday too." She frowned.

Des wanted to ask her more questions, but the Viking ran toward them. "Are you leaving the show early again, Ms. Nyland?" He looked frantic.

"My friend isn't feeling well, I need to get him home," she gave him an apologetic smile.

"I'm sorry," the guy patted Des shoulder.

Even if he wasn't as tall as the bouncer, the guy still had two inches and lots of muscle on Des. And yet, he still wanted to punch him.

He wanted to hit him for being condescending, for showing too much skin, for Nyland staring at his pectoral muscles, and most of all for Des not knowing what the fuck was going on. Someone should definitely get punched for that.

If Des didn't think he would projectile vomit if he opened his mouth, he'd say something. As it was, he had to just watch as the dude took Nyland's hands in his own and kissed them.

"Please make sure you come again, Ms. Nyland."

She pulled her hands away and gave the waiter a weak smile. "Sure, I'll try to do that."

Des looked over her shoulder and spotted the bouncer watching him from the exit to the outside. He had a manic look in his eyes. Then he did that thing with the teeth and the growl again. Was the dude high or something? Des wanted to talk to him, ask him some questions. But if the guy was on drugs, it wouldn't be of any use. Maybe that was the deal with this place. They were all on drugs.

He tugged on Nyland to get her to move.

They finally looked away from her and turned to Des. "Oh, and we'd love to have you come back too."

Des struggled with his wallet and handed over his credit card. "Just close out our tab, please."

"Absolutely, I'll be right back." The guy trotted away.

The giant guarding the door approached them. He grinned at Des.

"Can I help you," Des said. He tried to not make it obvious that he needed Nyland to remain upright.

The dude grinned, eyes bright bottle-green. "Maybe, brother. Maybe"

Before Des could say anything, the dude laughed like a hyena and walked out the exit. The door swung back, and Des lost sight of him. Yep, high as a kite.

He looked at Nyland.

"That's new," she said and cocked her head to the side.

"That didn't happen last Friday?"

"Not so much. Last week the Dakota was pissed off that I left early and stared after me with evil laser beam eyes as I drove away."

Des smiled. "Evil laser beam eyes? Sounds like maybe he was on drugs then too."

"I wouldn't know."

The waiter returned with Des's credit card.

"I'll drive," Nyland said.

Des handed over the keys without protest. He'd never let anybody drive his TTS before, but then again, music had never made him want to vomit before either. There was a first time for everything.

MOLLY WOKE up because the sun shone straight into her eyes. Did she forget to lower the shade? She rubbed her eyes before fully opening them and then winced. Instead of her familiar bedroom, she lay on a very uncomfortable black leather couch. Matching chairs flanked the sofa, and a glass and chrome coffee table displayed no less than three different remote controls.

Very masculine. Very bachelor.

Very Rankin.

He'd gotten worse on the drive home the night before. By the time they got to his place, he couldn't walk straight. Molly had half supported, half dragged him up the stairs to his apartment. Once she'd gotten him into bed, fully clothed, although she did take off his shoes, she'd turned him on his side in case he'd puke. Afraid to leave him alone in case he got even worse, she stayed the night.

Her bladder told her it was time to visit the facilities. The apartment only had one bathroom, attached to the bedroom. She'd hoped to sneak out in the morning without Rankin noticing. If he was still asleep, that might even be possible.

She creaked open the bedroom door.

A big lump under the covers rustled for a moment but then settle down again. Molly tipped-toed past the bed and into the bathroom. After she'd finished her business, she looked for something to help her bad case of bed head. One side lay plastered to her cheek while the other poked up as if looking for communications from outer space.

Rankin's bathroom cabinet revealed bars of soap, shaving foam, and spare razors. The only sign of his inflated ego and vanity was a jar of slightly expensive-looking hair gel. She stole some and tried to tame her now frizzy waves.

After returning the jar to exactly where she'd found it, Molly washed and dried her hands.

She opened the door to find Rankin sitting up in bed, leaning against the headboard with a cocky smile on his face. He had very little chest hair on top of well-defined pectorals. A tattoo decorated one of his bulging biceps, but she couldn't quite make out its design. When did he take off his shirt? Just now or during the night? Was he still wearing his pants from last night under those covers?

She blushed.

"Snooping in my cabinets?"

Molly avoided looking at his bare and smooth chest. What would it be like running her fingers down those rippled abs? "I was looking for some moisturizer."

"Sure, you were." He patted a spot on the bed next to him. "Care to join me so we can recap and perhaps finish off our under-cover evening?"

"In your dreams, Rankin."

Something dark flashed in his eyes but was gone so fast Molly thought maybe she'd imagined it.

"I better get going now that I know you won't drown in your own vomit."

"That's not a nice thing to say to the guy you spent the night with."

"I didn't spend the night with you, Rankin. I slept on the couch."

"Yeah, but when I tell this story to any of my friends, I'll only mention the 'spending the night' part."

Molly shook her head. Of course, Rankin would tell everyone. Clark had been the same. It wasn't enough that he turned the department against her after their breakup, he had done so by spreading lies about what they'd done together in bed.

Women were unfairly judged as the gossiping gender when that trait actually belonged to men. Her girlfriends could keep a secret, but give a man a locker room or a break room, and he had to spill every sordid detail about his sex life —most of it entirely made up. In Santa Clara, she'd ended up with a wholly undeserved reputation.

Time to leave. Let Rankin figure out on his own how he was getting to work when his car would, very shortly, be parked at her house. She pivoted on one foot and walked out of the bedroom.

"Hey, calm down," Rankin shouted after her. "I was only kidding."

Sure he was.

Molly heard him moving around in the bedroom, hopping around and muttering under his breath.

She paused by the apartment's door, and she scanned the room for her purse before finding it on the coffee table, next to one of the giant remotes. Seriously, the TV was less than five feet from the couch. Leaning over to change the channel or turn up the volume was too much of an effort for him?

She'd almost made it out the door when Rankin caught up with her.

"Hey, I'm sorry. That was crass. I don't kiss and tell, I promise."

"There's no kissing to tell about."

"Have you forgotten what happened in the bathroom at the club?" He grinned.

"Have you? I hurt your manhood and then gave you that mark that's still lingering on your cheek."

He rubbed his cheek. The palm made a scratchy sound as it caressed stubble. Why did he have to be so good looking?

"I remember." He pretended to wince and put his hand in front of his crotch. His checkered blue boxer briefs hugged his ass nicely. He needed to put some clothes on. She averted her gaze from where it had lingered, right where his hand was, and opened the door.

He leaned over her and against it, shutting it again. "Hey, let me at least make you breakfast."

"You cook?" Why was she even thinking about staying?

His grin turned sheepish. "Hey, let me at least *buy* you breakfast."

Her stomach growled. She hadn't eaten since lunch the day before. "Okay, fine."

"Give me two minutes to get some clothes on. He bounded into the bedroom, leaving Molly to second-guess her decision.

* * *

DES RUMMAGED AROUND in the bedroom, trying to find something that was clean and unwrinkled. He finally settled on a pair of old jeans and a black t-shirt. The top smelled fresh, and that was the best he could do since he'd been avoiding doing laundry since his move.

She'd been worried enough to sleep over. The thought shouldn't cheer him up, but it did. Fuck, he had it bad, and it was going to become a major problem.

He wondered if any of the other guys on the force had asked Molly out. He'd seen the looks she got from some of the officers. He should check on that.

Maybe Zedler had kept them at bay. He seemed very protective.

Fuck.

What would Zedler say if he found out Des wanted to date Molly? It'd probably be worse than when he'd broken up with the Sacramento PD receptionist, and she started hiding all the office supply from him. Mitchell had thought that was funny as hell.

He didn't want to think about his former partner. Not now when he was in a good mood and about to go out to breakfast with a woman who he couldn't stop thinking about. And she'd spent the night. Well, sleeping on the couch. Mitchell would have found that hilarious as well. But hell, it was better than nothing. Though usually when women went home with Des, they didn't sleep on the couch. They didn't do much sleeping at all.

He sobered. What he wouldn't give to hear Mitchell give him a hard time about one-night stands just one more time. But his best friend was dead because Des fucked up, which he was still trying to deal with, or at least figure out what the hell had happened in that warehouse. It was supposed to be a simple drug-bust, which instead turned into a cluster-fuck of gigantic proportions.

They'd acted on a tip and went in before backup arrived since they thought the perp was about to take off. But by the time the other officers arrived, Des had been coldcocked and his partner dead.

He jerked the t-shirt over his head. Time to go see what Nyland's take was on the events from the night before. He needed to solve this case. Maybe the forensic artist out in his living room would be able to help him. And once the case was solved, he could figure out what Mitchell and the botched drug bust had to do with Prairie Falls. His partner had written the town's name in his case notes, but not supplied any details.

Des shook his head. There was too much to think about. For now, he'd concentrate on taking Molly out for breakfast. It was the least he could do after passing out on her.

CHAPTER 11

olly swirled maple syrup in patterns of concentric circles on her short stack. Each sweep of her hand made a larger circle until she reached the edge of the top pancake. The liquid slowly spread out and saturated the stack. She waited for the food to achieve the perfect level of sweet saturation before taking her first bite. Carefully, she cut through the entire stack, loading the fork with a huge layered chunk before shoveling the whole thing into her mouth. She chewed with her eyes closed, savoring the sensation of sweet and warm comfort.

Heaven.

Opening her eyes to prepare another bite, she caught Rankin staring at her from across the table.

"What?" She asked.

He cleared his throat and shifted on the chair. "I have to take you out to breakfast more often. Pancakes are my new favorite food."

"You're eating eggs and sausage." She waved her fork in the direction of his plate where egg yolk and brown grease smeared together with tabasco sauce.

"Not to eat. It's my new favorite food to watch."

She blushed. "You're weird."

He just grinned in response.

"What are you going to do about Sinful Soul?" Molly said. "We don't exactly have proof of anything criminal going on other than weird acting personnel and audience responding unnaturally to the music.

"I'm pretty sure I could get a search warrant based on my suspicion of drugs being both taken by the bouncer and distributed to the audience."

"You think the audience was drugged?"

"How else would you explain their zombie-like attention to the stage? The music sucked."

She thought about any other possible explanations, but couldn't come up with any. "It was like that when we celebrated Nina's birthday as well."

"Were you affected?"

"No, that was the weird thing. Everyone but me was completely mesmerized by the music and the singer on stage."

Rankin smiled. "She was something."

Just like a man to be fascinated by a tight dress on a gorgeous body, even while ill. "I thought she made you sick."

"Her singing made me sick. If she'd kept her mouth shut, things would have been okay."

"Spoken like a true caveman."

He shook his head. "We're getting off-topic here. Tell me more about the night you celebrated your friend's birthday."

Molly described what had happened, including the weird interaction with Eric, the waiter, and Tasunke's reaction when she left the club. "Another weird thing is that Nina doesn't remember me being there."

Rankin rubbed his jaw. His stubble had grown out over

the night, obscuring the slight cleft in his chin. Even fresh out of bed, he oozed hotness.

She couldn't figure out what his deal was. Most of the time, he purposely pushed her buttons, but sometimes he made her want things she shouldn't. Working with him was more than a challenge, it was a freaking boot-camp obstacle course. One minute she'd be jumping over tires, the next crawling under fences in the mud, and then running smack into that wall with the ropes that she never seemed able to scale.

She loaded up another bite on her fork while checking him out through lowered eyelashes.

Rankin pushed a piece of sausage around in the mess on his plate.

Molly enjoyed flirting with him and, okay, she enjoyed making out with him as well. Judging from how she'd freaked out when he almost caught a glimpse of her scars though, she obviously wasn't ready for a relationship. Especially not with another cop.

Been there, done that, should have bought a gun and shot the bastard afterward.

No matter what Nina thought about Molly's lack of sex life, it was a lot less complicated than trying to figure out how to enjoy the physical part of a relationship without messing it up with emotional stuff. She'd never been good at separating the two of them. And with her scars, it wasn't likely that an encounter with Rankin would be more than a one-night stand.

She was on her third bite by the time Rankin spoke again. "So you never drank any of the wine that you ordered at your friend's celebration."

She shook her head.

"But last night, you had a drink, and you still weren't affected."

146

"What about your weird food poisoning?"

His gaze met hers briefly before flickering away. "Yeah, that's never happened before."

Why the weird look? "Why would you and I have completely different reactions to the show than anybody else?"

"And why were you getting so much attention from the people who worked there?"

She waved her fork around. "That was obviously a marketing ploy. Maybe they think I know a bunch of people and that I'll bring them to the club."

Rankin shook his head. "Why would they think that? And why visit you personally to make sure you came to another show? And how did they know where you lived?"

She swallowed the wad of pancakes she'd stuffed in her mouth. "I guess they could have gotten the address when I showed my ID. Or maybe from my credit card? You think they're giving me some kind of special treatment?"

He grinned. "Oh, there's something special about you, alright. Especially the special way you eat those pancakes."

Heat crept into her cheeks and put down her fork. "Stay serious. Do you think there's something weird about me, and that's why I didn't react like everyone else in the club?" She couldn't look at him while she waited for his answer, holding her breath.

"Why don't you tell me?"

She looked up.

He was studying her, holding her gaze.

She blinked and looked away again. Picking up the fork, she poked the pancakes left on her plate. "I don't think there's anything special about me."

"Do you think there's anything 'weird' about you?"

A chill trailed down her spine. "Everyone is weird in some way."

"True."

"I don't know what would cause me to react differently. But you reacted differently too. Is there something weird about you?"

"You tell me." His cocky grin was back.

"I think it's weird how much arrogance you have, and how charming you seem to think you are," she quipped.

He just widened his grin. "Most women like a confident guy."

"There is such a thing as too much confidence, you know."

"Nah." He shook his head, the grin never leaving his face. "Not in my book."

She snorted.

"Let's get back on topic," he said, looking serious again. "Is there anything you're not telling me about these guys' interest in you and the weird phenomena at the club?"

She crushed the remaining pancakes with her fork. "Not that I can think of."

He didn't look like he believed her, but before he had a chance to comment, his cellphone rang. "Rankin," he barked. His face fell as he. "Where?" He paused. "I'm on my way."

Molly raised her eyebrows inquisitively.

Rankin looked up, still listening to whoever was on the line. "No need. She's here with me. I'll bring her." He hung up abruptly.

"What's going on?" Molly asked.

"There's another body. A female this time."

* * *

POLICE CRUISERS FLANKED the empty lot Rankin had driven to on the east side of Prairie Falls. The neighborhood was known for easy access to drugs and prostitutes. Boarded up

148

buildings sat next to businesses advertising "All Girls, All the Time" and "Cheapest Beer & Cigarettes."

Molly and Rankin walked across the lot. He propelled her forward with a hand on her small back, and she wished she was in her running shoes instead of the brown boots she'd worn to the club. The heels forced her to take shorter steps, and it was hard to keep up with Rankin's long stride.

She actually wanted to change more than her shoes. Any outfit other than what she'd worn to the club would be more appropriate. In the faint morning sunlight, her slim pants and coat looked out of place and too much like something you'd wear going out. Not a work outfit. And arriving with Rankin early in the morning would get rumors started.

She needn't have worried. Other than a few curious looks from some of the uniformed officers that knew her, everyone's eyes were on the body. Three murders close together tended to put a damper on most things, even juicy office gossip.

The medical examiner crouched next to the body. He slid out a long metal probe from the victim's side and read the numbers on his handheld digital thermometer.

"Early estimated time of death would be between midnight and four am."

"That's quite a range." Zedler stepped out from behind the dumpster. He nodded toward Molly and narrowed his eyes at Rankin.

"The air temperature last night was warmer than normal, which may mess with my liver reading. I'll narrow it down once I open her up."

Molly looked down on the ground. The woman lay on her side and didn't look like she had ever been alive. Patches of waxy skin of an odd dull beige color peeked through strands of long blonde hair.

Rankin crouched down next to the ME and lifted a chunk

of hair off the cheek. He'd donned gloves while Molly had been gawking at the dead body.

"I can't see the face very well. Can we turn her over?"

The examiner nodded, and together, the two men gently rolled the woman over on her back.

Molly inhaled sharply. A whimper escaped her throat as Carol's lifeless eyes stared into nothing.

"Shit," Rankin said. "Are you going to hurl?'

She shook her head, but couldn't keep tears from welling up in her eyes. Dirty tendrils of her hair stuck to the side of Carol's cheeks. Her lovely features were distorted, the nose was swollen, and what looked like blood crusted her upper lip.

Molly tasted metal in her mouth, and her vision narrowed. She stumbled.

"Get her out of here," Rankin shouted, but nobody reacted. He cursed under his breath and grabbed Molly's arm.

She spun around quickly, her arms flailing.

He caught her wrists before she hit him by mistake.

"It's Carol," She shouted. "Who would do this to Carol?"

"Fuck, fuck, fuck," Rankin turned to Zedler.

"Major fuck," the older detective added.

Rankin angled Molly's body away from Carol. Dead Carol. Never-again-telling-raunchy-jokes Carol. She choked back tears. Don't cry. Never let them see you cry.

"Shh," Rankin whispered against her hair. He pulled off the gloves and slid his hands up her arms.

Molly shuddered as the rough material of her coat scratched the sensitive scars through the thin blouse.

Rankin hugged her, using his body to block the view of Carol's lifeless body.

Unable to resist his warmth, she leaned into his strong

body. He stroked Molly's hair as silent sobs shattered through her body.

"Let it all out," he mumbled and then repeated "sorry" over and over.

Briefly, Molly wondered how someone she wanted to slap most of the time, now felt like the most solid and comforting person in the world. Then she wondered how she would ever be able to tell Nina that one of her best friends was dead —murdered.

"Oh no," she pulled away from Rankin.

"What?"

"We have to go check on Nina." She fumbled in her purse for her phone, spilling lipstick, pens, and little pieces of paper on the ground.

Rankin grabbed her trembling hands and took the handbag away from her. "Slow down, Molly. Why do we need to check on Nina?"

Zedler walked up to them and put his hand on Molly's arm. "I'm so sorry. If we'd known who she was and that you knew her, we'd never allowed you on the scene."

Molly swallowed and then nodded. "I know."

Zedler studied her face with concern. "Are you up to telling me how you know her?"

Molly nodded again. "She's a good friend of my friend Nina." She turned to Rankin. "The two of them were together last night at Nina's apartment. We have to go see if she's okay."

"She's probably just fine," he said in a soothing voice. "Give her a call." He fished her phone out of the bag and handed it over.

She hit Nina's speed dial key. The line rang and rang while Molly held her breath.

Rankin and Zedler seemed to do the same.

"Hello?" A sleepy voice mumbled.

"Nina."

"Yeah, Molly? What's going on?"

"Oh, Nina—" she couldn't say anymore before her voice broke.

"Molly?"

She was trembling so hard, she could only nod.

"Molly, are you okay?" Nina's voice was worried.

"I'm fine," Molly choked out. "I'm coming over. Don't go anywhere."

"Honey, you have me worried. Tell me what's wrong."

She couldn't tell Nina about her friend over the phone. "I'm on my way." Molly hung up the phone.

"Rankin, I need to borrow your keys. I have to go see her."

His hand was still rubbing the small of her back. "You're in no condition to drive. I'll take you."

"Don't you need to stay here?" She glanced around the scene in the parking lot, avoiding the area where Carol's body lay.

Rankin gathered her closer. "I trust the team to get the evidence we need. I'm coming with you."

Molly shook her head. "Nina and Carol are very close. I have to tell her alone."

He looked at her with sadness. "This is a murder investigation. There is no more 'alone.' I need to learn everything that happened last night from Nina."

* * *

DES RANG the doorbell to Nyland's friend's apartment. She'd been withdrawn for most of the drive over, but he'd found out that her friend's name was Nina Hall and that she and the deceased had gone to school together. Some sort of fashion school, whatever that meant.

Hall opened the door dressed in black yoga pants and a pink t-shirt saying "My Mother's Daughter and Proud of It." She flashed a nervous smile, which changed into concern when she saw Molly's face.

"Honey, what happened?"

Nyland nodded but didn't seem to be able to speak. She swallowed several times. A lone silent tear slid down her cheek.

Des turned toward the tall brunette in the doorway. "May we come in, Ms. Hall?"

She narrowed her eyes at him. "That depends. Who are you, and what have you done to Molly?"

Suspicious and protective. Des liked Nina immediately but kept his face grave as he flashed his badge. "I'm Detective Rankin. Molly has had a bit of a shock."

When had he started thinking of her as Molly instead of Nyland? Maybe when he hugged her at the crime scene and hadn't minded that everyone saw. Or, when he found her in his apartment this morning and realized how good it felt to have her there. This wasn't the appropriate moment to figure that out.

"Oh," Hall said and stepped aside. "I'm sorry. It's just that Molly doesn't cry."

Des filed that away for later. "Is there somewhere we can sit down?"

She laughed nervously. "You are really freaking me out here, guys. What's going on?"

Des gave Molly a little push, and she walked down a short hallway and took a left. He assumed she'd gone to the living room and followed.

Hall trailed after. She grabbed his arm. "Seriously, what has happened to Molly?" She hissed.

"She's got some bad news for you and doesn't know how to tell you."

"Crap." She pushed him aside and ran after her friend. He could hear her talking to Molly down the hall. "What's going on? Are you sick? Has something happened with your scars? Your…special intuition? Please, just tell me."

Now that was interesting. *Scars? Special Intuition?* Molly definitely held out on him about something. Were the scars related to Molly's weird reaction in the bathroom at the club? Walking into the room, he found both women sitting on a red couch. Now was not the time to ask personal questions. He needed to get the details to establish last night's timeline for the vic.

Hall held her friend's hands. "Okay, just spit it out. What's wrong?"

"There's been another murder." Molly switched her hands so that she was gripping Hall's instead. "Nina, I'm so sorry. Someone murdered Carol."

"This isn't funny." Hall tried to pull her hands free, but Molly held on.

"I'm not joking."

"Why would someone kill Carol?"

"That's what we're trying to figure out," Des interrupted.

Hall turned toward him. "Tell me everything."

"Actually, I need to ask you some questions."

She opened her mouth as if to protest, but closed it again. "What do you need to know?"

Des led her through the standard line of questioning to establish a timeline of the deceased's last hours. As the last person who'd probably seen the victim alive, Hall might have crucial information that she didn't know she had. Sometimes the most mundane detail turned out to be the one that broke a case. He sincerely hoped that would be the case now. He did not look forward to explaining three open murder investigations to the lieutenant.

He copied down everything Hall told him and asked

details about where they'd gotten food poisoning, how long they'd spent together, and what they had talked about. If the deceased had exhibited any unusual moods, and finally when she had left Hall's apartment.

"I was pretty out of it for most of the evening. My stomach cramped, and I ran a temperature. Carol seemed normal. I mean, she seemed like she always was. Silly, funny, joking around."

"Wasn't she sick as well?" Molly asked.

Hall turned toward her friend. "Not as bad as I was. You know how Carol was, though, always cheerful no matter what was going on." Tears spilled down Hall's cheeks.

Molly nodded.

"Honey, I'm so sorry you had to see her like that." Hall patted Molly's knee.

"You're sorry? I knew her, but she was your close friend."

Hall shook her head, more tears running down her face. "We used to be very close, but the last year or so, Carol's been pulling away."

"How so," Des prompted.

"It's nothing obvious. She made some new friends and hung out with them a lot."

"Do you know who these friends were?"

"I wish I could tell you, but no. Carol loves—loved—to go out. I used to join her, but since I started my boutique, I can't afford to party every night. Financially or time-wise. So Carol found a new crowd who could." She shrugged. "It wasn't any conscious decision on her part, I think. We just didn't talk or hang out as much as we used to."

Des asked some more details about the victim's new friends, but Hall knew very little about them. "Do you know if she was dating anybody?"

Hall and Molly exchanged a look.

"What?" He wanted to know.

Hall studied the wall. "Carol liked to have fun—" her voice drifted off.

Molly cleared her throat. "What Nina is trying to say is that Carol didn't believe in committed relationships, but she very much enjoyed sex."

"Was there someone special she used to have sex with?"

Molly looked at Hall, who seemed uncomfortable. "Kind of," she finally said. "She liked to experiment, and she had some regular people that she saw, depending on what she felt like doing."

"Did she belong to any kind of sex club or organization?"

Hall shook her head. "I don't know if she was a member of anything like that. She never told me. As far as I know, she just had friends with benefits."

"But you don't know who any of these men are?"

"Not really. Or any of the women either."

Des paused his pen for a moment and then continued writing. "And were either of you one of her 'friends with benefits?'" He had to ask.

Both women met his gaze and shook their heads.

Molly stirred. "I think she might have hooked up with people from her work regularly."

"Why do you say that?" Hall asked.

"She talked about the pros and cons of workplace romances, and I just got the impression that she had first-hand knowledge."

Hall nodded thoughtfully. "You're right. She made a joke once about doing it in a supply closet while hiding from the custodian.

"Plus, there's the comment she made about how sleeping with the boss could be the best career move you ever made—as long as you learned the right moves." Molly smiled wistfully.

Des glared at her. She should put any thoughts about sleeping with her boss out of her mind right now.

Molly's face crumbled. "I know it sounds like a cliché, but she really enjoyed every day and made no excuses for having fun."

"I know, Honey, I know." Hall patted her leg, smiling through tears. She turned to Des. "What are you doing about contacting her family?"

"I'm afraid we haven't gotten that far yet. Do you have their contact information?"

"All I know is that she has a brother named Liam, who lives in Seattle. I think he owns a bar there and plays in a band or something."

"What about her work information? Did she work here in Prairie Falls?"

"She has—had—two jobs," Molly said. "She modeled for Vavoom and wrote copy for *Fit & Fabulous*."

"You say that like I'm supposed to know what those are." Des smiled. Her eyes were red. He still wanted to kiss her.

"Sorry, forgot you were new in town. Vavoom is a plus-size clothing line, and *Fit & Fabulous* is their sportswear catalog."

He felt his eyebrows hitch at the contradiction but wisely said nothing. He knew plenty of fit guys who were "plus-size." Although he wouldn't call them "fabulous" though, mostly because they would punch him if he did.

He stood. "I think I have enough for now. I may have more questions later."

Hall rose also. "Just give me a call if you think I can help. I want to find the bastard who did this." She still had tears trailing down her face.

Me too, Des thought. Me too.

CHAPTER 12

*D*es walked briskly down the hallway toward Zedler's office. He'd left Molly at her friend's place after she'd assured him she'd be okay and make it back safely to her apartment.

When he reached the older detective's office, he banged a quick sequence of knocks on the door and didn't bother waiting for a reply before entering.

Zedler looked up as Rankin entered, but pointed at the phone glued to his ear. He spoke through clenched jaws. "I'm quite aware that this is a top priority, Ma'am. No. No, I do know how this makes us look." He paused while the person on the other line spoke for well over thirty seconds. "Look, someone is out there killing people. It's our job to catch the criminal when a crime is committed, but at this point, I don't know how to prevent another murder."

Des cocked an eyebrow. "LT?" He mouthed to Zedler.

The older police detective nodded.

"No, Ma'am, I'm not disagreeing with you. We do need to work on prevention, but with the limited resources I have right now, I think the best prevention would be to find the killer before he strikes again."

Des heard a rapid string of words through the receiver, but couldn't discern their meaning. He looked around the office, which displayed its usual state of a jumble, but today it appeared a forlorn mess rather than an unconventional organizing method.

"I know they were related because all of them had similar stab wounds and appear to have been killed in a similar manner." Zedler's pallor had taken on a gray hue, and the bags under his eyes looked unusually large. He raised his voice. "Taking the time to drain victims of their blood qualifies as 'similar manner' to me."

Des sympathized but was happy he wasn't the one getting his ass reamed. The LT's standard mode of operation was to attack. Des didn't mind. As a woman in a male-dominated field, she'd have to be hard-nosed to survive. Lieutenant Lewis might not be an excellent communicator, and maybe she yelled a little too much, but she was consistent in her abuse. She treated all officers the same, and they never had to worry about what she thought about them or their cases. The LT would tell them straight to their face, in clear and loud expletives.

He moved a pile of cut-out magazine articles and a yo-yo from the visitor chair and sat down.

The older detective frowned when Des put the stuff on the floor, but there was no other place to use. Finally, the call ended, and Zedler slammed down the receiver. "That woman is hard to please."

"That's how she gets results."

Zedler just shook his head without looking up. He looked preoccupied.

"Are we going official with the murders being related?" A serial killer would definitely throw the town into a panic.

Murders became hard to solve when the public was hysterical. Sometimes mistakes were made, details missed if eager cops wanted to close a case quickly and get out from being under the media's scrutiny.

A few seconds ticked by before Zedler lifted his head. "The three victims died of stab wounds from a similar weapon. All were drained of blood after they were killed. The only difference is that Wymer and our last victim were not killed where we found them. They were moved. I don't see how we can keep that out of the media for much longer."

Des stomach sank. A feeling of dread permeated his body. "Fuck."

"That about sums it up," Zedler agreed.

"It's going to be mayhem out there when the good citizens of Prairie Falls realize they have their first serial killer." Des scratched his jawline. "We need to grab this sick fucker quick, but make sure we get the right sick fucker."

"Yup. The question now is, how?"

"Call in the feds?" Des had had both good and bad experiences working with the suits. Basically, it came down to whether they sent good or bad investigators, the same as working with any other cop.

"There's a small bureau office in town because our town is popular with the witness protection program. I've already been in touch with them."

"And?"

"They are short on resources like everybody else but will help out any way they can. It might take a few days before they can free up some man-hours."

Silence permeated the air.

Des shuddered, lost in the horror of knowing they had a madman, or madwoman, on their hands. Who would be killed next if the PFPD didn't find them first? He pulled out his notebook. "I interviewed the latest vic.'s friend and got some information."

"Anything solid to go on?"

"Not really. She was sexually active with multiple partners of both genders."

Zedler raised his eyebrows. "And she was a close friend of our Molly's?"

Des quirked an eyebrow at the "our" in that sentence, but let it go. "Yes, Molly knew her. The vic. is closer to Molly's friend Nina Hall, but all three of them socialized. They were at Sinful Soul together last Friday."

Des realized he hadn't told Zedler about the strange evening he had experienced at the club. He'd bet a year salary on the club, or someone at the club, being involved somehow, but to what degree?

"So the club may be a factor in this." The older detective leaned back in his chair. "The third victim visited the club, and the bouncer was seen in the vicinity of the second crime scene."

Des shrugged. "Yes, but we need more than that to get a search warrant."

"But it may be enough to bring in the bouncer for questioning." He tapped his fingers on the desk. "Although I'd like to have more information before we talk to him." He grimaced. "Don't' have much to ask him right now, though, other than what he was doing in the park and if he saw something."

Des noticed a yellow stain on Zedler's tie. Mustard? Egg yolk? He checked his own shirt for remnants of his breakfast. Nothing. An image of Molly eating pancakes flashed through his mind. She'd been smiling through most of the breakfast. He liked her happy. He wished he could keep her shielded from things like finding your friend murdered.

Zedler turned his way, interrupting his thoughts. "Did you get a chance to chat with him last night?"

"Not really, although I did observe some strange behavior —from him and the club patrons."

"Tell me."

Des watched Zedler while he debated how to describe what had happened and how to reveal that Molly was somehow immune to the weird drug effects if there were drugs involved. Fuck it, might as well jump into the deep end. "What do you know about Molly's intuition?"

Zedler threw him a skeptic look. "What are you talking about?"

Des looked down and turned a page of the notebook. "I overheard her friend asking about her intuition. I assume it has something to do with her sketching." He looked up. "You must have noticed how Molly has an uncanny ability to ask just the right questions when she's interviewing a witness."

The other detective shrugged. "She's a great forensic artist. Always available when we call, and she produces more accurate sketches than anybody I've ever worked with. She's also phenomenal at making the witnesses feel comfortable while she interviews them." Zedler looked Des straight in the eye while delivering the monologue, but his gaze was too solid, too direct. Like when someone had trained to tell lies, or at least not the full truth.

Des kept his own gaze steady. "I realize that you want to protect her, but I think I have a right to know what's going on."

"I don't know what you're talking about, but if I was keeping secrets, they are not mine to tell."

"Does Molly know that you know her secrets?"

Zedler hesitated, then shook his head once.

Fuck. It was going to be harder than Des thought to get Molly to open up to him. She hadn't confided in anybody—

except for Nina Hall. He doubted she would ever tell anyone without Molly's consent. Hall had been fiercely protective of Molly while they'd talked that morning.

Time to level with Zedler. "Okay, hear me out before you decide not to tell me anything. Molly is somehow connected to the weird stuff going on at the music club."

Zedler moved as if to interrupt, but Des held up his hand. "Let me finish. I don't think she's a willing participant. The bouncer and one of the waiters were a little too appreciative of her visiting. They singled her out."

The older detective leaned forward in his chair, scowling. "They may just have flirted with her. She's pretty."

Des remembered his own jealousy over the men's attention to Molly but knew their interest was more than just appreciating a beautiful woman. "The bouncer visited her apartment and gave her the VIP passes. He was very insistent that she'd go. Plus, the audience behaved bizarre last night, almost as if they had been drugged. Molly was the only one acting normal."

Zedler leaned back in his chair. "You better start talking. And don't leave anything out."

By the time Des had finished describing their evening at Sinful Soul, and what Molly had told him about her visit the previous week, Zedler had broken two pencils and annihilated several paper clips.

"Shit, shit, shit. This is worse than I thought," the older detective said as he twisted the thin silver metal wire.

"This is why I want to know everything about her. If there's something in her background that connects her to this case...if this intuition she supposedly has is somehow involved, I need to know."

"It's not my place to tell you," Zedler said. "All I have are third party rumors. As far as I know, she just has an incredible rapport with the witnesses."

Des grew angry. "Fuck your place."

Zedler smiled. He swept a hand around the office. "You're welcome too. See if you can make it a little cleaner while you're at it."

Des rubbed his face. How was he supposed to protect Molly from the creeps at the club if nobody would give him the information he needed to do so?

Zedler took pity on him. "Look, Son, go talk to her, and maybe she'll tell you."

"I've tried to get her to open up to me since I first met her."

"You've tried to get in her pants since you first met her. It's not the same thing. "

Des grinned sheepishly. "Did she tell you what happened in Sacramento?"

"No, she didn't." Zedler didn't return the smile. "What happened in Sacramento?"

The smile drained off Des face. "Nothing. Nothing important."

Zedler leaned forward with the speed of a striking snake. "If you do anything to hurt her, I will hunt you down and make you wish you'd never come to Prairie Falls. Understood?"

Des reared back as far as his chair would allow. "Very much so." In protective mode, Zedler was one scary dude. They needed to change the subject quick. Des cleared his throat. "Any other news?"

Zedler held his gaze a moment longer, but then dug around in a pile of papers on his desk. "Yeah, I got two things going for us. I meant to tell you, but then we ended up with a third body." He pulled out a document. "The vic. is a transient from Denver, Charlie Pratt. He's a forty-five-year-old veteran who likes to ride the trains. Has been classified as homeless for the last ten years."

"That's tragic. Does Mr. Pratt have any family?

Zedler nodded. "A sister. She lives in Denver too. Once the ME is done, she's asked for the body to be shipped back to her."

Des sighed. "So no known enemies or any involvement in any cults?"

"Not that the sister knew."

"What's the second piece of news?"

Zedler retrieved another document. "The knife. The lieutenant sent pictures to someone at the university. The letters are Armenian."

"What do they say?"

Zedler traced a line on the paper as he read out loud. "From eternal pain comes eternal blood becomes eternal life."

"What the fuck? So we are dealing with some nut job, who believes they can live forever by killing people, maybe even a cult that thinks this, great—just great." Des leaned forward.

"We don't have any information indicating more than one perp." Zedler put the paper back on one of his piles. He slammed a hand on top of the document. "And this stays between us for now. I don't want any of this leaked to the media."

"It's easier to hold down a victim and drain them of their blood if you have help."

Zedler shook his head. "I don't even want to think about that until we have proof that there's more than one person."

Des understood, the town would become a total circus if the press found out about a serial killing cult. Fuck.

MOLLY RETURNED HOME LATE that afternoon. Nina had assured her she'd be okay and that Molly didn't have to stay with her overnight. She had arranged for her staff to take care of the boutique for a few days while she drove north to go stay with her grandmother and great-aunt. The two sisters always complained that they didn't see Nina enough and were ecstatic over the visit, even if it was during sad circumstances. Molly half wished she'd gone with Nina. The coming workweek would be hell. Working on the Marvelous Melon campaign already reminded her of Wymer's death. And now she had the image of Carol's lifeless body lying abandoned next to the dumpster in her mind as well.

Why had Carol been in that part of town? Carol was— had been—adventurous when it came to sex, but she didn't think she would be the type to venture out in that neighborhood to scratch her itch. Maybe she was, Molly hadn't known precisely how adventurous Carol's tastes had been. Not that there was anything wrong with a healthy or diverse sex life. It was just so opposite from her own experiences that made it hard to reconcile.

Molly's only regular sex partner was Mr. Vibrator. Maybe if she took him for a spin more often, she wouldn't be so bothered whenever Rankin was near.

She blushed when she recalled what had happened in the Sinful Soul bathroom. With Clark, she had liked sex. Although, she'd been self-conscious about her scars and hadn't always relaxed enough to truly enjoy the act. But even when the sex had been good, Clark never turned her on as much as Rankin did.

When he'd kissed her, her knees actually buckled. This was new territory, scary territory.

She was hyper-aware of him whenever he was near her. Her body always knew his exact location without her having to look. The smaller the distance between them, the louder her hormones hummed. In that bathroom, they'd practically shouted, "take me, take me now."

He'd been comforting at the crime scene and understanding at Nina's place. Did he actually have a nurturing side, or was that just manipulation to get them to divulge information about Carol? She couldn't be sure. Last time she'd trusted a cop enough to date him had not ended well. It was best to remain cautious.

Briefly, she thought about calling Rankin, but he must be super busy working on the case. She looked down at her clothes. The outfit she so loved the night before now felt uncomfortable and very unfresh. Wearing it for twenty-four hours contributed, but she also felt unclean after seeing Carol's body. The outfit would forever be associated with Carol's death. She felt like lighting the top and pants on fire and wished the act would get rid of the images of Carol's dead body that were forever burnt onto her retina. A sob escaped her throat.

In the bedroom, she peeled off her clothes and chucked them in a corner. She'd soak in the bath for an hour or two. Hopefully, that would relax her enough to go to sleep later.

Half an hour later, she lounged up to her neck in soapy suds when a faint knock rapped on the front door. At first, she thought she'd misheard it, and someone was knocking on her neighbor's door. She ignored it, but by the third time she heard the sound, she got out.

Maybe her neighbor, Mrs. Coolridge, had some juicy gossip she needed to share or complain about. "I'm coming," she called to the front of the apartment as she toweled herself off. She threw on her bathrobe, a powder-blue fluffy monster of terrycloth.

A glance through the peep-hole revealed the waiter from the Sinful Soul. What was his name again? It took a moment, but she remembered he'd introduced himself as Eric when he took Rankin's and her order. She stepped back and considered pretending she wasn't home, but she'd already called out. Slowly, she slid the security chain in place before opening the door. She positioned her body slightly behind the door so that only her face and neck appeared in his line of vision.

"Ms. Nyland, it's essential that I speak with you." He looked over his shoulder as if he was afraid someone had followed him.

"Okay, I'm listening."

"Will you invite me in?"

Molly had a flashback to Tasunke asking the same thing a few days ago. "No, I don't think so."

Disappointment marred his beautiful face. "I understand, but I really do need to speak with you."

"You can tell me whatever it is you need to from there."

He hesitated for a moment, then shrugged quickly as if he'd made up his mind. "You need to stay away from the club. You may be in danger."

Molly stared at him. Was he crazy? "Why am I in danger?"

He rubbed his forehead. "Look, I can't give you any details. Just be careful."

"Is this somehow related to Sinful Soul?"

He looked away. "It may be hard to believe, but Dakota and I are actually trying to protect you."

She snorted.

He straightened to his full height. "I assure you, Ms. Nyland, you will not be harmed on my watch."

"What are you talking about? Are you following me?"

"Things are complicated, and I'm afraid you're going to have to trust me. I can't talk about this here in the hallway. I took a big enough risk coming here."

Molly studied the man for a while. She believed his

sincerity but didn't want to be in the apartment alone with him. "I'm sorry, I still can't invite you in."

"I understand. Could we perhaps meet in a public venue?"

"Sure."

They agreed to meet at a café on the outskirts of town the following day.

Eric looked relieved when he left, but Molly felt anxious. She needed to talk to someone, and her first instinct was to reach out to Nina. But her best friend was heading out of town to be with her family. Molly didn't want to bother her, but she should tell someone about Eric's weird visit.

She went to search for her cell phone and finally found it in the pocket of the brown pants she'd chucked before her bath. She scrolled through her contact list. Rankin would overreact and insist on coming over.

She kept scrolling and settled for the very last one in the list and hit the call button.

"Zedler," the detective barked after the very first signal.

"It's Molly Nyland." She wasn't sure how to continue.

"Are you feeling better, Nyland?"

"Much better, thank you. I've never seen a dead body before."

Muffled expletives reached her ears. It sounded like the detective was cursing while holding a hand over the mouthpiece. "Rankin shouldn't have brought you to the crime scene."

"He didn't know."

"Well, he should have found out. That's what detectives do, we find out what we don't know."

She decided to change the subject. "Listen, something strange is going on at Sinful Soul."

"Yeah, Rankin filled me in on your night out together. He shouldn't have brought you there either."

Molly smiled at the gruff protectiveness in the detective's

voice. "Actually, I brought him. I would have gone whether he came along or not. I had plans to go with friends."

Zedler just grunted, so Molly continued. "The waiter that served our table yesterday, and my friends the week before, just stopped by my apartment." She paused.

"What did he want?" the detective barked.

"He says he needs to warn me about something."

"Did he threaten you?"

"Not really, but he did say that I might be a target and need to be careful. I didn't get the feeling that the threat would be from him, though."

Zedler was quiet for a long time.

"Are you still there?"

"So now two people from Sinful Soul have been to your apartment?"

"Yes, isn't that a little weird?"

"Nyland, I think it's time we got together and talked."

"That's actually why I'm calling. I'm supposed to meet Eric, the waiter, at Coffee Grounds tomorrow. Will you go with me?"

"Absolutely, give me the time and address. Actually, I'll come by and pick you up. I don't want you walking in there alone."

She didn't realize how tense she'd been until her body relaxed. "Great, thank you so much."

"Nyland, has anybody threatened you lately? Have you gotten any weird phone calls or messages?"

"No. Why do you ask?"

"I can't really explain everything right now, not over the phone. Will you do me a favor, Nyland?"

"Sure."

"Don't go anywhere on your own. Stay in tonight and lock all doors and windows."

"You're freaking me out a little." She laughed nervously.

"Sorry, I'll explain everything tomorrow. Right now, I have to take care of some stuff."

Molly hung up the phone, confused. She'd always trusted and respected the older detective, but it sounded like he knew something about Sinful Soul that he wasn't sharing. She sunk down on the couch. I'm second-guessing everything and everybody. She cursed her grandmother and Clark for teaching her that people couldn't be trusted, not even the ones who appeared to be friends.

* * *

DES WAS WORKING on tracking down Liam Perry, the brother of the diseased when Zedler barged into his office. The older detective hadn't bothered to knock and swiped Des' jacket off a chair before he sat down.

"You've exposed Nyland to things she shouldn't be involved in. Thanks to you, she's now on the radar of people who she shouldn't even know."

"You're not making any sense," Des felt his temper rising. Was this about him and Molly going on a date? Zedler wasn't her father.

"You have to stay away from Nyland. Don't wine and dine her. Don't take her with you to question suspects. Don't bring her along to crime scenes."

"That's not your call to make." Des could feel his jaw tense up.

"For fuck's sake Rankin. She'd never seen a dead body before, and you took her to see one lying next to a dumpster. A body of a friend of hers."

Des flushed with guilt, but let Zedler think it was anger that made his face red. "I didn't know it was going to be someone she knew."

Zedler quirked an eyebrow.

"Okay, so I didn't know she'd never seen a body before," Des admitted. "But the officer who called me asked for her."

The older detective rubbed his face. "That may be my fault. I mentioned her name before he made the call. But you still need to stay away from her. I don't want her involved in this anymore."

"I'm not staying away from her, I can help protect her, and she's already involved."

"You don't understand—"

"You're right, I don't," Des interrupted. "And the reason I don't understand is because you won't explain what the fuck is going on."

Zedler opened his mouth and closed it again. "I can't tell you. I'm not even sure where to start explaining what I don't fully understand myself." He stood up and walked out without looking back.

"At the beginning," Des shouted. "You start at the fucking beginning." But Zedler had already left, and Des was hollering at a closed door.

CHAPTER 13

*M*olly clicked on the Norah Jones playlist on her computer and turned up the volume. She selected a second shade of blue from the graphics software palette and applied it to the sky of the gritty city-scape displayed on the monitor. The Urban Fantasy campaign for Marvelous Melon turned out to be the most fun project she'd worked on. Usually, advertising campaigns were about making life seem happier and brighter than most people experienced. These drawings were darker and bleaker with shifters and vampires creeping along deserted sidewalks and foggy alleys. Thank you, Harry Potter and Twilight, she thought. Not only did the popular book series get kids to read again, but they also created whole new sci-fi and fantasy related markets for consumer goods.

She grinned bitterly. As a little girl, she'd been fascinated with anything paranormal and devoured the Goosebumps books before tackling Harry Potter and Twilight. In secret, of course, her grandmother would never allow those "devil books" in her home. Molly had read them in the library. But after the lightning strike, her childhood had turned darker than most. Reading about a magic school and then pretending to be a wizard now seemed so innocent. The reality of being labeled an evil witch by her grandmother had been far from the marvelous adventures of Harry Potter. The woman had been convinced Molly's scars were a sign the devil had entered her body.

Over the years, she'd researched her abilities. The science studies said that lightning victims often experienced altered behavior or enhanced senses. The most feasible theory said the lightning strikes probably rewired their brains. One neurology paper showed that in animals exposed to extreme electric shock, the brain's pathways changed after the current zapped through the gray matter. The electricity blocked some of the regular neurological pathways, while it fused others to create super-synopses highways. In some cases, the therapy also created new communication pathways shaped in intricate patterns not previously observed in any mammal's brain.

She hadn't found any human case studies, but something like what that had described probably had happened to her. The animals in the studies had shown increased sensibility for things like touch and smell. She figured that the lightning had enhanced her neural pathways for periphery input, such as body language, voice frequency, and word choices. At times, she'd played with the thought of finding a neurologist willing to examine her brain.

But every imagined scenario ended up with Molly being laughed out of their office. She'd read enough of the medical community's attitude toward psychics to know that explaining about her enhanced abilities and tingling sensation would not warrant a scientific study. More likely, she'd be sent to the psych ward, even if she presented her heightened senses theory and showed the research papers she'd read.

Besides, as a child, she'd had enough of being experimented on. Her grandmother had treated her like a lab rat during attempts to lure the devil out of Molly's body. The most extreme methods involved Molly spending hours in isolation without food so that the devil would leave her for a better host.

She shuddered at the memory and pulled her robe tighter in the neck. She preferred to not know precisely how her senses worked and keep them a secret. Her life worked just the way it was. Her day job paid well, the freelance gig with the police fulfilled her, and she loved her condo.

This moment right now was a great one. A Saturday night couldn't be spent better than drawing unique and exciting designs while listening to good music and drinking excellent wine. Especially if you got to do it in your pajamas and fluffy robe.

Thoughts of Carol's lifeless body made her pour herself another glass of sauvignon blanc and concentrate on the image on the screen. Three teenagers battled a wolfman that had enormous claws. The two girls and boy had created a gigantic bubble of Marvelous Melon bubble gum as a buffer between them and the creature. With his arms and legs tangled up in the gum, the wolfman struggled to get to the humans. They danced around him as the sticky residue slowed him down.

Molly sipped her wine. There you go, Raymond, in the end, you got kids blowing bubbles after all.

Would Wymer have liked the designs? Probably not. Especially not if Molly had drawn them. She hoped his family was okay. Although she couldn't remember if she'd ever known anything about his family members, or if he actually had any.

A loud knock at the front door startled her. The computer clock showed just after ten, and she hesitated to get up. Maybe the person would think the music came from a different apartment and eventually go away.

"Open up, Molly. I know you're in there. I can hear your stereo."

Of course, Rankin. Molly sighed loudly. She really didn't want to deal with him tonight. Their sizzling attraction was too complicated. She wanted to drink wine, draw, and mellow out to Norah. Uncomplicated at its finest.

Detective Rankin took up too much space. And he messed with her hormones. She took a big gulp of wine before she went to the door and carried the glass with her.

As she had with Eric, the waiter, she only cracked the door open as much as the security chain would allow. "What do you want? It's late."

"It's time for you and me to talk. Let me in."

She wondered what had happened to make him so intense. His eyes glittered, almost sinister, and he held his body coiled tight. Letting him into the apartment didn't seem like a good idea. Plus she'd been drinking. She took another gulp from the wine glass. "It's too late. Let's talk tomorrow."

"Molly, open the fucking door and let me in. I'm tired of these games," he growled.

"I'm not the one playing games," she countered.

He closed his eyes and leaned his forehead against the door. "Open. The. Fucking. Door," he said between clenched teeth.

"I'm not supposed to," she tried.

"Says who?" His eyes flew open.

"Zedler."

"Fuck, Zedler. It's because of him that I'm here. And because I'm tired of being the only one who doesn't know your fucking secrets."

Molly gasped.

"I'm dead serious. I need to know what's going on so I can

find the fucker who killed your friend and Wymer."

"You think it's the same person?"

"I'm not having this conversation in the hallway. You have to let me in."

"I don't have to do anything I don't want to. Go home, or I'll call the police."

Rankin let out one long-suffering sigh. "I am the police."

Well, he had her there. Molly took another long sip of wine. Maybe she better let him. Mrs. Coolridge might go looking for her cat and catch them arguing in the hallway.

If that happened, there would be no end to the complaints. Plus, she needed to fill up the glass. Rankin might break down the door while she walked to the desk, where the bottle was.

"Fine, you can come in. But only because you represent the fine and upstanding police department of Prairie Falls." She had some trouble pronouncing *represent* and *prairie*, but he probably understood.

"You're drunk," Rankin said when he stepped through the door.

"Whatever." She waved her hand in the air but stopped when she had to concentrate on pouring the bottle.

Rankin marched right in and threw his jacket on one of the armchairs in front of the TV. He then went to the fridge and helped himself to a beer.

Next time she'd tell him he couldn't come in unless he brought his own beer. And some wine for her.

He crowded the kitchen and the nook with her workstation. She needed room to breathe and to pour. Picking up the glass and the bottle, she walked to the couch and sat down. With her center of gravity lower, it was much easier to maneuver the liquid from the bottle into the glass. *Look at me doing my own scientific study. Don't even need fancy PhDs in white coats.*

Rankin sat down next to her.

Why did he have to hog all the space and air in the room?

"Have you eaten anything since breakfast?" He asked.

She thought about the question for a while. "I had an apple when I came back from Nina's," she finally said, triumphantly.

"Maybe you should slow down a little."

She poured more wine just to prove her point, but since the glass was already full, it sloshed mostly on the table.

"Whoa, that's it. I'm cutting you off."

"After this glass."

"Okay, fine, finish your glass."

"After this bottle."

He sighed. "It's your headache in the morning."

"That's right," Molly said. "I can do whatever I want because I'm a grown woman, and I can drink my own wine."

Rankin made a point of leaning closer. "You are indeed a 'grown woman.' Where did you grow up?"

Molly leaned away while concentrating on drinking her wine. She swallowed a big sip. "Oh no, you don't."

"Don't what?"

"You don't get to ask me personal questions about my past so you can go and investigate me later on. I'm keeping my deepest darkest secrets." She looked at him over the top of her glass.

He moved closer, reached up, and played with a strand of her hair by the temple. "And do you have many of those? Are they very dark?"

She pulled away, so he had to release the hair. "I'm not telling you."

He sighed. "Of course not," he mumbled under his breath. "Molly, I'm trying to be respectful of your boundaries, but I think you may have information that is key to this case. Maybe information you don't know that you have."

"Yeah, right," she snorted.

"Alright, keep your secrets, but tell me why you freaked out in the bathroom at the club."

"You were crowding me."

"You seemed to like it at first."

"I did, but then I didn't."

"Why did you stop liking it? What did I do wrong?"

Molly looked out the dark window. She could still make out one of the branches of the tall tree that stood outside. WWND, she thought. What. Would. Nina. Do. She looked down in her lap and picked at a loose thread on her robe. "*You* didn't do anything wrong. I'm just…wrong."

Rankin grabbed the hand that was picking the thread and held tight. "You're not wrong. You're perfect. Please tell me what I did to make you feel uncomfortable."

Exhaustion seeped into Molly's bones. She was tired of worrying about what to wear and how to move to not reveal the scars. Always keeping part of herself hidden was exhausting. She did it to not get hurt but never sharing all of herself with people hurt too. "You touched my shoulder," she mumbled, not looking at him.

"I touched your shoulder," he repeated, clearly baffled.

"I don't like having my shoulder touched."

"I think we've established that. But why?"

"If I tell you, will you promise not to tell a soul? Nobody at the precinct? Nobody at all, even though you think they may not be connected to me?"

Rankin looked confused but nodded. "I solemnly swear not to tell anybody why you don't like to have your shoulder touched."

"Okay then," Molly said. She reached for the wine glass and drained it before she walked over to the other side of the coffee table.

Rankin and her was a bad idea. They didn't have any kind

of future together, but there was definitely chemistry between them. She was tired of fighting the attraction. Better to show him her deformities now so he could bail early before things became more complicated. And after seeing Carol tonight….

She swallowed.

Carol had been so full of life. She never shied away from sex and never apologized for enjoying it. If Carol could keep sex uncomplicated, so could Molly. She owed it to Nina's friend to not miss out on the good things in life.

To live as fearlessly as Carol.

She let the robe slip off her shoulders and down to the ground. She reached for the waist of her pajama top and started to pull it over her head.

* * *

DES CHOKED on the sip of beer he'd just pulled from the bottle as Molly pulled her top past her waist and navel. Coughing, he stared at the smooth and creamy skin covering her belly. She revealed the tantalizing lower curves of her breasts and tears gathered in his eyes as he tried to suck air into his starving lungs. This was not what he'd expected, but he liked this secret very much.

She stopped and let the pajama top drop back down.

No, he shouted silently. Don't do that.

"Are you okay," she asked, big gray eyes solemnly studying him.

"Fine, fine," he wheezed. "Please continue."

She pulled the shirt over her head in one swift swoop and stood before him in her pajama bottoms and bra.

Glorious.

The pajama pants hung just below the hip bones. Des's fingers ached to touch the silky smooth skin of her stomach and rib cage. A lacey pale pink bra hugged full, firm breasts. The rosy outlines of her nipples peeked through the fabric.

And then there were the freckles in all their glory. The bra obscured some of the patterns, but Des could make out most of them. His gaze trailed the line of dotted little stars up to her collar bone. Her left shoulder was covered in intricate white scars. The fern-like pattern spread out down her arm like a unique tattoo.

She stood with her arms straight down her side, watching him watching her.

His mouth felt dry as a dessert. His cock drummed against the crotch of his pants, so hard it hurt. He shifted on the couch.

"Well?" She asked.

He had to take a swig of the beer before he could answer. "Well, that was surprising." His gaze caressed her from top to toe. "You're so beautiful."

"You don't have to lie. Now, do you get it?"

"No, I have no fucking clue what your secret is." He took another swig as his eyes roved. "But please continue to explain it to me."

Maybe she would take off her pants next. Des couldn't wait to get a glimpse of those muscular legs of hers. He'd checked them out when she wore skirts but desperately needed to see more of them.

She gestured to her left shoulder with her hand. "This whole side is scarred."

His underperforming brain finally got the connection between her not wanting him to touch her shoulder and said shoulder having scars. "Did I hurt you when I touched you?"

"Not really." She blushed. "I just don't like people knowing how disfigured I am."

Des stared. Disfigured? What the hell? She was absolutely

181

gorgeous. If he'd ever seen anything sexier, he couldn't remember. "Molly, you are beautiful."

She glared at him and snapped up her top. "Don't lie to me." She stormed into the kitchen, clutching the garment in front of her. Her back was covered in the same intricate web pattern. "And don't try that pretend to kiss me shit, only to tweak my nose," she threw over her shoulder.

Somehow he'd missed large chunks of the conversation. Apparently, he'd gone deaf when Molly went bare. "Wait," he said and followed her.

She was struggling with the top, trying to turn it right-side-out.

"Molly, I'm sorry I've upset you. I apologize for the nose tweaking, but I was freaked out over the heat between us. It was the only thing I could think of to not screw you right here in the kitchen."

"And now?" Moisture gathered in the corners of her eyes.

"Now, I want to kiss you, touch you, and screw you right here in the kitchen." Desperation made his voice shake. "If you'd let me." Please don't put your shirt back on. Please don't bolt from me again.

"I'm not good with this stuff," she said.

"Neither am I." He walked closer. Slowly. "Maybe we can practice and learn together."

That earned him a smile.

His fingertip traced her collar bone. "I love this trail of freckles. I can't stop looking at them. It's very distracting."

Her smile grew broader.

His hand traced closer to where her scars started. "Does it hurt when I do this?"

"No," she whispered, closing her eyes.

"What happened to you?"

"I was hit by lightning when I was twelve."

He continued tracing the faint lines. "People die from

that. You were lucky."

"I know that now. When I was little, I didn't think so." Her voice was hoarse. "My grandmother used to lock me in the chicken coup because of the scars."

Des frowned. "Why did she lock you up?"

"Because I was a bad, bad girl who made a deal with the devil."

"What?" Completely shocked, he stopped touching her.

She waved her hand, dismissively. "That happened a long time ago. I'm totally over it."

Obviously, she wasn't, but Des wasn't going to press her about it tonight. Not while she stood in front of him with all this glorious bare skin as a temptation. He remembered how she'd rubbed her shoulder while taking Mildred Bunsig's statement. He pressed his lips to the top of her shoulder.

She shuddered but didn't pull away.

"Am I hurting you? Do you want me to stop?"

"No and no."

He wanted to ask about the connection between her shoulder and sketching. He struggled to find the words to phrase the questions. His dick told his brain that talking could wait.

His brain agreed.

Des continued tracing the faint white lines with his lips. Stopping every so often to nibble her skin. She tasted of melons and honey.

* * *

LIQUID FIRE TRICKLED down Molly's shoulder and arm. Whenever Rankin's lips touched her scarred skin, that spot sent out flames igniting the nerves along their path. Her brain short-circuited. She'd drunk too much wine but also experienced sensory overload.

This must be what it feels like to be beautiful.

She'd seen the desire in Rankin's eyes when she pulled off her shirt. He wasn't a good enough actor to pretend he didn't notice the scars, but they didn't disgust him.

As he kissed her collar bone, her knees melted. Heat pooled between her legs. She moaned. It was too much, but she needed more.

Much more.

Impatiently, she tugged on his head until his lips met hers. With the kiss, she tried to convey the pent up frustration her body needed to release.

"Slow down," he whispered. "I've been waiting a long time for this. I want to savor it."

Molly whimpered her protest and pressed her hips closer. Through her pajama pants, she felt the rigidness of his shaft. She wiggled to maneuver that glorious hardness to just the right spot between her legs.

"Christ," Rankin hissed. "You're killing me."

His hands cupped her breast. When his thumbs found her taut nipples, she thought she'd expire from the sweet torture.

He unclasped the back of her bra and released her mouth as he slipped the shoulder straps down her arms. "All the constellations of the heavens," he whispered and stared down on her chest.

She grabbed his head and kissed him again.

His tongue darted in and out of her mouth, mimicking the rhythm of his hips pressing his hardness into her softness. Increasing the tempo, he grabbed the back of her head. He sucked her tongue, devouring her mouth.

She clasped her hand behind his neck and pressed her whole body into his. She wanted him to possess her. She wanted him inside her. She wanted him inside her *now*.

His hands trailed down her neck and back to rest on her waist. Guiding her hips so that they matched his tempo.

Pressure built between Molly's legs, in her nipples, and all down her shoulder and arm. Heat engulfed her. She needed to cool down.

She wanted more heat.

"Sweet heaven," Des mumbled as his hands found her ass. He squeezed and pressed his still restrained bulge between her legs.

Molly wanted to tell him to pull her pants off, but that would require him to stop moving. She couldn't take him stopping.

He molded her ass with his hands through her cotton pants before moving them to the front and undoing the drawstring. The pants fell to the floor, and he lifted her up on the counter.

Molly gasped as the cold granite hit her ass and the back of her legs.

Rankin trailed kisses down her cheek and collarbone, leaving a path of fire in his wake. When his lips found her nipple, she arched off the counter, but he steadied her by grabbing her hips and holding her in place. One of those clever hands slipped lower, tracing the outline of her panties before dipping below the fabric.

Heat liquefied Molly's bones as Rankin's teeth grazed her nipple, and his finger entered her heat. He stroked her with a rhythm matching his firm lips on her breast.

Moaning loudly, Molly leaned back and gripped the edge of the counter behind her for balance.

Rankin slipped a second finger inside her and moved his mouth to her other breast. Pressure built to an uncontainable level, and she screamed out as her only choice was to release it.

Supernova, she thought as white spots danced in front of

her eyes. She rode the pleasure waves that hit her, over and over again.

Rankin's body stiffened and then relaxed, just as a loud groan escaped his lips. "Fuck," he sighed. "That has not happened in a long, long time. But it was way better than with Jamie Heraldfield."

Molly rested her head on Rankin's shoulder. "What?" she mumbled.

"Never mind."

She sighed. "I don't' know what to say. Thank you?"

With one finger under her chin, Rankin lifted her head and gazed into her eyes. A warm smile, very different from his usual cocky grin, grazed his lips. "It was my pleasure."

"I want to…," Molly hid her face in his shoulder. "I want to take care of you. Make you feel good."

His chest rumbled as a chuckle passed through. "Already been taken care of. I can't believe I blew my load still dressed." He kissed the top of her head. "You're incredible."

"Next time, we'll undress you too," Molly said and then wondered what possessed her to plan for a next time. She couldn't get involved with Rankin. This should only be for fun.

"Deal," he said and swept her up in his arms. "Let's get you to bed for now, though. You've had one hell of an emotional ride today."

In the bedroom, he lowered her down on the soft mattress and covered her with the down comforter.

She tried to open her eyes. "Stay," she whispered and felt the bed dip beside her.

"I'll wait for you to go to sleep, but I don't do sleepovers, never have really." Rankin traced the side of her face. "I can't sleep when someone else is in the bed. It's pissed off most of my girlfriends."

"I don't care," Molly mumbled before slumber claimed her.

A few hours later, her bladder insisted she'd wake up. She squirmed to get out from under the covers and was surprised over how heavy they were. Even more surprising was the hand clamped on to her right breast. She turned her head.

Rankin snored beside her, his body half draped on top of hers. Heat rushed to her cheeks when she remembered what they had done. It had been fabulous.

Beyond fabulous. She'd come harder from Rankin's fingers than she'd ever done when making love with Clark.

Not that she would tell Rankin that, of course. His ego was already too big. She smirked as she swung her legs over the edge of the bed.

As soon as she stood up, she gasped. Sweet mother, someone had opened a rock query in her head and was busy pounding the stones into sand. She definitely needed to lay off the wine, or at least not drink most of a bottle on an empty stomach.

As quietly as she could manage with the hammers in her head, she tiptoed into the bathroom and took care of business. She stared at the shower. Maybe the massaging jets of her super expensive designer shower would restore some peace in her head. If not, then she'd at least be clean while she waited for the pain to go away.

She turned the faucets on full. As she entered the steam-filled shower stall, she remembered the admiration and desire she'd seen in Rankin's eyes when she stripped. Neither had ever been present in Clark's gaze. Not when they were intimate and not when her sketches closed a case for him.

And she'd never wanted Clark as much as she wanted Rankin.

She craved Rankin's body.

She was in trouble. Major trouble.

CHAPTER 14

*D*es held open the door to the Coffee Ground café and gestured for Molly to step inside. She gave him a disgruntled look before stomping through. He'd found her dressed and ready to go out when he woke up. At first, the pleasure of having slept a full night without nightmares had distracted him from where he was, and the fact that he'd slept that soundly with someone else in the bed.

When he'd heard her rummaging around in the kitchen, he'd gone to investigate. He still couldn't believe she thought she'd sneak off to some secret meeting with the Viking from Sinful Soul without him. She'd explained she was meeting with the waiter in public, so it was safer. Like that backward logic would mean he'd let her go alone. When she said Zedler was supposed to pick her up, he'd made her call the detective to cancel the ride.

He scanned the café, automatically evaluating anyone and anything that might become a threat. A familiar figure sat at a table in the back.

Zedler.

Even on the weekend, he wore slacks and a button-down.

At least he'd taken off his jacket and loosened the tie. The blue strip of fabric hung in a wrinkled noose over an even more wrinkled white shirt.

Molly headed straight to Zedler's table.

As Des lengthened his stride to catch up with her, the older detective glared at him, "I told you to stay away from her."

"And again, not going to happen."

Zedler tried to stare him down, but Des matched the detective's hard glance. After a few seconds, Zedler broke eye contact and instead turned to Molly. "You shouldn't have brought him."

She blushed. "Rankin brought himself," she mumbled. "I tried to leave without him."

Zedler shot Des another ice-cold look through narrowed eyes.

Des cocked his head. Let the other detective figure out why he happened to be with Molly this morning. Des was not going to share the details, but Zedler needed to know he didn't get to dictate whether they saw each other or not.

The older detective turned back to Molly. "So this Eric Enfrid will be here soon. We need to figure out how to play this."

Molly sat down next to Zedler, and Des pulled out a chair with more force than necessary. Molly had discussed the meeting with Zedler but didn't bother to tell him. After a night with him, she should be sharing this kind of stuff with him. Even if they had only slept next to each other, the session in the kitchen counted.

She was his now. Wait, not exactly his, but he definitely didn't want her to be with anyone else.

Fuck. He was so screwed.

Frustrated, he decided to take the lead. "Okay, how do you want to do this?" He addressed his question to Zedler but held up a hand before the detective could answer. "And before we even start talking strategy, it's time for you two to tell me what the hell is going on."

Molly finally looked up. "What do you mean?"

He wanted to shout at her, but instead, he took a deep breath and struggled to keep his voice even. "Tell me why I got a splitting headache at the club, and the rest of the audience turned into zombies while you were just fine. Tell me how you know to ask just the right questions while sketching a composite. Tell me why the staff from Sinful Soul traipses by your apartment regularly."

Molly opened her mouth as if to protest, but Zedler stopped her by placing his hand on her arm. "Why do you think Molly and I know any more details than you do," he said.

"Don't treat me like I'm stupid." Des glared at Zedler.

"Listen," Molly interjected. "We're just here to listen to why Eric thinks I'm in danger."

"He threatened you?" Des's voice was loud enough for the other patrons to swivel their heads in their group's direction. He lowered his tone. "Why the fuck am I only hearing about this now?"

Molly glared at him. "He didn't threaten me. He warned me."

"Warned you about who?" His blood pressure was rising so fast he had to grip the table to not slam a fist through it.

"I don't know. That's why we're here," Molly shot him a death stare.

"Look," Zedler interrupted. "We need to figure out what the threat is and what kind of protection Nyland will need." He grabbed Molly's hand. "Maybe you should leave town for a while."

Her answer came lightning quickly. "I'm not leaving."

Des sighed. Of course, she wouldn't. He couldn't blame

her, though. In her shoes, he wouldn't either. He'd confront the threat and eliminate it. It didn't surprise him that stubborn Molly had the same instinct.

"I'll protect her," he heard himself saying.

Two pairs of eyes pierced him.

"Excuse me?" Molly said. "I can take care of myself. I have for a very long time."

Zedler glared at Des before turning to Molly. "It might not be a bad idea to station a patrol outside your house, and at Berker Studios. Just until we figure out what's going on."

Des clamped down to keep a loud profanity from escaping. "I'll stay with her."

"No," Zedler and Molly said in unison. What the fuck?

Molly shook her head. "I don't need anyone to stay with me."

"You need someone to keep you safe," Des said, and then quickly added "for now," when Molly hit him with another scalding look.

Zedler leaned back. "And you will keep her safe?" He traced the tabletop with a finger.

Des held the other detective's angry glare. "I will."

"Like you kept your partner safe?"

Major low blow.

Although Des was less surprised than expected. He'd wondered when Zedler would bring up Marshall's death. And Des had pushed just about all of Zedler's buttons by showing up today. After the detective had told him to stay away from Molly.

"That's harsh," he said, still holding Zedler's gaze. The other detective looked away first.

"I'm just laying it all out there," Zedler said, holding up his hands.

Out of the corner of his eye, he saw Molly looking back

and forth between himself and Zedler. "What are you two not telling me?"

Cold seeped into Des' stomach. He looked up at Zedler, who just shrugged.

Fine.

She'd find out eventually, and it was better if he told her himself. "I made a bad judgment call in Sacramento, and it cost me everything. My partner, Mitchell, was killed."

"I'm so sorry." She grabbed his hand from across the table. Warm fingers caressed the top of his hand.

He grabbed them and held on tight. "Thank you." He should tell her how it was his fault Marshall had died. But he couldn't stand her looking at him with suspicion, or worse, disgust. The way his former colleagues eventually had when the investigation into Mitchell's death went nowhere. It was still open.

Molly squeezed his hands back. "I don't remember anyone named Mitchell from when I worked with Sacramento PD."

"You wouldn't have met him. He was working undercover during the short time you were there." Des still didn't know the details about what his partner had been up to during that operation.

"Tell him about the wolf," Zedler said suddenly, turning toward Molly.

"What wolf?" she asked.

"The one in your parking lot." The older detective turned toward Des again. His eyes were intense and hard.

"Was that a wolf? I thought it was a dog. Did you find it then?"

"No. But it was a wolf. Tell him." Zedler continued staring at Des.

Des met Zedler's gaze with a straight face, but cold seeped into his stomach, and he could feel his gut cramping.

He wondered if the older detective had managed to dig up details about what had happened in Sacramento. He forced himself to speak. "What wolf."

Out of the corner of his eye, he saw Molly's head swivel between himself and Zedler. "There was a big dog…a wolf in my parking lot the other day. It scared me."

Shit. Fuck. Des had to look down. "What did it look like," he whispered.

Molly frowned. "It was big, tawny-colored, with weird amber eyes. I thought it was going to attack, but then a car came, and it ran away."

Des let out a breath of relief. Light-colored. Not black. Not the same animal as in Sacramento. He held on tighter to her hand. "I'm glad you're okay." His voice sounded hoarse.

"What's going on?" Molly asked. "What are you not telling me about the dog…the wolf?"

Des looked up at Zedler. The other detective shrugged.

"I had a bad experience with a wolf in Sacramento. But it was black." Des watched Zedler's reaction closely while he spoke. The detective's face didn't twitch a muscle. Des made a mental note of never playing cards with him.

"What kind of experience?" Molly asked.

Des closed his eyes. Images of red blood splashing as white teeth ripped into Mitchell's throat played on his retina. His partner's scream and the animal's growl pierced his eardrum. His fingers twitched as he remembered reaching for a dropped gun he couldn't find. And then the blackness. The impenetrable darkness that wiped out all other memories.

Molly put her hand on his arm. "Are you okay?"

He opened his eyes and found her gray eyes watching him solemnly. "I will be," he said, trying for a smile, but it came out a grimace. "My partner…my best friend, Mitchell, was killed by a huge wolf."

"I'm so sorry." Her warm fingers caressed the top of his hand.

He grabbed them and held on tight. "Thank you."

Zedler stood up, startling Des and Molly.

Des dropped her hand.

"Look, Enfrid doesn't know who I am. He's never met me. I want to keep it that way," the older detective said. "I'm going to go sit at another table and observe." He stalked off.

"What was that about?" Molly asked.

"Probably feels bad for blaming me for my partner's death. He knows all the facts and where things got fucked," Des said. He stood. He needed to move. "I'm going to get some coffee. Do you want anything?"

"Tea, please."

* * *

Molly watched Rankin's back as he walked up to the counter to order their drinks. She wondered what he and Zedler weren't telling her. There were undercurrents that hinted at more secrets than the death of Rankin's partner. And both of them were super protective of her all of a sudden.

She didn't like it.

She'd been on her own since she ran away from the farm at fifteen, she didn't need any protectors. Rankin or anybody else.

That morning she'd tried to not wake him. He'd slept like a dead man. Obviously, he needed the rest. But he'd heard her in the kitchen and stomped out in full interrogation mode, shooting questions at a rapid speed. What was she doing? Where was she going? Why didn't she wake him?

He'd said he wasn't going to spend the night, and now she wished he hadn't. What had happened before that was nice.

More than nice, incredible. She blushed when she thought about how her body had hungered for his caress. Her body responded to Rankin on a level she'd never experienced, but if it made him go all protector-mode on her, they'd have to have a talk.

The door opened, and Eric Enfrid walked in. The denim jeans and black t-shirt he wore outlined his body perfectly. The fabric molded his impressive pecs and quads. Molly let her gaze sweep over him appreciatively as he strode toward her table.

She caught Rankin's gaze as he leaned back against the counter, waiting for their order. His eyes narrowed.

She blushed.

He'd caught her ogling, but she only appreciated the esthetics of the other man's body, like a piece of art. Her body didn't respond in any way like when she watched Rankin.

Or when he touched her. Her body tingled, and her neck and cheeks grew hot. She quickly stopped thinking about Rankin's touch.

"Molly, I was worried you wouldn't come." Eric grabbed her hands as he sat down across from her.

Molly glanced over at Rankin again.

He'd taken a step toward their table, hands fisted at his sides.

She quickly slid her hands out of Eric's grip. Too late.

Rankin stomped across the coffee shop and slid next to her, forcing her to move over one spot. A perfect maneuver to make sure he sat across from the blonde waiter instead.

"She didn't come alone," he growled.

Eric smiled, but his eyes narrowed, and his gaze hardened. "So, you're her protector."

"Something like that." Rankin leaned back, putting an arm around Molly's shoulders.

"And do you think you can protect her against unknown threats?"

"I'll do what's necessary."

"You're a big talker. Can you back that up?"

Rankin's body tensed. "You care to find out personally?"

Molly rolled her eyes. Enough of this shit. "For the record, I can protect myself. When you are done comparing the size of your dicks, maybe we could talk about exactly what it is I should be on the lookout for?"

The two men blinked at her as if they'd forgotten she was there.

She sighed. Testosterone overload had fried their brains. "Why do you think I am in danger," she addressed the question to Eric.

"I cannot say for sure, but there are signs that *vargar* is after you."

Molly started to ask what exactly *vargar* was, but Rankin interrupted her. "Enough of this shit. Spit out what you know. Otherwise, I'll arrest you for threatening a police employee."

Eric grinned. "You are fierce, Mr. Protector. I cannot tell you any more than I know. *Vargar*…what you would call wolves are hunting in the area. They are rogue wolves. Dangerous."

"We'll call the animal control people," Des said.

Eric laughed bitterly. "These are not ordinary wolves."

"What kind of wolves are they?" Molly asked.

The blonde Viking looked at her for several seconds before answering. "This will not be easy to understand. These are intelligent wolves."

Molly nodded. "I saw one in my parking lot."

Eric sat up straight. "One of them appeared at your home."

Molly nodded again.

"This is not good. Things have progressed further than we thought."

"Who are 'we' and what 'things' are you talking about?" Des asked, his tone tinged with impatience.

Eric studied both of them. "I will tell you what I know, but you must stretch your minds. Think beyond what is ordinary in this world."

Molly wanted to ask what he meant by those cryptic words, but Eric held up a hand when she was about to speak. "Let me speak. Then ask your questions."

She nodded.

"These animals are only in their wolf-shape some of the time. Other times they are in their people-shape. They are shifters."

Des snorted.

"You do not believe me."

"That werewolves are running around the streets of Pine Rapids? No, I don't believe that."

Molly put her hand on Des leg to quiet him. "Let him finish."

Des shot her a curious look but kept silent.

Molly nodded to Eric to continue.

"Not all shifters are evil, but these wolves are shifting through blood magic. They require an offering to shift, a violent death. One victim will last for a few transformations, but each shift requires more violence, more blood."

Des interrupted again. "Are you saying the murders in town are related to these wolves?"

Eric looked at Molly when he answered. "Yes. For now, ordinary people have died to fuel the shifting. The wolves are harnessing power, but they will run out of supernatural energy. And after a while, ordinary deaths will no longer fuel the shift. They will need to kill people with unusual gifts."

Molly squirmed and studied her hands in her lap. Eric

obviously believed in what he was saying, but she had a hard time buying his story. There was no such thing as shifters. She looked up to see what Rankin's reaction was. The detective's gaze was directed at the blonde man across from him. Eric was studying Molly.

"I know you have a gift." He phrased it as a statement.

"Why do you say that?" Molly kept her tone breezy. Casual.

"Because you resisted the shroud."

"What the fuck are you talking about?" Rankin wanted to know. "What shroud?"

"You fought it too, but it made you ill." Eric looked at Rankin.

Molly interrupted the detective before he could curse again. "Please explain what the shroud is?"

The waiter paused yet again. "I'm not sure I can. When Isa sings, her voice spins the shroud. The audience forgets everything but their admiration for Isa. They are enraptured."

Molly felt a headache start. She massaged her temples to ease the pain. "Are you telling me the singer at Sinful Soul is some kind of witch? That she puts a spell on people?"

Eric shook his head. "No, she isn't forcing their will. Her voice enhances what they already feel."

"Why does she do this?" Molly asked.

Eric avoided her gaze. "That is not my place to say. She has her reasons. She doesn't hurt people."

Rankin shifted in his seat. "Can we get back to these rogue wolves? Who are they, who are committing these murders?"

Eric turned toward him. "That I don't know."

"But you know they are responsible."

The waiter got a far-away look in his eyes. "Yes, I have

seen this before. A long time ago." He seemed lost in thoughts for a while. "Someone I cared for was lost to me because I didn't react fast enough. I do not want that to happen again."

"How much exactly do you care for Molly?" Rankin's voice was hard.

Eric grinned. "I do not know her well, yet. But I am sure that if I spent time with her, I would come to care for her very much."

"Not going to happen." Rankin put both his hands on the table as if he was bracing himself.

"Do you care to wager on that, Protector."

Molly rubbed her temples again. Good grief. These two were like roosters circling each other, comparing plumage. She looked across the café toward Zedler. He seemed to watch the posturing with interest. When he caught her looking his way, he winked. *Men, they're all the same*, Molly thought.

"Do I get a say in who I may or may not spend time with?" she asked.

"No," Rankin answered immediately.

Eric just grinned.

She'd had enough. "Look, can we come up with a plan for how to catch these wolves, or at least catch the murderers?" Molly looked at Eric. "Do you have any clue as to who killed these people?"

"No, I only know what Tasunke found at the places where the bodies were placed."

"What are you talking about?" Des asked.

"Tasunke is *varg jägare*, wolf hunter. He sensed the animals in the park when the first murder happened and went to investigate."

"I'm losing you here, buddy," Des said. "What does Tasunke do?"

"He can sense shifters. He tracks rogue wolves and eliminates them."

"What did he find at the crime scenes?"

"Large paw prints, wolf hairs, and a strong scent of wolves just coming into power."

"Fuck."

Molly raised an eyebrow when Des cursed. He shook his head. "One of the things the crime scene technicians couldn't make sense of was that there were animal hairs at both scenes and tracks."

"You didn't tell me this before." Molly was hurt.

"It didn't seem important." Des shrugged. "Plus, it took a while to examine the hairs at the first scene. The farmer had kept goats and dogs in that field."

Molly's headache struck out in full bloom. She'd had enough of overprotective men. Men who thought they knew what was best for her. Men who needed to work on their communication skills and dial down the testosterone. She pushed at Rankin to get him to move so she could get out from behind the table. "I need to go home."

Rankin pushed back, refusing to let her out. "You're not going anywhere alone."

"He's right," Eric said. "You should not be alone. I will arrange for someone to stay with you."

"Not going to happen," Rankin said through gritted teeth. "I'll make sure Molly is protected."

"For fuck's sake. Snap out of it," Molly growled.

The two men froze, staring at her wide-eyed.

"I'm a grown woman. If I need protection, I will arrange it on my own. Stop treating me like a child."

Rankin stroked her arm. "I just want to see you safe."

She shrugged him off. "If I want your help, I will ask for it."

Eric watched their exchange, an amused smile playing on his lips. "If you need my help, you may ask for it too."

Rankin stood up. "Not going to happen."

Molly pulled him down again. "Thank you, Eric. I'll keep that in mind."

* * *

DES GLARED at the man in front of him. The Viking had a couple of inches on him, but Des was pretty sure he could still take him. The guy was huge, but in his experience, giant dudes moved slowly. He wanted to test how quick the guy was by clipping him one on the jaw. Just for that self-satisfying grin, he got on his face when Molly said she'd let him know if she needed help. She was with Des now. She didn't need any help from anybody else. He opened his mouth to say so, but before he could let the words out, the door to the café opened. Over the Viking's shoulder, she watched as the long-haired bouncer from the club strode toward them. He wore his usual black leather, black hair streaming behind him, bottle-green eyes boring into his own. When he reached the table, he grinned at Des.

"Brother Wolf, we meet again."

Des now wanted to punch both of the giants. "I'm not your brother and shut the fuck up about the wolf crap. I've had enough of it."

The bouncer bowed his head slightly. "If you say so." He turned to Eric. "We must leave for Sinful Soul. Isa needs you."

The blonde guy stood up and looked at Molly. "This is a lot take in, I know. However, please listen with your heart, as well as your mind as you think it over. Trust your instincts."

"I will," she said.

The two Sinful Soul employees turned toward the door.

Tasunke's nostrils flared suddenly, and he turned toward the table from which Zedler was observing them. The two men took a step toward the old detective, but he shook his head as if to warn them. They both froze.

"The wise one has arrived already," Tasunke mumbled.

"Is he fully aware," Eric asked.

Tasunke lifted his head and sniffed the air. "I do not know," he said. "He is old magic, and his scent is harder to decipher."

With a short nod to Zedler, both men swiftly strode outside, leaving Des baffled, and from Molly's expression, she felt the same. They both looked at Zedler.

He was studying the door as it closed behind the other two men, a thoughtful look on his face.

Des walked over to his table. Molly trailing behind after him.

"Care to explain that little show, oh wise one?" Des asked.

Zedler ignored him. "What did you find out?"

"Why don't you first explain how you know those guys?" Des shot back as he pulled out a chair and sat down.

Molly did the same but didn't say anything.

"I don't know them," Zedler said.

"They sure think they know you."

The older detective sighed. "I swear I don't know them. I've worked with their kind...with people like them in the past. They know me by reputation."

"People like what, like who?" Molly wanted to know.

Zedler studied her for a few seconds before answering. His gaze searching her face. "I can't tell you. You just have to trust me for now. Trust that I am on your side." He held out his hand.

Molly placed hers in his, palm to palm. "I do. That's why I called you."

Des cleared his throat. "Can we cut this mumbo jumbo crap and do some crime-solving? The Viking and the Bouncer are obviously involved in these murders somehow."

"What did they tell you?" Zedler asked.

Des looked at Molly and raised his eyebrows.

"Fine," she said in response to his unspoken question. "I'll tell him." She proceeded to relay the conversation—if you could call it that—to Zedler. Let the older detective try to figure out what the hell all that doublespeak and riddles meant. Des had no idea how to sort it all out or whether any of it was true, or just delusional ramblings. Sure the people at the club had all turned into zombies, except for him and Molly. And it was true he'd gotten a major headache, but there was probably a reasonable explanation for all of it.

"—and so, apparently I'm in danger because I have some sort of special gift," Molly concluded, shrugging.

"Did they say what the gift was," Zedler asked.

Molly looked down in her lap, her face flushed. "No, just that it enabled me to resist the shroud."

Zedler placed his other hand on top of Molly's, encapsulating her smaller palm between both of his. "We both know you have unusual abilities."

Molly shook her head. "There's nothing special about it. I just know how to read body language better."

Des wanted to hug her, she looked so forlorn. He must have made a move because Zedler stopped him with a look, shaking his head. He turned to Molly again. "I think it is time for you to embrace what you can do, who you are. You are putting yourself and others in danger by denying your powers."

A tear trickled down Molly's cheek.

Screw Zedler. Des put his arm around her.

She leaned into him. "Now you sound like Nina," she said, sniffling a little.

Zedler nodded. "She's a wise woman. And a good friend. You should listen to her more."

"What do you know about my 'ability?' You've never asked me about my sketches." She used air-quotes.

"True," Zedler said. "But I have worked with others like you. I recognize the gift when I see it."

Des felt like he'd fallen down the rabbit hole. This was too much to process. And it made him think about Mitchell's death because the victims here in Prairie Falls had a large-predator connection, even if their bodies hadn't been torn apart limb-by-limb like his partner's.

He didn't want to think about Mitchell. Didn't want to remember the blood, the teeth marks, the mauling.

His cop instincts were screaming out that he had to, though. He tuned back into the conversation in front of him.

"It's not a gift," Molly was saying. "It's a curse."

"Don't say that. You are helping people," Zedler said. "Can you tell me how it works?"

Molly took a deep breath. Her shoulders slumped. "I don't exactly know how it works. I just feel a tingling sensation in my damaged skin when someone doesn't use the right words to describe something."

Bloody hell. Fuck me. This was what she'd been holding out on Des with. He'd thought her secret had been that she suspected someone from Sinful Soul. This was so much bigger than that little omission. The woman used magic mojo while she sketched. He was too stunned to speak.

"Does it work outside the interrogation room? Can you tell when people are lying when you're not drawing?" Zedler prodded.

"No, it only really works when I have a sketch pad in front of me."

The older detective nodded. "That's good to know."

Molly looked up, her chin held high. "I'm not a freak. This is just something I can do. It doesn't change anything."

Zedler patted her hand again. "Of course not. Having special abilities is normal. It's a lot more common than you think."

Des wanted to ask the detective on which planet it was normal to detect when people weren't accurate in their descriptions through tingles in your skin but still couldn't get his mouth to shape any words.

Molly was looking at him, expecting a response, but he didn't have one. He opened his mouth, but there were no words. All Des could do was look at her. He took in her sweet face, the slightly upturned nose dusted with freckles, her red curls. She seemed so normal. He watched her eyes clouding over as he struggled to say something, anything. Finally, she avoided his gaze, shutting him out.

"Could you please give me a ride home," she asked Zedler.

The other detective studied Des for a few seconds before smiling at Molly. "Of course." He rose and helped her by pulling out the chair as she also stood.

"Wait," Des said in a weak voice as the two of them walked toward the door.

Zedler turned around and gave him a look filled with pity.

Molly didn't react at all, she just kept on walking. As she opened the café door, her glorious red hair and curvy body were illuminated by the bright sunshine for a brief second before the door closed behind her.

Des felt the thud reverberating through his chest.

Fuck. He could have handled that so much better.

CHAPTER 15

*T*ired and disillusioned, Molly walked into the office of Berker Studios the next morning. Zedler had driven her home after the disastrous meeting at Coffee Grounds. He'd only let her spend enough time at the apartment to pack a bag and grab her laptop and then drove her to a hotel.

She'd insisted she wasn't scared to spend the night in her own bed, but he'd just looked at her like she was five years old and told her not to be stupid. "Don't tell anyone where you are," he'd said as he dropped her off. "Not even Rankin."

Unnecessary warning, she thought as she dragged herself down the hallway toward her office. It wasn't like she'd be speaking to him any time soon. She couldn't shake how shocked he'd been in the café. So much for the passion and desire she thought had been in his eyes during their erotic gymnastics in the kitchen. Now that he knew everything about her freak intuition, he couldn't even speak to her.

She shouldn't be as hurt as she was, it's not like she'd expected a commitment. Sex with Rankin was only supposed to be fun and casual, and yet, she'd lain awake most of the night, obsessing about his shocked face in the café. By morning, that worry had turned to anger.

She unlocked her office door and stashed her purse in the bottom desk drawer. In an hour, she had to present the final designs to Marvelous Melon. Maybe she'd be more awake by then, or at least less upset. But as pissed off as she was with Rankin, she was even more angry—furious actually—with herself. She knew better than to fall for another good-looking cop who had no problem screwing her but couldn't stomach who she really was.

A small voice in the back of her mind pointed out that Rankin hadn't actually screwed her yet, but she refused to listen. What they had done in the kitchen was close enough. She was entitled to hold it against him.

That same voice also tried to convince her that there was no way Rankin could fake how turned on he'd been, but she squelched that too.

After he dumped her, Clark had confessed how hideous he found her scars. How he had to fantasize about someone else to get an erection. She hadn't had a clue anything was wrong between them in bed.

Rankin's reaction when she told him about the connection between her scars and her enhanced intuition had been visible, though. If she'd lead up to the revelation, he'd probably have been able to hide how he really felt. Put on the spot, he'd been at a loss for words.

She swallowed the lump she refused to acknowledge had formed in her throat. It was better this way. Better it ended before she got more attached. More hurt.

Molly turned on the computer and stared at the phone next to her monitor. The message light blinked an irritating red. Rankin had left several messages on her cell phone. She hadn't listened to any of them and didn't want the risk of hearing his voice now. There was too much to do before the presentation. She didn't have time for another emotional meltdown.

Forty-five minutes later, she rewrote the closing sentence of her speech for the third time when there was a knock on the door. Anthony let himself in before she had a chance to answer.

"How's it going, Molly? All set?" His smile was just as blinding white as usual.

"Sure," Molly said, giving him a grin back. It might be insincere, but Anthony's charm still cheered her up today. "I uploaded the slide presentation to the network a while ago. We're all set to go."

"You decided against the traditional poster boards?"

"The designs are sharper if projected on the screen, and I want them as big as possible." She didn't tell Anthony, she also wanted the designs viewed frame-by-frame with sound effects. The element of surprise would make them more impressive.

"I'm fine with whatever you decide. I trust your judgment." Anthony sat down in the chair across from her.

Molly tried not to be obvious when she glanced at the clock in the lower corner of her computer screen. She needed a few more minutes for the finishing touches on her narrative.

"So," Anthony drawled. "I understand there's been another murder."

Molly's head snapped up. That was a segue she hadn't anticipated. She waited for him to continue.

"And you knew this victim too?"

Molly's shoulder itched. "She's a friend of a friend," she said cautiously. She'd never before had a reaction from her injuries when someone asked her a question.

"Aren't you worried that two murdered people are both connected to you?"

Molly's shoulder tingled like crazy, and she had to mentally force herself to not rub it. This was really weird, why did he want to talk about this? "Prairie Falls is not a very big town. Most people are somehow connected to everyone by only a few degrees of separation." She wasn't used to having uncomfortable conversations with Anthony. Except for the one several years ago, when he'd asked her bra size. It had been during her first Christmas party. Anthony had been very drunk. Since then, they both pretended it never happened.

"Do the cops have any leads?"

"I don't know. I'm only a part-time sketch artist. The investigative detectives usually don't share that kind of details with me." She was a lousy liar, but Anthony didn't seem to notice her fib. When Molly worked on a case, the detectives usually filled her in. It probably wasn't standard procedures, might even violate a few. More than once, though, she'd found that some minor thing from the investigation could be used when she questioned a witness about a description. Especially if she was working on a crime scene sketch.

She was pretty sure Rankin kept a lot of his investigation from her, though, so maybe she wasn't lying to Anthony.

She forced the thoughts of the detective out of her head.

Her boss scrutinized her for a while. "Sorry, I asked." He stood up in one smooth motion. "Good luck on the presentation," he threw over his shoulder and exited her office.

Molly sat back in her chair. Something peculiar had just happened, but she didn't have time to figure it out. She quickly copied the files she needed to a thumb drive, just in case the network would go down.

One quick peek in the small mirror on the wall next to her file cabinet showed she looked as presentable as could be expected. She put on some lipstick, but there was nothing she could do to hide the bags under her eyes. She stuffed some business cards and the thumb drive in the pockets of her jacket before snapping the cuffs in place. Taking a deep breath, she exited and headed down the hallway.

An unusually large number of people had squeezed into the firm's largest conference room. The polished solid oak table held eighteen people, and only two of the high-backed leather swivel chairs were empty. Five of the occupants were from Marvelous Melon, but the rest of the chairs were all employees of Berker Studios. Many of the company's junior designers had joined the meeting, which was usual since they were encouraged to learn from senior designer presentations.

Fred being there was a surprise, though. He had been clear about how he felt about Molly leading this account. He threw her a fake smile, looking very pleased with himself for some reason. Unease trickled down her spine as she walked along the table to stand in front of the flat screen hanging on the wall. She mentally shook herself to clear the disquiet.

Showtime.

She nodded to the Marvelous Melon marketing team and pressed the on-button on the remote control to the projector in the ceiling. A muted whir filled the room as she logged on to the laptop in front of her. She clicked on the icon for the network drive and then the folder with her name.

Empty.

Every file she'd ever copied to the network had disappeared.

What she saw on the monitor also projected on the screen behind her. The faces in front of her displayed various levels of worry: from the Marvelous Melon team's vague puzzlement to her coworkers' high anxiety.

Except for Fred. He watched Molly with feverish eyes, a smile of triumph playing on his lips.

Anthony entered the room and shook hands with each of the clients before standing beside Molly. "Ready?" he asked her.

Molly reached into her pocket and pulled out the flash drive. As she popped it into the USB connector, she gave Fred a quick nod. It wasn't hard to figure out he was to blame for the disappearing files. *Game on, sleazeball.*

She faced Anthony and smiled big. "Absolutely."

He turned toward the table. "I give you our own Molly Nyland, the lead designer on this campaign." A smatter of polite applause followed as Anthony claimed one of the empty chairs.

Molly nodded to the junior designer closest to the light switch, and he dimmed the lamps in the ceiling. She took a deep breath. "This presentation mixes the valued traditions and brand integrity of Marvelous Melons with current trends among teenagers." She smiled nervously. "I hope you enjoy watching the designs as much as I did creating them."

Clicking the play icon on the laptop, she took a step to the side so everyone could see the screen.

Vampires, wolfmen, and other creatures of half-human-half-beast variety fought with human teenagers in an urban environment. As each slide progressed, a new battle formation displayed, giving the impression of flipping through a stack of papers to make a still movie. Music similar to the soundtrack of original Marvel TV cartoons played. Molly had timed the auto-play slide show such that a loud pop sounded when a scene containing a burst Marvelous Melon bubble appeared. The bubbles either trapped or disarmed one of the paranormal creatures.

The presentation lasted only a few minutes but contained over fifteen designs. When the last slide faded, Molly signaled for the lights to be brought up to full intensity again.

She glanced at Anthony.

He watched her with a peculiar expression as if there was something he was trying to figure out. His eyes narrowed slightly as he continued to scrutinize her.

Uncomfortable, Molly quirked her brow at Fred instead, who mouthed the word "bitch."

She responded with a beaming smile. Advantage, Nyland.

The senior marketing executive from Marvelous Melon clapped enthusiastically. "That was amazing."

"Thank you." Molly's shoulders relaxed as the anxiety over whether the clients would like her work drained from her body.

One of the two women on the team spoke. "Yes, very impressive. Could we please see each design again by itself?"

"Certainly." Molly busied herself with bringing up a second file. She clicked through each slide—this time without music—and jotted down notes as the clients discussed the strengths and weaknesses of each graphic.

Anthony dismissed the rest of the Berker Studios personnel, before joining Molly's and the Marvelous Melon representatives' discussion. A few of her coworkers gave Molly thumbs up as they walked out of the room. Fred slunk out without looking her way.

At the end of the meeting, the clients had picked out eight scenarios they wanted to build the campaign around. Options of TV commercials and internet ads had been discussed, and the marketing team left with satisfied smiles.

Molly gathered her notes. Before she had a chance to leave, Anthony grabbed her left wrist. A shock shot up through her arm, all the way to the nape of her neck.

Startled, she met Anthony's eyes.

"So you *do* feel it too?" His smile turned predatory.

Molly opened her mouth to ask what he meant, but he waved his hands and interrupted her.

"Never mind. It's not what we need to discuss right now." He released her wrist. Molly rubbed where he'd gripped her.

"That was one heck of a presentation." Anthony's most charming smile was back on his lips. "I'm taking you out for lunch."

"I'm not sure—"

"It isn't a question." Anthony studied her again.

She couldn't tell if he was trying to figure something out about her, or if there was something he wanted her to figure out about himself.

"We need to finalize the next steps of the campaign," he continued, "and I need some fresh air."

"Okay." Molly shrugged. She didn't know what these new undercurrents meant. But, free lunch was free lunch. "Do I get to pick the place?" she asked.

"Sure, as long as it has margaritas and is within walking distance."

That narrowed the choices down to one Mexican restaurant around the corner. It was one of Molly's favorites, though, so she didn't mind.

"Meet me by the elevators in five," Anthony said before leaving the room.

Molly had just enough time to drop off her stuff, and do a quick restroom stop before catching up with Anthony at the elevators. Samantha's desk was curiously empty.

"Where's Sam?" She asked.

Anthony just shrugged before stepping onto the elevator.

They rode down to street-level in silence, which lasted as they walked to the restaurant door. Too early for the lunch crowd, it wasn't long before they were seated in a booth in the back of the restaurant. Molly had first walked toward a window table, but Anthony steered her toward the back.

"Tell me how you came up with the ideas for your designs," he said after they'd given the waitress their order.

Molly stopped a salsa loaded chip midway to her mouth. She put it on her side plate. "I'm not sure." She thought for a while. "It kind of just came to me."

"Where you watching something that made you think of vampires and werewolves?"

"No, not really."

"Reading a book about them?" He watched her closely.

"Is this important?" Molly shifted in her chair. "I don't always know where my ideas come from."

Anthony looked away. "I guess not. I'm just curious. They're very different from what you've done for us before." He paused. "Very otherworldly."

"I know, right? But also so on-trend right now." Molly told him how inspired she'd been when she'd worked on the very first drawing. How one had led to several others until she felt she was drawing a story. Almost like a graphic novel. "Oh, maybe that's it," she said. "Nina and I were talking about how today's graphic novels are so much darker and edgier than the comics we grew up with."

Anthony's shoulders relaxed. "You were a comic book reader?"

Molly bristled at the incredulous tone he used. "What's that supposed to mean?"

He shrugged. "I just don't picture you as a superhero fan."

"There are more to comics than just superheroes."

"Spoken like a true geek." Anthony chuckled.

Molly relaxed. He was teasing, not insulting her. "Fine, you got me. I was an utter and total geek."

"Did you wear glasses?" He popped a chip in his mouth. "Short plaid skirt, with a white shirt and school tie?"

"You're such a pervert," Molly said but smiled to take the sting out of the words.

"I assure you, I've only pictured you in your school uniform while at legal age."

Molly squirmed in her seat and tried to cover the flush in her cheeks to hide how uncomfortable she felt. This side of Anthony was new. He'd never really flirted with her, not since she'd told him off after the awkward Christmas party question about her bra size. He wasn't her type. She couldn't stop thinking about Rankin, so her kind was apparently cocky and arrogant. Even now, she compared the detective to her boss, and Anthony came up short, but she could see why women were attracted to him.

Leaning back in the booth, one arm casually draped over the back of the seat, he looked relaxed, confident, and charming.

It was unsettling to be on his radar all of a sudden. Molly could feel the weight of his gaze as she pretended to look for the one perfect chip in the basket on the table. Had Samantha ended things?

"It's cute when you blush," he finally said. "Does your cop make you blush?"

She looked up. "My cop?"

"The detective that came to the office, whatever his name was. He's definitely into you."

Anthony didn't fool Molly. He remembered Rankin's name, but this explained the sudden interest. Another alpha male had marked his territory, and her boss didn't like it. What an ass. "I thought we were going to talk about the campaign," she said.

"Message received," Anthony countered. "The cop is off-limits. Just tell me if you are seeing him or not."

"Not your business," Molly growled before she could stop herself. She cleared her throat. "About the designs," she said. "Which one do you want me to start finalizing first."

Anthony obliged her change of topic. They spoke of nothing but design work and marketing strategy during the rest of the meal.

Since her boss had a client meeting, Molly rode the elevator up alone. When she stepped out on Berker Studios' floor, Samantha ambushed her. "Where's Anthony?" she grabbed Molly's arm.

"He had to go across town." Molly carefully extracted herself from Samantha's grip. The office manager looked nothing like herself. Her clothes were wrinkled, and her eyes were red-rimmed. "Are you okay, Sam?"

A big tear traveled down Samantha's cheek. She sniffed. "Anthony and I had a big fight, and now he won't talk to me."

"I'm so sorry."

The blonde looked at her with wide eyes. "Are you going out with him?" Several more tears threatened to spill out of her eyes.

Molly shook her head. "No, of course not. Anthony and I have a professional relationship. That's all it's ever going to be." She gave Samantha a hug and stroked her back. "What did you fight about? Is there anything I can do to help?"

Samantha stiffened. "You're sweet. But I think I have to figure this out with Anthony." She smiled bravely. "Thanks for listening, though." She walked back to her desk and took a moment to compose herself before concentrating on her monitor.

Molly watched her for a moment and then mentally shrugged. She couldn't help unless Samantha gave her more details. Meanwhile, she had enough of her own problems. Both personal and professional.

She ignored the stab of pain she felt in her chest when she thought of Rankin. For now, she'd concentrate on how to solve the mess she had at work. At least she could handle that without any emotional pain. What exactly should she do about Fred? Glancing at Samantha one last time, she walked back to her office.

The design team had always been cutthroat. More than a

little backstabbing occurred as people vied for better assignments and better offices. Fred had crossed the line, though. By sabotaging the presentation, he'd jeopardized the account.

She wanted to talk to Fred herself before she brought it up with Anthony. Going straight to the boss could lose her the other coworkers' respect. No one liked a tattletale.

Molly had barely sat down in her office chair when the door flew open. It hit the wall with a bang, and Fred stormed into her office. He kicked the door shut and flung himself in her visitor chair.

"You think you're so clever, don't you?" He snarled. His face glowed beat red, and his eyes narrowed into small slits.

She'd never seen Fred this worked up. Had he been drinking? He wasn't slurring his words. She didn't smell alcohol, but he was acting crazy. Carefully she watched to see what he would do next. "What can I do for you?"

"Who do you think you are?" Fred sneered. "You're nothing special. You have no talent."

Molly stayed as still as she could in her seat. This wasn't at all what she'd planned when she thought of talking to Fred.

"I was here first. The Marvelous Melon account should have been mine. And if you hadn't scampered around in short skirts and flashed your tits in Anthony's face, it would have been."

The first flush of annoyance cramped Molly's stomach. She knew Fred resented her, mostly because she was a woman, but he'd never been so obvious about it.

"Me being female had nothing to do with why I'm the lead on that account, I—"

Fred snorted and interrupted her. "It has everything to do with you being female. Do you think Anthony would pay any attention to you if he couldn't also look down your blouse while reviewing your designs?"

Her annoyance rose to anger and traveled up Molly's esophagus, heated her cheeks, and erupted through her mouth. "You fucking jerk." She stood.

Shock widened Fred's eyes. He leaned back so quickly the chair almost toppled before he shifted his body weight and flopped the front legs back down.

"Who do *you* think you are?" Molly said, advancing on him. "Sabotaging *my* presentation. Coming into *my* office. Attacking *my* career. Criticizing *my* designs, which by the way showed more talent than you could even dream of."

Fred scooted the chair further back.

Molly wasn't done. "If you think I'm just going to take your misogynistic crap, you are so fucking wrong." She leaned over the chair and put her face close to Fred's, lowering her voice to a deep growl. "If you even breathe another word about me getting preferential treatment because I'm a woman, I will rip you a new one and report you for harassment." Her scars burnt, heat radiating down from her shoulder across the skin of her arm. She leaned back, crossing her arms. "Do you understand what I'm saying?" Her hand felt hot, so hot.

Fred's face drained of all color. He nodded.

"Now, get out of here before I call security and have them throw your scrawny ass out."

He shot out of the chair, which tipped over as he bumped into it during his hasty retreat.

"Oh, and I'm documenting this incident, so don't try to deny it, if these issues come up again," Molly shouted after him.

She watched as the door fell back into place. To his credit, he didn't slam the door but didn't shut it softly either. She straightened the chair Fred upturned on his exit and took a deep breath.

She rarely got angry. More accurately, she rarely expressed her anger.

She could still feel the heat in her cheeks. But what had happened with her scars? Her nerve endings were still sizzling.

She retrieved a bottle of water from her mini-refrigerator and sat down behind her desk again. Placing the cold bottle on her forehead, her skin cooled, as did her temper. Her hand finally returned to its normal temperature.

Had she gone too far? If Fred had planned major sabotage because he felt cheated out of an account, what would he do to get back at her for threatening him? Hopefully, he'd understand she was serious and leave her alone. If not, she would go to Anthony.

She took a swig of the water, and her eye caught the blinking message light.

Sighing, she flopped back in her chair. She'd already dealt with two unpleasant situations today. Three if she included the lunch with Anthony, but that had been more weird than unpleasant. Might as well do all of them in one day. Besides, the messages couldn't all be from Rankin. There might be some client calls, as well.

She still hesitated and reached for the mouse to check her email first. It only took a few minutes. After ignored the four messages Detective Rankin had sent, there were only a few she had to respond to. Several of them were from the Marvelous Melon team, congratulating her on a job well done. Two were from junior designers asking her if she'd review some of their work.

Part of the asking was just brown-nosing, but the company did encourage senior artists to mentor new design school graduates. She wrote both of them back and told them to meet with her together. Maybe if she encouraged junior designers to work in teams and bounce ideas of each other, there would be less backstabbing.

Molly hit the send button on the last email. No more stalling.

She could delete Rankin's phone messages without listening to more than the beginning of each. That should tell her whether they were about the case or not.

She dialed her message system and punched in her pin.

The unemotional electronic voice informed her of five new messages.

She closed her eyes and kept her finger hovering over the delete button, ready to punch it when she heard Rankin's voice.

Instead, she heard a woman's voice, high pitched, and sobbing. Molly's eyes flew open, and her breath caught.

"I'm so sorry. I didn't know. I just wanted to find out what he was like. I didn't—" The voice stopped abruptly and instead screamed. A horrible wail traveled down the line before the message ended.

A sharp pain fired through Molly's mind, making her gasp out loud.

Carol had left her a message. Right before she died.

CHAPTER 16

*D*es threw his stapler across the office. He'd spent the last ten minutes trying to open the fucker so he could clear a jam. The stapler hit the wall with a satisfying thump, then bounced on the floor, busted open, and spilled its guts. His report would not get stapled any time soon. Not that he had expected to be able to do something as simple as connecting two pages with a tiny piece of metal. The rest of his life had turned into a shit parade, the broken stapler was just an added float.

Des rubbed the stubble on his chin with both palms. He cleared cases because he had to. Unsolved problems kept him awake. He had to find a solution or an answer. Which was why he hadn't slept properly without prescription drugs since Mitchell died.

Except for the night he stayed in Molly's bed.

Molly.

He'd screwed up and needed to fix it. Needed to solve the problem. But she wouldn't return any of his calls. She wouldn't even return his emails. He couldn't apologize if she wouldn't talk to him.

She'd disappeared completely. He'd gone to her apartment and knocked until one of her neighbors came out to yell at him. The crazy old lady ignored his badge and had stood in the hallway until he left.

He returned thirty minutes later and picked the lock, only to find out that the neighbor had been right. Molly was spending her nights somewhere else. Maybe with someone else.

The thought hurt, but he just wanted her safe. Wanted to know she was safe.

He'd gone by her friend Nina's apartment too, but that had been empty as well. After that, he didn't dare picking any more locks. A breaking and entering didn't look good on a detective's resume. Molly could be anywhere, in or outside Prairie Falls. Des tried to think of whom else she had talked about. Nothing came to him. He couldn't recall a single friend she'd talked about other than Nina. And Carol, whose dead body she had to see thanks to him.

He'd pressed Zedler for answer, but the detective wouldn't budge. He just said Molly wasn't staying with him. He'd looked at Des like he was scum. Which he was.

If he hadn't been so stunned, he'd have handled the whole situation at the café differently. Finding out your date had weird talents because she was struck by lightning as a child was not covered at the academy.

He was still a little freaked. A lot of what Molly had said didn't make any sense to him. When she sketched, an untruth caused a ripple in the scarred skin of her back. If the witness were heading in the right direction, her shoulder and arm felt it. He had so many questions.

How could a lightning strike give someone enhanced interrogation skills? Was it just a huge fluke? A string of coincidences?

And if he hadn't been such an idiot—a mute fucking idiot

—when she shared her secret, he could ask her all of those questions, and more.

Zedler refused to talk about Molly's ability at all. Said it wasn't his place. Probably also thought Des didn't deserve to know any details. Which he didn't. But he needed to find out if Molly was okay.

Zedler probably had a working stapler. It would serve him right if Des borrowed it and broke it while he stapled this fucking report. Not that there was any hurry. He'd been catching up on paperwork while hoping for a break in the murders.

No such luck.

The man Ms. Bunsig had seen in the park had come forward when the brass released the sketch to the media. He was a Native American—not Asian, just like Molly had suspected—and a local business man out for a jog. He hadn't heard or seen anything unusual that night, mostly because he'd not been wearing his glasses and had blasted music through his headphones. The man did remember Ms. Bunsig and her dog though.

Apparently, Blitz had disliked the jogger and gone for his ankles. Mildred Bunsig disputed all such allegations.

Des got a headache just thinking about it. About the lady and her dog. About the break he'd hoped would happen when they found the man in Molly's sketch.

About Molly avoiding him.

Restless, he stood and then paced the office.

The door flew open and Zedler sprung through.

"Get your stuff."

Des grabbed his shield and weapon from the top desk drawer. "Where are we going?"

"Berker Studios." Zedler left as fast as he'd entered.

Des caught up with him and grabbed his arm. "Is Molly okay?"

Zedler gave him a dirty look and jerked his arm free. "As okay as you can be when you find your dead friend's left you message on your voicemail."

Fuck.

Des didn't waste any more time. He took off down the hall. "I'll drive," he said over his shoulder.

They found Berker Studios in chaos and way too many people in Molly's office. The first person who needed to leave was her asshole boss.

THE DOUCHEBAG HELD Molly in his arms, stroking her back. She turned around and looked at Des with red-rimmed eyes.

His jaw clenched. He should be the one comforting her. Not that slimy bastard rubbing his hands all over her while she silently shook. Hands that slipped lower and lower down the small of Molly's back and actually touched her ass.

Des' fist twitched.

At least Molly noticed the slip of the palm. She pulled away and pushed away from Berker, now looking disgusted, as well as distraught.

Des wasn't the only one who had noticed the indiscretion. The amazon blonde with the silicon rack glared at Molly and her boss from one of the corners.

He did not want to be the man who explained grabbing another woman's ass to that woman. She had murder in her eyes, although at the moment she was staring at Molly.

His Molly.

Des stepped between the two women and broke the blonde's stare. The sadness in Molly's eyes broke his heart.

He took her hand. "You okay?"

She shook her head, wiping her eyes.

He wanted to hug her, but this was official business. Lamely, he squeezed her hand. "What happened?"

She gestured toward the phone. "Carol left me a message," she whispered.

"For heaven's sake." The blonde muscled her way to the middle of the room. "I can't take the drama." She executed an impressive hair toss and exited the room.

He turned back to Molly. "What about Carol," he said gently.

Zedler took command of the room and shooed the slimy boss out of Molly's office. "Find me a conference room to keep these people in," he ordered one of the uniforms. "Keep them separated. No one talks to anyone."

Once the room emptied, Zedler closed the door and walked over to Molly. He pulled her out of Des loose grip and enveloped her in a big bear hug.

Fuck. Des should have done that.

Molly's body shook as she soundlessly leaned into the older detectives arms.

Des felt useless as he watched Zedler rock Molly.

Eventually Molly calmed and she extracted herself from Zedlers embrace. Reaching for a box of Kleenex she smiled bravely at the older detective. "Thanks," she said. "I'm sorry for being such a baby."

"No worries," Zedler said, stroking her chin with the back of his knuckles.

Des would have had to punch the man if the gesture hadn't been so fatherly.

He would have to think about what that meant later. Right now he needed to know what had made Molly so upset.

Zedler wouldn't give any details on the ride over. He'd said Molly was too upset to relay any.

Des cleared his throat. "Molly, you think you're up to answering some questions?"

She nodded and slunk down in the chair by her desk. "I

procrastinated checking my messages today." She blinked furiously and wiped her eyes again.

Des felt like a bastard. She'd avoided checking her messages because she didn't want to hear the ones from him.

"There was too much to do this morning. A big client meeting, then lunch with Anthony, then Fred—I just didn't get to the phone until this afternoon.

Des made a mental note to find out who Fred was. He also wanted to know how often Molly ate lunch with her boss, but this wasn't the time to ask. Instead, he nodded encouragingly and propped his hip against her desk.

Zedler took the chair across from Molly's and nodded too.

"I guess I could just play it for you." She pulled the phone closer, punched a button, and keyed in a pin.

A woman's voice pleaded and called out for Molly before dissolving in horrendous screams as a wail echoed down the line. The message ended abruptly.

Cold seeped into his bones.

Those screams.

He'd heard them before. Mitchell had made ones similar while Des futilely searched the ground for his dropped gun.

And he'd heard that wail too. He broke out in a cold sweat. Images flashed through his head. Too fast to make any sense out of them. There were the familiar pictures from his nightmares. Images of white gleaming teeth and blood. Too much blood.

Had someone growled? He shook his head.

Someone had held Des down.

He hadn't dropped the weapon, someone had taken it from him. Held him so he had to watch Mitchell dying. Someone much stronger than Des. Unnatural strength. A vice grip.

And then he'd remembered his backup piece in the ankle holster. He'd reached for it and—

White light exploded behind his eyes and the horrific images disappeared.

And there was nothing.

* * *

MOLLY GASPED when Rankin sank to the floor. Zedler reached and caught him just before Rankin's head hit the sharp corner of the desk and gently lowered him to the floor.

"What happened," Molly said as she kneeled next to Rankin and checked his pulse. Strong and regular.

She let out a sigh of relief.

"I don't know," Zedler said, "but we should get him to the hospital."

Molly nodded. "I'll call for an ambulance."

Zedler checked Rankin's pulse too and bent closer to check his breathing. "I think he'll be fine if I take him in the squad car."

"I'm coming with you." She grabbed her jacket and collected her purse.

Zedler stopped her as she headed toward the door. "Before we do anything, we need to secure that recording." Molly stopped mid stride and must have looked appalled, because the detective continued, "I'm not taking any chances with the evidence."

She understood. Their voicemail was stored digitally on a central server. It could be tampered with. "What do you want me to do?"

"Can you send or forward that message?"

"I think so, but probably only to another mailbox in the system."

"Damn." Zedler whipped out his cell phone and stabbed

the keys with his fingers. "Yeah," he barked at whoever picked up on the other end. "I need to get a voice message into evidence. What do I do?" He listed for a while and then looked up at Molly. "What kind of system do you have?"

"Nortel."

The person on the phone spoke rapidly, but Molly couldn't make out any words. Zedler put the phone between his chin and shoulder. He signed that he wanted a pen and paper.

Molly found both and handed them over.

"Okay, okay," Zedler repeated while scribbling furiously.

He hung up. "We're going to email the voice file digitally to the station. The tech guy gave me instructions."

"Okay," Molly said. She didn't really care what they did with the voicemail. She never wanted to hear it again. It was evidence, and she should care more, but Rankin passed out for no reason. She checked his pulse again. Still steady.

Zedler pushed buttons on her phone while mumbling to himself. "What's your security pin," he asked at one point.

Molly gave him the number combination and continued to monitor Rankin.

Some color had returned to his cheeks and his breathing seemed more even. His eyelids fluttered.

She stroked his forehead. Sweeping the dark blonde hair off his face. It was a little too long, but she liked it. His trim body and permanently clenched jaw exuded need for control and perfection. She liked that a little part of him was unkempt.

A small sigh and then a mumble escaped from his lips. She leaned closer to hear what he was trying to say.

* * *

DES CAME TO GRADUALLY.

He felt like a Mack Truck had ran over him. Every muscle in his body ached and he had a splitting headache.

He opened his eyes and saw Molly's concerned face looming. He really loved those freckles on her nose. A blinding white pain shot through his head.

Fuck. Let's not do that again. He closed his eyes.

Molly's cool hand stroked his forehead. "Rankin? Can you hear me, Rankin?"

He bristled at her still using his last name. He'd given her an orgasm in her own goddamned kitchen. The least she could do was call him by his first name.

He opened his mouth to tell her so, but then stopped when he felt the floor vibrate as someone walked over and kneeled on the other side of him. Another person was in the room.

Before he had a chance to wonder who it was, strong fingers pried his eyelids open and shined a light in his eyes.

Des hissed in pain when the light hit his retina. "Fuck," he screamed.

The light disappeared and instead Molly's hand cradled his face. "Rankin. Wake up Rankin."

"I am awake," he growled, and then immediately regretted saying anything when Molly's hand disappeared.

"Can you open your eyes?" she asked.

"His pupils respond normally to light. I don't think he has a concussion," Zedler's voice said.

That explained the flashlight sadist.

"He didn't hit his head, so how could he have gotten a concussion?"

"Who knows?" Zedler didn't sound particularly interested. "The man puts his body parts where they don't belong. Someone's bound to hit him on the head sooner or later."

Rankin bristled. He still didn't know why Zedler was so

protective of Molly, but he'd find out. "I can hear you, you know," he said, eyes still closed.

"I know."

"Rankin, can you sit up? Can you open your eyes?" Molly's arms encircled his shoulders and helped him lean back against the desk.

"Call me Des," he said.

"What?" She fussed with the collar on his button down.

"I want you to call me Des. After what we shared, you shouldn't call me by my last name. It just doesn't sound right."

There was a long pause. Then smack, her palm hit the side of his head.

Des' eyes flew open.

"Careful," Zedler hollered. "Just because he doesn't have a concussion, doesn't mean there isn't something wrong with his head."

"Oh there's something wrong with his head alright," Molly grumbled her eyes stormy. "There's something wrong with a lot of him."

Des grinned, but when he caught Zedlers look, the smile died.

The senior detective's face looked carved in stone. His eyes were coal-black, staring into Des' as if he tried to stare into his soul.

Des swallowed the lump that formed in his throat. Zedler could be one scary dude when he wanted to.

Molly scrambled to stand.

He caught her hand. "I'm sorry. That was uncalled for."

She looked down and nodded, and then withdrew her hand from his and stood.

Des struggled to sit up straighter. "Look Molly, I'm sorry about a lot of things. I just—"

Zedler interrupted. "If you're done having the vapors, could we concentrate on the case for a few seconds?"

Des cursed under his breath.

Vapors? Fuck Zedler.

He didn't know what had happened, but fainting wasn't it. He tried to remember what had happened before he passed out. "The tape," he said. "Carol's voicemail." He struggled to get on his feet.

Molly rushed forward to help him.

He pretended to be a bit weaker than he was and leaned on her. She smelled so good. Vanilla and citrus, and a scent underneath that. It was uniquely hers. A Molly smell.

Maybe he had hit his head on something. Since when did he notice a woman's natural scent?

Since Molly, a voice in the back of his mind answered.

He told his subconscious to shut the fuck up.

Zedler watched him from the other side of the desk. Arms crossed, he wasn't buying Des' performance as a weakling.

"What happened?"

"We listened to Carol's call and then you hit the floor," Zedler said.

Des struggled to remember. "Her voicemail." The sounds were the same as when Mitchell had died. A stabbing pain shot through his temple and he stumbled.

"You need to go to the hospital," Molly said. "I don't care what the police still have to do here, but you're going to the emergency room right now." She propped her shoulder under his arm and walked toward the door.

"Wait, just one minute," Des protested.

She stopped.

He looked at Zedler. It wasn't really important how much the older detective knew anymore, or how he had found out. What mattered was that Mitchell's killer might be in Prairie

Falls. "That message," Des said. "The sounds on that message is exactly what I heard when Mitchell died."

Zedler straightened, ultra-alert. "Same sound. Are you sure?"

Des nodded. "One hundred percent."

The older detective patted his pockets. "This changes things."

Rankin swayed a little.

"You need to get checked out," Molly said. "People don't just pass out for no reason."

Zedler nodded. "I'll take care of things on this end if you drive him to the hospital."

When they got to the car park, Molly stowed Rankin in the passenger seat. She slipped into the driver's side and tried to start the car.

Her hand shook. She needed two tries before she got the key into the ignition.

Rankin leaned over and covered her hand with is. "Easy. It's going to be okay."

Molly blinked rapidly, obviously refusing to cry.

He turned her slightly toward him and nudged her to hug him back.

Molly straightened up. "We better get you to the hospital." She started the engine.

"Look, Molly," Rankin said. "About what happened in the café."

Molly shook her head. "Not now. Let's just get you checked out."

Rankin moved his arm from her shoulders and took her hand in his. She tugged to get it back, but he held on. "I handled you telling me about your gift poorly. I'm sorry about that."

Molly sat ramrod straight, staring out the windshield at nothing but a big concrete wall.

Rankin stroked her hand. "I should have been a lot more understanding."

Molly looked down into her lap, she picked at a small stain on her skirt. Salsa, maybe?

"Now that I've gotten over the shock, I have so many questions, I won't ask them now, you've had a crappy day." He tugged on her hand.

She refused to look at him. "Again, thank you for sharing it with me." He forced as much sincerity as he could into his voice. Molly remained silent, but glanced at him out of the corner of her eye. When he saw her looking, he spoke again. "Is there anything you'd like to say?"

Molly shook her head. She pulled on her hand again so she could change gears, but he held on.

"So ah, can I have another chance?" he asked.

She slumped down in her seat.

"I see," he said and pulled his hand away.

Molly quickly faced him. "I don't handle rejection well," she said.

Rankin took her hand again. "I didn't reject you. I was stunned. I didn't know what to say." He grinned and put his hand on her thigh. "I've never been with anybody who has super powers before."

She didn't smile back, instead she shook her head. "I don't have super powers," she said. "It's just something weird that happens. A feeling I get."

"It's not weird," Rankin said.

"I'm taking you to the hospital now." Molly put the car in reverse and backed out of the parking spot. "I want to know you're right in the head before we talk about this."

"Molly, I'm fine." The blinding pain he'd felt was gone and he'd much rather straighten out how badly he'd hurt her. "Your ability does not make you weird. It's an asset."

She threw him a skeptic look and threw the gear shift in drive before stomping down on the gas.

Des' body pressed into his seat. Message received. No more talking until he'd been examined by a doctor.

* * *

DES HAD WAITED for a long time. He really wanted to leave. The place smelled fucking awful of antiseptics and bleach, and there was a draft up his bare crotch. The hospital gown was too short and wouldn't close properly in the back. His ass was cold too.

Before the white-coats put him in this room to wait, they'd poked and prodded him for hours. He'd had enough.

He needed to figure out what was going on with that voicemail. He needed to catch the killer. He sighed. But right now, the short-term goal was to get dressed, go home with Molly, take a shower and then take her to bed.

Not necessarily in that order.

She sat across from him reading some magazine with a bunch of movie stars on the cover. At least he thought they were movie stars. He'd never really had the time to keep up with celebrity news. Neither had Molly apparently, because she was engrossed in whatever she was reading. Or maybe she just didn't want to talk to him.

"You okay?" he asked, brusquer than he'd intended.

She looked up, her eyes slightly unfocused. "Fine. Why?"

"I need to get out of here. Where's my cell phone?"

Molly pointed toward a pile of clothes on the chair next to him.

He jumped off the hospital bed and bent down to pick up the clothes. Too late he remembered the gaping hospital gown. He turned around and caught her smile, a pretty blush creeping up her cheeks before she quickly returned her gaze to the magazine. He opened his mouth to explain how cold it was in the room, but one of the doctors entered the room before he had a chance.

Her name tag listed her as part of neurology. "Mr. Rankin, we've ran every test we can think of. Your levels are all normal. You're free to go."

"But what happened?" Molly wanted to know.

The doctor tapped her pen on the journal. "We can't actually say for sure. It could have been a visual migraine."

"A migraine can do that?" Molly sounded skeptical.

He liked that she spoke for him and doubted the doctor's prognosis as much as he did.

The doctor glanced at Des. "Well," she hedged.

"Spit it out," Des demanded.

With a glance at Molly, the doctor continued. "What you described sounds very much like what we see in our veterans with PTSD. When they have a particular violent flashback, they can pass out or have a seizure."

PTSD. Fuck.

"That makes sense," Molly said calmly. "He just flash-backed on a traumatic event."

Des stared at her. She must not have heard the doctor. They were talking about PTSD. Post. Traumatic. Stress. Disorder.

This was so fucked up. He'd seen how some of his army buddies had behaved with PTSD. Distancing themselves from their friends, sometimes experiencing violent episodes of rage.

The doctor's lips were moving, but Des hadn't been listening. He tuned back in.

"—and so we'd like for you to come and see a counselor so you can learn the tools to deal with the flashbacks and the emotions they may trigger."

Molly nodded and took the card the doctor held out when Des just stared at it.

The doctor tilted her head. "Any questions, Detective Rankin?"

He shook his head. He couldn't look at her. She waited a little longer before she left the room.

"Well," Molly said. "That's a relief."

"A relief?" Didn't she understand that he was now seriously damaged goods?

"Yeah, you could have had a seizure disorder or a brain tumor."

He tried to clarify, "But I *have PTSD*."

"Don't we all?" No judgment, no look of horror, no big deal. Molly patted his arm as she walked past him. "I'll get the car while you get dressed. Meet you up front."

He watched her ass as she walked toward the door. He'd never get tired of that view. She was amazing. He should have tried harder to find her after she'd run out on him in Sacramento.

He was pretty sure he was falling in love with her, but now was not the time to tell her, or even think about that.

He needed to solve this case and unscramble what his brain had revealed before he could commit to a relationship. She deserved better than him, she deserved the best.

His cell phone rang as he buckled his pants. The caller ID showed a big Z.

"Yeah," Des said.

"We've got a problem," Zedler whispered.

Why the fuck was he whispering. "What kind of problem?"

"Is Molly with you?"

"She's getting the car, why?"

"Go get her right away and stay with her. Don't leave her alone."

"Tell me what's going on." Des heard the other detective talk to someone in the room, then some footsteps before Zedler came back on the line. This time there was less background noise.

"Look," Zedler said. "The LT found me as soon as I returned to the station. She had a warrant covering the whole firm, but especially Molly's office.

"What?"

"An anonymous call to the stations questions Molly's connection with two of the victims and why the police aren't investigating that angle."

"That's bullshit," Des said. "There isn't enough of a connection between the vics and Molly to get a search warrant.

Zedler cleared his throat. "The LT is under pressure and got some judge to see things her way." He paused. "That's not the worst part. They found some stuff in Molly's office."

Des felt a headache coming on. "What kind of stuff."

"Bad stuff. A woman's scarf and a man's glove, both with stains that appear to be blood." They're being sent to the lab as we speak. He paused. "They want you to bring her in for questioning."

"Fuck." Des ended the call and rushed out to find Molly.

CHAPTER 17

*M*olly tried to estimate how many times she'd been inside of an interview room and came up with around fifty times. Sometimes she sketched out in the field, but most of her cases had been with a witness in a room just like this one. Drab walls painted an indeterminate color somewhere between beige and gray. Utilitarian furniture made of steel, usually a table and a few chairs. Fluorescent lights that emphasized the hollows and wrinkles of people's faces.

She'd never sat on this side of the table though. Well, technically she'd probably been on this physical side of the table, but not as a witness. A suspect actually, she corrected herself, while glancing at the red light of the video camera aimed at her.

She wondered if Rankin and Zedler were watching. Probably, it was after all their case. Unless higher command would take it away from them. Maybe they would be in trouble for personally knowing Molly.

She tried to take deep breaths, but panic rose in her chest. Rankin wouldn't tell her why they needed to interview her.

He'd come out of the hospital stone faced and quiet and asked her to drive to the police station. All he'd said was that the lieutenant wanted some answers about items found in her office.

When she'd asked him what kind of items, he'd slumped in the seat, his shoulders hunched and just told her he wasn't allowed to say.

Molly squirmed in the chair and fiddled with her sleeves. She was glad she'd brought her jacket. The room was chilly. At least they hadn't Mirandized her. At least she wasn't under arrest. Yet.

The door opened and detective Martin Faurk entered the room.

Molly greeted him with a smile. They'd worked some burglary cases together last spring. He didn't smile back and she felt silly grinning by herself. She quickly relaxed her lips.

"Ms. Nyland, can I get you anything?"

Formal address, this was serious. She shook her head in answer to his question.

The detective sat down and placed a folder and some plastic bags on the table.

She leaned forward to see what was in the bags, but he covered them with some papers before she could make out any details.

"Do you understand you have the right to have legal counsel present?" Detective Faurk's blue eyes were serious, but not unfriendly.

"Yes," Molly said. "I don't need a lawyer." Legally, it would be more prudent, but cops took "lawyering up" as a sign of having something to hide. If things got serious, if they charged her with something, she'd ask for counsel.

The detective nodded and clicked a pen. "How long have you worked at Berker Studios?"

"About five years." She studied him to see if he'd give her a clue as to where this was going. He didn't so much as twitch a muscle and wouldn't meet her eyes.

"How did you know Raymond Wymer?"

"He was a client." If she kept her answers short, she minimized the risk of incriminating herself by mistake.

"A good client?"

Molly frowned. "I don't understand the question."

Detective Faurk glanced at her. "Would you say he was easy to work with? Someone you enjoyed working with?"

"No."

It was the detective's turn to frown. "'No' to which question?"

"Both of them."

"Would you care to elaborate?" He sounded frustrated.

Weirdly, the sign of emotion calmed Molly. She thought for a while. "I didn't enjoy working with him because he would often change his mind after we'd already started on a design, using his earlier specifications. He wasn't easy to work with for the same reason."

"I understand you had a fight with Mr. Wymer the last time you saw him."

"Yes."

The detective sighed. "Ms. Nyland, please tell me about the fight?"

"Am I in trouble?"

"Just answer the questions."

Molly paused, but then decided she wasn't telling them anything they didn't already know. "Mr. Wymer was unhappy with the designs I had done for his company. He threatened to have me fired."

"And did that make you angry?"

"No."

When it was clear she wasn't going to say anything else, Faurk continued. "Did it make you worried?"

"A little."

"You were afraid you would lose your job?"

Molly made a point of looking the detective in the eye when she answered. "I was worried I might get in trouble with my manager and taken off the account."

"And that made you angry." It was a statement, not a question.

Molly answered it anyway. "No." She kept her tone as unemotional as the detective's. She was starting to get pissed off. Faurk was just doing his job, but if he would just tell her why she was sitting here answering these questions, things would go a lot quicker. It was painful how long it would take before he'd get to the point.

"Tell me about Carol Perry."

"What would you like to know?"

"How close were you?"

"She was a very good friend of my best friend Nina's."

"But not one of your good friends." It was again phrased as a statement.

"No," Molly said, and then decided to elaborate. "I like—liked—her, but we never saw each other unless Nina was there."

"Why was that?"

Molly shrugged. "Don't know. Neither of us made the effort, I guess."

"So you didn't have anything against Ms. Perry."

"No, she was a hard person not to like. She was funny and full of energy." Her voice cracked at the end of the sentence. A lump formed in Molly's throat when she thought of how full of life Carol had been.

Faurk cleared his throat and fiddled with his papers.

Inwardly, Molly sighed. Blood and violence didn't bother Faurk. But the possibility of her crying made him uncomfortable? She waited for the next question.

He made a point of looking at his notes before clearing his throat again. "When was the last time you saw Ms. Perry?"

Molly had to think. "At Nina's birthday celebration. Friday before last, about a week and a half ago."

"And what did you speak about?"

"Nothing really." She tried to remember and then blushed when she did. Carol had been teasing her about Anthony coming on to her. Molly hadn't believed her, but judging from how Anthony had behaved yesterday, Carol had either been uncanny in her guessing or a better judge of character than Molly was.

Detective Faurk watched her. He arched an eyebrow when she looked up.

"She was giving me a hard time about my boss," Molly clarified.

The detective shuffled his papers around and glanced at a couple of them. "This would be Anthony Berker?"

"Yes, he has a bit of a reputation and Carol gave me a hard time about him asking me to work late on a Friday night."

"What kind of reputation?" The detective clicked his pen.

Molly hesitated. "He has a lot of girlfriends."

"Were you ever one of them?"

"No."

The detective's eyebrows quirked again. "Why not?"

"Is this pertinent to the case?" Molly shot back.

"Let us determine what's important, Ms. Nyland. Please answer the question."

Molly bristled. She was not part of "us" on this case. She was on the other side, the civilian side, or worse, the suspect side. "He is my boss, that's all." She shrugged, trying to keep her irritation out of her body language and voice.

"Did he ever try to be more than your boss?"

"What do you mean?"

Faurk gave her a patient look, as if she was a little dense. "Did he ever ask you out? Flirt with you?"

Molly shrugged again. "Anthony flirts with everyone. It doesn't mean anything."

The detective scribbled on his pad for a while.

Molly cocked her head, trying to see what he wrote, but his handwriting was atrocious. She was avoiding the question, but didn't see what her relationship with Anthony had to do with Carol's, or Wymer's death. More likely, Faurk was just trying to get some gossip to spread around the station. A few of the officers had asked her out when she first started working there. She'd turned them all down. Until Rankin that was.

Everything that had to do with him was irrational and confusing. She'd never had trouble resisting attraction to the opposite sex, but with Rankin it was like there was a force field around him that dragged her in. She shook her head.

That relationship was in the toilet now anyway. With Molly as a suspect, he wouldn't be allowed anywhere near her. So far there hadn't been any charges, but even if she was a "person of interest" he would have to stay away from her. She sighed.

"Who else did Mr. Berker flirt with?"

Molly looked up, startled, and found Faurk studying her. "How would I know?"

"Did he flirt with anyone at the office?" The detective clarified.

"He used to. But when he and Samantha became involved, he slowed down."

"That would be the office manager of Berker Studios?"

Molly nodded, wondering why they were asking so many questions about Anthony.

"To your knowledge, did Anthony Berker and Carol Perry have a relationship?"

"I don't think so. I don't think they've ever met."

"So it would surprise you to know that Ms. Perry had Mr. Berker's phone number stored in her cell phone?"

Molly tried to read Faurk's face, but the detective just calmly looked at her. "Yes," she finally said. "I know they'd met at least once, but I didn't know they spoke beyond that."

"And how does it make you feel if I tell you that they had a relationship?"

Molly shrugged. "Why would it have anything to do with me?"

Faurk leaned forward. "It wouldn't make you jealous?"

Molly shook her head. "No, why would it? Anthony and I weren't involved."

"Were you involved with Ms. Perry?"

"No."

"But you knew Ms. Perry dated both women and men?"

"I didn't find that out until after she was killed." Molly calmly met his eyes. If he thought she would be rattled by Carol being bisexual, she wouldn't give him the satisfaction. Martin Faurk was a good detective, but he was a gossip. She didn't want to give him any reason to start spreading rumors about Carol, or about herself.

The detective studied her for a few seconds, then reached for the two plastic bags and threw them down in front of Molly. They landed with a double thud. "Ms. Nyland, what are these?"

Molly picked up the bags and tried to figure out what she was holding in her hand. It looked like a scarf and a brown leather glove. "I don't know, wait." She swallowed. "I've never seen the glove before, but that's the scarf I gave Nina for her birthday."

The detective scribbled fast. "Why would they be in your office?"

"You found these in my office?" Molly thought hard while

looking at the items again. "These aren't mine." There were some brown crusty spots on both of them. Like dried up ketchup. Suddenly she knew what it was, blood.

She swallowed. "Was this with Carol?" she held up the scarf.

"Please just answer the question, Ms. Nyland." The detectives voice was hard and his eyes intense blue as they scrutinized her.

"I don't know why they would be in my office." Molly's eyes stung. Thinking about Carol and the jokes she'd made about the scarf. There had been such joy in Carol, she didn't deserve to die.

Detective Faurk slapped his folder shut.

Molly startled, jerking back in her chair.

"So you gave this scarf to Ms. Perry?"

"Yes…No…I mean, I gave it to Nina. Carol must have borrowed it."

"Ms. Nyland, now would be a good time to come clean. When we find your fingerprints on these items and the lab matches the blood on them to Ms. Perry and Mr. Wymer, it won't look good if you don't cooperate with us."

A tendril of fear trickled down Molly's spine. The police couldn't possibly think she had anything to do with these murders.

Shit, someone was trying to frame her.

It had to be someone she worked with. Nobody else would have access to her office. Her thoughts tripped over themselves. Were they just out to get here or were they themselves the killer? Shit. Was she working with a serial killer?

Faurk interrupted her thoughts. "If you confess, maybe I can put in a good word for you with the district attorney. Ask him to be lenient."

Molly stared at him, her thoughts all jumbled up in her mind. No words would come out of her mouth.

* * *

DES WATCHED Faurk interrogating Molly on monitor in the observation room. He wondered if she knew he was there. Zedler stood next to him, a grim look on his face, which probably matched the one on Des' own face. Both of them had their arms crossed and jaws clenched. It was agony to watch Faurk trying to trip up Molly and not be able to do anything to help her. This was all bullshit. No way had Molly killed Carol Perry. He couldn't logically explain how he knew that. There was no evidence that showed her innocence. He just knew she was, in his gut.

In his heart.

Fuck. What a mess.

He glanced at Zedler. The detective hadn't said a word since the interrogation started. Maybe because they weren't alone in the room. Another detective, Faurk's usual partner, was also observing. It was only because Zedler had pulled the seniority card that he and Des were allowed to watch. When Des brought Molly through the doors of the precinct, she'd been whisked away immediately and he'd been called into the brass' office where Zedler had been waiting.

Lieutenant Lewis informed them both that they were off the case. She didn't say it straight out, but it was understood it was because both detectives had a personal relationship with Molly.

Since neither Molly nor he had advertised their involvement, someone must have guessed it on their own. That was the police for you, a bunch of fucking gossips. Worse than old women.

Zedler being pulled off made more sense. He'd never

made a secret of the fact that he looked out for Nyland. The whole precinct knew it. When Des had discreetly asked around about Molly dating anyone in the precinct, he'd heard that a few of the officers had tried to hit on her, but been "persuaded" otherwise by Zedler. As a result, the cops treated her like a little sister instead.

Des didn't blame them. The older detective was fucking scary when he turned on the protective mode. At the same time he was grateful that Zedler had scared off the others. Des would have had to punch anybody who had dated Molly, which may cause some problems when you were the new guy at the precinct.

He would definitely punch Berker the next time he saw him. That guy had it coming big time. Molly had avoided a straight answer when Faurk asked her if her boss had hit on her, but it was clear enough that he had. Fucking slime ball.

Faurk was still trying to get Molly to break but she insisted she'd never given the scarf to Perry or seen the glove.

Even though Des knew she was innocent, he'd held his breath when the two bags landed in front of her on the table. She'd been genuinely surprised and puzzled. He'd noticed Zedler letting out a sigh of relief when he saw the same thing. Not because he suspected Molly, but because he, like Des, knew the other officers would register her reaction as genuine as well. Even more importantly, so would the camera.

"She's been set up," Des said.

"No shit, Sherlock," Zedler growled between clenched teeth.

Des turned to Faurk's partner. "When those fingerprints come back, you better compare them to every employee at that design firm."

"Already in progress." The guy gave him disgusted look.

Zelder turned around, surprise registered on his face.

"Did you think you were the only one who cared about Molly?" Faurk's partner asked Zedler. "She may be a little weird. It's crazy how accurate her sketches are, but she's one of ours. I've worked with her on two cases and they were both cleared thanks to her drawings."

"Good to know," Zedler said and turned back, facing the monitor again.

Des did the same.

Molly wasn't budging and Faurk finally wrapped things up. He stood and mumbled something to Molly. She looked up, surprised, and then nodded.

After Faurk exited the room, she slumped down in the chair. Des ached to go and comfort her, but as much as it irked him, he couldn't. If it became public that he and Molly were an item, the little sister vibe might change into jealousy. Right now he wanted the entire precinct looking out for Molly.

Before she left the interview room, Des slipped out and down the hall to his office. He wanted to review the statements of the other employees at Berker Studios. One of the people Molly worked with was out to get her. He didn't know why, either this was office politics or they were dealing with the actual killer. Either way, Des would make sure he got them, before they got Molly.

* * *

SITTING IN HER CAR, Molly rested her head on the steering wheel. Physically, she felt drained, but her head buzzed with questions. She couldn't imagine anybody hating her enough to frame her for murder. Sure, there was jealousy, as evident by Fred's prank during the Marvelous Melon meeting, but murder was a whole new level.

The thought of someone hating her that much made her

stomach ache. The thought of Carol dying because someone hated Molly was even worse. She started dry-heaving.

A staccato of knocks on the windshield startled her.

Zedler.

She unlocked the passenger door.

"You okay?" he asked as soon as he sat down.

"I've been better." She tried for a smile, but it came out a grimace.

Zedler took her hand. "Molly, this will all be cleared up. You got people on your side."

"I know. Faurk said as much. He almost apologized before he left."

Zedler nodded. "I wondered about that. He wasn't as tough on you as he usually is on suspects."

"He's normally tougher?" Molly asked. "I was breaking into a cold sweat having him interrogating me. His ice-blue eyes are unnerving and somewhat scary."

Zedler chuckled. "He's one of the best. Got more confessions than anybody at the precinct."

"And you guys sent him after me?"

Zedler turned serious. "We didn't. The LT wanted everything by the book so nobody can complain later about us looking out for one of our own."

Molly had to swallow the big lump that stuck in her throat. "I didn't know the guys thought of me as a one of them," she managed to squeeze out around the lump.

"Are you kidding? They love having you on the force."

The lump had gotten bigger. She could only nod.

Zedler cleared his throat and let go of her hand. "So, you and Rankin," he said.

Molly jerked around to face him. "What do you mean?"

"It's pretty obvious there's something going on between you. Is it serious?" When Molly hesitated, Zedler hurried on,

"I know it isn't any of my business. Feel free to tell me to take a hike, but I'm here for you Molly."

She thought about his question. Zedler had always been there for her, a mentor, and almost like a father figure. "I don't know what it is," she finally said. "I've never felt this way before and it's a little scary." She looked down and fiddled with her seatbelt. Not only was he like a father figure, she felt as uncomfortable talking about her boyfriend as if he actually was her father. She smiled a little and looked up again.

The detective nodded, and then looked out the front windshield of the car. "Molly, your empathy with witnesses—"

Startled Molly sat up straight and waited for him to continue.

"It's something special," Zedler finally said. "You have to be careful who you share it with, but you shouldn't be ashamed of it. You should own it, test it, and try to expand it."

Molly looked down in her lap. "How much do you know about what I can do?"

"Only what you told Rankin and me in the café."

"But you knew about it before I told you guys, you encouraged me to open up."

"I knew there was something unusual about you, but not exactly how it worked."

She held on to the quiet for a while. Wondering how much she dared telling him about her history. "I was hit by lightning when I was little," she finally said. "Afterward, I somehow connected more strongly with people. When they describe things, it's as if I see the pictures in my head. When they don't use the right words for the details, the picture is unclear." She turned toward Zedler. "I don't like to talk about it because the lighting strike also gave me scars running down my arm. I already felt like a freak."

"Who made you feel like a freak?"

Molly knew how bitter and brittle the smile playing on her lips was. Her mouth hurt as her lips stretched in the grimace. "My grandmother and great-uncle were convinced the devil had entered my body to devour my soul. They tried to beat him out of me. When that didn't work, they tried to starve him out."

Zedler squeezed her hand.

She looked up at him. "It wasn't until I started working as a forensic artist that I knew that excess intuition could be useful."

"I'm sorry that happened to you." The detective studied her face. "What happened to your parents?"

"They died when I was a year old. I don't remember them at all."

He nodded.

Molly wanted to change the topic. After the interrogation she already felt raw and exposed. Thinking about her childhood brought up too many emotions. She couldn't handle it.

"Why didn't you ever ask me about this before?"

He shrugged. "I figured you would tell me when you were ready. There are a lot of unusual things in this world." He smiled. "Special people with abilities we label as 'weird' because we don't yet have the science to explain them, but we'll get there."

She returned the smile. "I'm nothing special. Thank you though."

"You're welcome." Zedler looked out the front again. "There's a lot more going on in the world than our regular senses pick up. Some cops clear cases on hunches they can't explain. We try to explain it using words like 'luck' or 'coincidence,' but it doesn't matter what we call it."

"What do you call it?"

The detective turned back and studied her face. "I call it a gift. And that's how you should think of it Molly. You are gifted."

"That's what Nina says."

"Then you should listen to your friend."

Molly nodded. "I will. She's due back in town tonight."

They sat in silence for a little while. Then Zedler stirred. "I better get back in there. Once they figure out who put that scarf and glove in your office, all hell will break out."

"How will they find out?"

"I'm hoping our perp. left a fingerprint or two." Zedler smiled reassuringly. "Don't worry, Molly. We'll find out who did this." He opened the door. "Before I go, Rankin wanted me to give this to you." He handed her a note.

Molly stared at the small square of folded paper. Did Rankin feel like he needed to tell her why he had to stay away from her? She already knew that.

"Aren't you going to open it?" Zedler loomed in the open door.

She looked up. "Don't you know what it says?"

Zedler glanced out the front window. "Look, I may not like you seeing each other, but you're old enough to make your own decisions. Just be careful." With that he left and closed the car door.

Molly stared after him. Did Zedler pass the note because he knew Rankin was breaking up with her? Did they even have a relationship that merited a breakup? Things were so confusing. Her head buzzed with questions, but at least she didn't feel so alone anymore.

She needed a plan. She should go back to the hotel room nobody knew she was staying at, call Nina, and then maybe Rankin, depending on what the note said.

Even if talking with her best friend wouldn't create a solution, at least it would make her feel better.

She fingered the folded paper in her hand. She hadn't had

a chance to ask Rankin how he was handling the PTSD diagnosis, or if he remembered anything else about his partner dying.

Taking a deep breath, she opened the note.

We need to talk, was all it said. Freaking Rankin, not helpful at all.

CHAPTER 18

*L*ater that evening, Molly opened the hotel room door, and Nina entered in a flurry of colors and fabric. She wore a long flowing skirt and a peasant blouse. Unusual attire for someone who usually looked more like she belonged on Fifth Avenue in New York City than Main Street, Prairie Falls, where her boutique was located. Nina had insisted on coming over as soon as Molly called her and told her about Carol's voicemail and the interview at the police station.

She hadn't called Rankin yet. She wasn't sure if that would get him in trouble with his lieutenant, so she figured she'd just wait until he got a hold of her.

"Holy shit, Molly. Are you okay?" Her friend cupped Molly's face. "I can't imagine what it was like to listen to Carol's voice, never mind being interrogated right after."

"It was intense, but at least I wasn't arrested." Molly studied Nina closer. She wore less makeup than usual, and instead of the elaborate updo she favored, her hair rippled down her back in a straight, shiny sheet. "Are you wearing flats?" She'd never seen Nina in anything lower than two-inch heels. Sometimes she'd worried her friend's footwear would give her altitude sickness.

Nina frowned. "Are we changing the subject?"

Molly pinched the bridge of her nose. "I'm sorry. I'm completely scatterbrained and don't know how to process all of this. All I can think about is that awful voicemail and that someone hates me enough to want to frame me for murder."

Nina pulled her in for a hug. "It's completely surreal. Do you want to talk about it, or just take a break from it altogether?"

"Let's talk about your shoes first and then ease into serial killers."

Nina smiled and then threw herself in the plush sofa lined up against one of the walls in the room. She held out her feet, showing off bejeweled leather sandals. "Grannie and I went shopping at the flea market. What do you think?"

"You bought shoes at a flea market?" Molly couldn't keep the incredulity out of her voice.

"I know, right?" Nina grinned. "They're handmade and don't even have a designer tag."

"Well, they go with the rest of your outfit."

Nina looked down and held out her blouse and skirt. "I got these at the market too."

"They suit you," Molly said. Nina's dark hair and olive complexion matched the peasant outfit perfectly. She looked like she should be picking olives in Italy, or tell fortunes in a carnival tent.

"I had a great time with Grannie and Auntie. Instead of hassling me about finding a husband and getting married, like they usually do, they showed me their herb books."

"Herb books?"

"Did I never tell you they are healers?"

"Yeah, but I thought that had more to do with having the sight and laying hands on people."

Nina let out a peal of laughter. "They do some energy healing, but that's more for show than anything. The real treatment they offer is through herbal brews." She patted the cushion next to her.

Molly took a seat next to her friend and absorbed the goodwill and kindness radiating from Nina. She'd always had the ability to calm her down. Molly's mind struggled with anything that wasn't rational or logical. Nina, the exact opposite, navigated through life based on intuitions and "good vibes."

"The interrogation wasn't as bad as it could have been," Molly finally said. "The guys at the precinct are looking out for me and are unofficially looking for who might have framed me."

"Honey, of course they are. You're one of them."

Molly didn't want to tell her that she'd never known what her police colleagues thought of her until Zedler told her. It seemed too self-involved. Instead, she just smiled. "How are you holding up? You were much closer to Carol than I was."

"I feel awful for not knowing where she was going after she left my place. If I'd taken the time to ask…" Nina paused. Awkward silence permeated the room.

Molly turned sideways on the sofa. "You can't blame yourself for Carol's murder."

Nina's eyes welled up. "I would be of more help finding her killer if I'd known a little more about what she'd been doing the last couple of months."

Molly hugged her friend.

"Look at me, I'm a mess," Nina said, pulling away and reaching for a tissue from the box on the coffee table.

"You look beautiful, you always do," Molly said. It was true. Her friend was a gorgeous crier. The kind you saw on the big screen.

Nina dabbed her eyes, then blew her nose. "Okay," she said, "got any wine in here?"

Molly went to the mini-fridge and pulled out a bottle of chardonnay. "Is white okay?"

"Bring it on over. Let's toast Carol properly."

Molly retrieved two wine glasses and the bottle opener before returning to the couch. She handed the bottle and opener to Nina. "Do the honors, please."

Her friend popped the cork with great flourish and filled up the two glasses. "To Carol," she said and held up a glass.

Molly grabbed the other and clinked Nina's. "To Carol," she repeated. She took a deep sip. "What's your happiest memory of Carol?"

Nina's eyes welled up again, but she smiled. "There are quite a few." She put her glass down, folding her hands in her lap. "One of my earliest ones is from a few months after I had just met her. In one of our design classes, we were supposed to create ball gowns and show them off at a contest fashion show at the end of the semester." She reached for her wine glass and took another sip. "So, every week, the instructor is riding Carol's butt because her dress is a plus size. He's saying things like 'designer labels don't go beyond size 8' and that Carol will end up working for a catalog company in the Midwest if she doesn't wise up."

Nina waved her free hand in the air while rolling her eyes. "To him, that was like the biggest insult. Anyway, Carol ignores him the whole semester. And when it's time for her to step on to the stage, she looks amazing in her hot pink silk dress. She's wearing this feather headdress in the same color. Gloria Gaynor's *I will Survive* blasts through the speakers, and as she takes the first few steps down the runway, two drag queens step out behind her. They're super tall, at least six-foot-five, wearing the same dress and headdresses, but in neon green."

Nina put the wine glass down and jumped to her feet. "So, the three of them strut their stuff in formation to the end of the runway." She demonstrated a catwalk on the hotel carpet. "They execute a perfect pivot, but before they head back to the curtained area, they all pause where the instructor is sitting in the audience. All three cock a hip and snap their fingers, perfectly synchronized. One of the drag queens leans down and says, 'Suck it, prof.'" Nina threw herself back down on the couch, convulsing in laughter.

Molly joined in. "Did she pass the class?"

Nina quirked an eyebrow. "Our grade depended on where we placed in the contest."

"And," Molly urged on when Nina paused.

Her friend reached for her wine, took a long drink, and made a big deal out of drying the corners of her mouth.

"Nina."

"Okay." She grinned big. "Carol won the whole damn contest. Someone posted a video on the internet, which went viral. A company specializing in women's clothing for men sees the footage and offers Carol a contract."

Molly laughed loudly. "For real?"

Nina nodded. "Yep, that was Carol. She never did anything half-assed." She smiled wistfully. "I'm going to miss her so much."

"I'm so sorry. I wish I'd taken the time to know her better."

Nina put her glass back down on the table. "And I wish I had spent more time with her these last few months. Maybe if—"

Molly interrupted her. "You can't think that way. Nothing you could have done or said, or didn't say or do, lead to her murder."

"I know, I'm just…" Her voice broke.

Molly grabbed her hand. "I know."

Nina gave her a brittle smile. "Let's talk about something else. What else did I miss while sequestered in the country?"

Molly swirled the butter-yellow liquid in her glass. "I told Rankin and Zedler about my…about my talent, with all the details."

Nina's head snapped up. "Honey, that's great news. Don't you feel better now that you don't have to keep secrets anymore?"

Molly smiled at her friend. Leave it to Nina to cut to the chase. "I do feel better. At first, I thought Rankin freaked out, but it turns out he was just stunned. I guess finding out your date is a little different take some time getting used to."

"Wait, you went on a date? This we must celebrate." Nina reached for the bottle and filled up their glasses. "You must really like this guy."

"I do. Rankin was fine with my scars when he first saw them, and he seems to accept my intuition."

Nina stopped her glass halfway to her mouth and held up a finger. "Hold on, when did he get to see your scars?"

Molly fidgeted in her seat. "I'm not going to give you any details."

"Oh, that's too bad." Nina made a pretend, sad face. "Seriously, though, you slept with him. That's huge."

Molly's face was on fire. "We didn't exactly sleep with each other."

"But you were naked?"

"Almost."

Nina groaned. "You're killing me here. Please tell me you were…satisfied with the outcome."

"Very satisfied." Molly couldn't help the grin stretching her lips.

Nina reached for the bottle and filled their glasses. "Well, I'll be damn," she said with an exaggerated southern accent. "He won you over with an orgasm. I'll drink to that." She insisted they'd clink their glasses in another toast.

"That's all I'll tell you," Molly said after they'd drunk.

"Fine." Nina pouted, but then looked at Molly more seriously. "Are you ever going to tell me what happened in Sacramento?"

Molly cocked her head. That memory didn't seem as shameful as it had. "I was in a mess because of the breakup with Clark. There was this strange attraction to Rankin, and one night, after some drinking, I went home with him." She took another sip of wine, cursing the heat creeping into her cheeks. "We had sex, but I kept my shirt on. He started to take it off. I freaked and ran away." She looked up.

Nina shook her head. "The man's hot. No wonder you went home with him." She flashed a quick smile. "But it takes some serious trust for you to show him your scars. Does this mean you want to take the relationship beyond just physical?"

Molly sighed. "I don't know. I trust him, but I'm not sure if there's a chance for a relationship. Especially not now, when I'm a 'person of interest' in an ongoing murder investigation."

Nina took her hand. "That will be resolved soon." She squeezed Molly's finger. "What can you tell me about the case? I know I'm a civilian, but maybe it will help to talk about it."

Molly hesitated, but then decided she needed to talk to someone and she trusted Nina. "Do you remember when we went to the club for your birthday?"

"That was the last time we saw Carol." Nina's eyes grew serious.

"I'm sorry to remind you."

"No," Nina waved her hand. "Just tell me what you were going to."

Molly took a deep breath and filled her friend in on what she knew about the singer at Sinful Soul enchanting the audience and feeding on their admiration and about rogue wolves showing up in her parking lot.

Nina held up her hand when she mentioned the wolf. "What do you mean it was stalking you?"

"It felt like it was toying with me. Like it was laughing at me."

"Grannie and the aunts talk about wolves who are actually people."

"Like werewolves?"

Nina shook her head. "No, as if the spirits are mixed up somehow. They wouldn't tell me the details."

Nina frowned.

"Shit. I can't believe how much has happened while I was visiting the grannies."

"How are they?"

"As crazy as usual, and as secretive. I swear those two women thrive on confusing me." The fond smile playing at the corner of Nina's mouth belied her words. She loved her older female relatives.

At times Molly had been jealous over how much support Nina had, her own grandmother being a bat-shit crazy religious nut and all.

Molly's phone chirped, and she checked her text messages. "It's from Zedler," she said, frowning as she read."

"What does he want?"

"He's asking me to talk to the bouncer and the waiter from the club."

Nina looked up quickly. "The hot Latino and your Viking?"

"I think he's Native American." Molly shook her head. "That's not what's important here. Zedler calls him Wolf Hunter."

"That's strange too," Nina said. "Granny said the wolf hunter had come early."

"What does that mean?"

Her friend sighed. "Again, I don't know. The old woman throws out these cryptic sayings and then won't give you the details." Nina stood. "I think we should go find Wolf Hunter and ask him what all of this means."

"Are you crazy? We can't go anywhere tonight."

"Why not?"

"Well, we've been drinking, for starters."

Nina sat down again in a huff. "Oh, I forgot about that part. Can we call him?"

Molly hesitated. "I guess so, we could call the club."

"Great." Nina went to the phone, punched a number, and then asked for information.

Molly listened as her friend got the number for the club and got connected through. She wasn't sure this was such a good idea. Zedler had told her to go with Rankin. They didn't really know Tasunke. Then she shook off the notion that she needed male protection. They were grown women. They knew how to take care of themselves. The little voice in the back of her head reminded her that Carol had been a grown woman too. Molly silenced it. Carol had been out on her own, she was bringing Nina.

"That's it then." Her friend picked up her purse and headed for the door. "We're off to see the wizard." She grinned.

"I'm not sure going to that club is a good idea."

"It isn't, and we're not. I asked the bouncer to meet us at the diner a few blocks from here."

At least they could walk over and not worry about taking a cab. Molly closed the hotel room door behind them.

"What does Tasunke mean anyway," Nina asked.

"It's a Dakotan word for horse."

Her friend turned around, eyes as big as the oversized hoops she was wearing in her earlobes. "You're kidding me. He's tall, built, and—"

Molly interrupted. "Let's not go there."

Nina giggled as they waited for the elevator. "Whatever you say. But I thought you were past your prudish ways now that you've shown Rankin your scars and everything."

Molly sighed. She might be in for a very long night.

* * *

DES SLAPPED some papers on the left pile on his desk and pulled a small bunch from the collection on the right. He'd been reviewing Berker Studios employee statements for hours. So far, nothing stood out. Somewhere in all this ink, there should be a clue. Someone said too little, or too much about Molly, or her designs, or about another coworker.

He scanned the documents. Nothing.

Technically, he shouldn't have access to these reports. He had to bribe Faurk. Next time the guys went drinking, the first five rounds would be on Des. He hoped Faurk liked cheap beer.

A quick staccato beat on the door, and then Faurk opened the door.

"Got preliminary lab reports," he said.

"Already?"

Faurk turned slightly pink. "I asked for a favor."

Did Molly know how much the guys on the force cared about her? Probably not. "Let's have it then. What do they say?"

"The outside of the glove was wiped, but the perp wasn't able to clean the inside completely. The scarf had some partials, but they were too smudged to get a match. Plus, silk is often hard to process. Leather is much better to lift from than cloth."

Des wanted to shake the guy. He took a deep breath and tried to reach for patience. "And who used that glove?"

"Don't know. The person is not in any of the criminal databases. We're checking private and government now. But it will take a while."

Des pinched the bridge of his nose. "What *do* you know then?"

"We know they're not Nyland's."

Des let out a breath he didn't know he'd held. "Not Molly's," he repeated.

Faurk smirked but tried to hide it when Des threw him a sharp look. The guy cleared his throat. "It doesn't mean she's clear, but it means someone else has touched these items."

"Could it be the vics?"

"We checked those. It's not Wymer's."

Excitement stirred in Des' chest. Finally, a break in the case. He could tell in his gut that whomever these prints belonged to would lead to the killer.

Faurk was studying him. "So," he said. "We've compared them to Berker's prints as well."

Des jerked his head up. "And?"

Faurk shook his head. "Not his."

"Fuck, it would have been nice to have a reason to bring the douchebag in."

"Precisely how I feel."

Des quirked his head. He knew why he didn't like the guy. Berker's hands had a tendency to roam where they didn't belong, like on Molly's body. But what did Faurk have against him?

The other detective picked up on the unspoken question. "I just don't like him. He's too good looking and too charming."

Des nodded. "I agree. Did you tell Zedler about the prints?"

"On my way to his office now." Faurk hesitated. "I thought maybe I'd call Molly first and let her know."

"I'll tell her." Des looked down at the papers. "How long until we might have a match?"

"Depends, we only fingerprinted the employees of Berker Studios that said they'd been in Nyland's office in the last two weeks."

Des thought for a while. "Double or nothing, it's one of them."

"I'm not taking that one," Faurk said. "I'll hold on to my five pints."

"Worth a try," Des shook his head.

Faurk moved toward the door. "You're going to pay for my beer, several of them. Just accept it." He reached for the handle and paused.

Des waited for him to say something else.

Faurk faced Des. "If you hurt her, there's going to be a lot of people that'll want a piece of you."

Des froze for a second and then nodded. Obviously, he and Molly had not been as discreet as they thought.

With a nod of his own, Faurk left.

Even if Des hadn't yet defined his and Molly's relationship, the rest of the precinct had decided they were a couple. Looked like Zedler was the father figure, and Faurk was the big brother. More like she had several big brothers to come to her rescue. He liked that they were looking out for her, but it was also intimidating.

He probably shouldn't pile more emotional complications on top of flashbacks of Mitchell's death and PTSD. But somehow it felt right to think of Molly as his. He reached for his phone and sent her a text, asking where she was. It didn't take long before she wrote back.

Having dinner with Tasunke.

He read the display a second time before reacting. Jerking his jacket off the hook on the back of the door, he slung it over his shoulder. Time to go and tell Molly who she should be having her meals with.

* * *

TWENTY MINUTES LATER, Des walked through the door to the fifties-style diner on the other side of town. The booths were lined with beige vinyl, and Happy-Days-like paraphernalia covered the walls. He spotted Molly in the back of the place. She waved to him, smiling big.

Nina sat next to her. "Well, hello there, detective," she said as Des approached, his jaw clenched, hands fisted.

Molly rolled her eyes and elbowed her friend. "Rankin, you remember Tasunke."

Silently, Des vowed to make her use his first name before the end of the week. He turned to the bouncer, jerking his chin up once to acknowledge him. The fucker took up most of the booth across from the women. His shoulders spanned almost half of the back of the seat, and his legs were braced wide open. With his bronzed skin and the shadows cast by his chiseled features, the guy looked like an extra from some gladiator movie.

Des pulled up a chair and sat on the short end of the table.

Grinning, Tasunke held out his hand. "Good to see you."

Des slapped his palm in the one offered and shook once, struggling to not wince when a vice grip met his. He'd forgotten how powerful the dude was. *So, it's like that.* He squeezed back.

Nina sniffed the air. "Molly, can you smell all that testosterone in the air."

"Sure can. It reeks." She frowned at Des. "Good thing Eric couldn't make it, or we'd suffocate."

Tasunke arched an eyebrow at Des.

"Just ignore them." He shook his head. "Catch me up on the wolf hunting."

"I haven't found either of the rogues yet. I think they are a mated couple."

"What exactly is so special about these wolves?" Nina asked.

"Other than the fact that they scare people in parking lots? And that wolves don't belong in the city?" Molly said.

Nina patted her friend's hand. "I know one of them scared you, sweetie. I'm wondering why *the* Wolf Hunter is in town to catch them."

Tasunke studied Nina. "I am not the Wolf Hunter," he finally said. "I'm just a wolf hunter."

"That's not what my granny and aunties say."

"Your grandmother? What is her name?"

"Dueña Moreno."

"The bronzed mistress." Tasunke bowed his head. "She and her sisters are descendants of sage women."

"I guess so." Nina changed position in the booth, a frown on her forehead. "I've never thought of exactly what her name means. How do you know her?"

"I have never met her, but of course I know her name." He stared at Nina as if memorizing her face. The atmosphere around the table shifted, and the air felt denser.

The hairs on the back of Des' neck stood up. He turned around to see if anybody had walked behind the chair. The space between then and the rest of the patrons were as empty as it had been before.

Nina squirmed again.

Molly watched Tasunke, mesmerized.

267

Des cleared his throat. "Okay, then. Maybe we should change the topic—"

"Wait," Nina said. "I want to know more about my gran and her sisters. They are always so mysterious and never share anything about my parents or my grandfather." She grabbed Tasunke's sleeve from across the table. "Please tell me what you know."

The man put his hand over Nina's. "I cannot. I do not know anything, and if I did, it would not be my story to tell."

Nina pulled her hand back and slumped back in the booth. "You're as bad as them."

A small smile played in the corner of Tasunke's mouth. "Maybe one day, you would honor me and take me to visit your grandmother." His eyes were locked on Nina.

Des noticed that even if his face appeared relaxed, Tasunke's body was tight as a coiled spring. He frowned.

The women didn't seem to notice anything.

Des pulled Molly's hand into his own. She looked up, startled, then smiled and gave his hand a little squeeze. He was glad he'd used his left. The right one still ached from the handshake with Tasunke.

Nina watched Tasunke with a puzzled frown on her forehead. "Sure. I can take you to see granny."

"I don't know if that is a good idea," Des interjected. "You should ask her before you bring Tasunke." He didn't like how important this visit seemed to be to the giant.

Tasunke shot him an annoyed glare. "I would never harm the Duena."

Nina nodded. "She did talk about you as if you were a good guy."

Tasunke bowed his head. If Des didn't know any better, he'd say the guy was blushing. It was hard to tell with that bronzed skin and the shadows cast by his chiseled features.

Fuck, the guy looked like he should be an extra in some gladiator movie.

"Can I share my news now?" he asked, and jumped a little with the others when his voice came out a few decibels louder than intended.

"Share away," Nina said.

Des turned to Molly. "We found fingerprints on the glove that are not yours."

She frowned. "Of course they're not. I've never seen the thing before."

"I know, Sweet. But now everyone else knows too."

"Whose fingerprints are they?" Nina asked.

"We don't know yet. They're not in the system, but we're comparing them to the prints we took from Berker Studios' employees."

"I can't believe anybody I work with might hate me that much." Molly's voice broke.

Nina rubbed her friend's shoulder. "Don't think about it, Hon. It's got nothing to do with who you are or what you've done."

Des tugged on Molly's hand to get her attention. "Is there anybody at your work that has been hostile toward you?"

Nina snorted.

Molly found her lap fascinating, all of a sudden. She tugged to release her hand from his grip.

He held on. "Tell me," he said.

"You should tell him," Nina said.

"Fine." Molly stopped trying to pull her hand back. "Before the meeting with Marvelous Melon, Fred Mueller erased my files from the server and giggled with Samantha about it when I was about to open the presentation."

"Do you think he could be involved in these killings?"

"No." Molly almost shouted, then lowered her voice when

the other patrons swiveled their faces their way. "I can't imagine anybody I work with being capable of murder."

Des nodded. Most people couldn't. Unfortunately, he'd seen enough dead bodies to know that quite a few people were able to kill without much remorse. "Hold tight," he said. "I'll just give Faurk a heads up."

* * *

MOLLY WATCHED Rankin walk across the restaurant toward the bathrooms. She liked his leather bomber jacket and the way his faded jeans hugged his butt.

As sharp pain hit her side. "Ouch." She rubbed her rib where Nina had elbowed her.

"I said, isn't that good news?" her friend said. "If you'd not been so absorbed in ogling your boyfriend's butt, you'd have heard me the first time."

Tasunke chuckled.

"He's not my boyfriend," Molly said.

"Could have fooled me." Nina quirked a dark eyebrow.

"I think the detective would disagree too," Tasunke said, but he wasn't looking at Molly or Rankin. He was watching Nina, a small smile playing at the edges of his mouth.

"Who asked you?" Molly shot at him, then regretted being so rude.

Nina barked out a burst of loud laughter, and Tasunke joined her.

Great, I'm back in high school talking about boyfriends. "I don't want to talk about it," Molly said. It just made her table companions laugh louder.

Rankin chose that moment to return to the table. "What did I miss?"

"Nothing," Nina giggled.

At least Tasunke had the decency to swallow his laughter.

He cleared his throat several times. Mirth still twitching his lips.

"I think I'm ready to go," Molly said.

"I'll drive you," Rankin interjected.

"It's only a few blocks to the hotel. Nina and I will be fine."

"I can take Nina home," Tasunke interjected.

Molly looked at her friend. Nina shrugged. "That's fine by me. I took the bus to the hotel, so I'd appreciate a ride."

"Call me tomorrow?"

Nina nodded. "Absolutely." She shot Rankin a wicked grin. "I'll want a full account of the rest of your evening's events."

Molly shook her head and walked out with Rankin. The chill of the night hit her out on the street, and she shivered. She wrapped her fleece tighter around her.

"Cold?" Rankin asked, slipping his arm out of the sleeve of his jacket.

"I'm fine," Molly hurried to interject. "It's just the temperature difference."

He grabbed her hand and pulled it into the crook of his arm.

At first, she resisted, but then gave up. The man couldn't help but being alpha.

All alpha, all the time. And in this instance, she liked it a lot. He and Tasunke had a lot in common. "Do you think it's okay to leave her alone in there?" she asked Rankin.

"She's not exactly alone. There are other diners with her."

"You know what I mean."

"She'll be fine. We would only have been in the way anyway."

"What do you mean," Molly turned toward him.

He traced her jaw with the back of his knuckles. "I think there might be something between them that the two of them have to figure out." Rankin's caress trailed down her neck. "Let's not worry about them. I'd rather talk about us."

Molly shivered again, but not from the cold this time. The sounds of traffic and other pedestrians faded into the background. She swallowed. "Aren't you going to get in trouble for being seen with me?"

"Probably. I'm not planning on being seen, though." His eyes looked like emeralds with gold flecks.

Molly's breath caught in her throat.

Rankin tugged on her arm and made her move again. "Come on. Let's get you back to the hotel."

They walked quickly, not uttering a word.

Molly felt equal parts excitement and trepidation. The attraction she always felt when Rankin was near was dialed up tonight. Three other people joined them in the elevator on the way up. Standing side by side with Rankin without touching was agony.

She unzipped her coat to cool down.

Aware of every breath Rankin took, every shift of his body, she closed her eyes to calm herself. Instead, she smelled his scent that sandalwood aftershave blended with pure male, and her body went on full alert.

The scars on her shoulder and arm tingled. The hairs on her neck stood on end.

Her nipples ached for his touch and she gasped. This had never happened before.

Rankin turned, his pupils dilated as he studied her face. His gaze trailed lower, to her breasts. A smirk of pure male satisfaction grazed his lips when her nipples tightened in response.

Finally, the elevator stopped on her floor.

Rankin grabbed her hand and squeezed through the doors before they fully opened. "What number?" His voice was hoarse.

Molly pointed mutely to her door and gave him the keycard.

"Fuck, fuck, fuck." Rankin slid the card several times, but the light wouldn't beep to green.

Molly grabbed the card, turned it over, and unlocked the door.

He kissed her before the door closed behind them. His lips devoured hers, tongue plunging into her mouth.

Standing on her toes to reach and holding on to his jacket for balance, Molly matched him thrust for thrust.

She pressed her body into his and felt his gratifying hardness pressing against her belly. She couldn't get close enough.

"Fuck Molly," he growled and grabbed her ass while lifting her against the wall.

Yes, that's the right spot. She rubbed herself against him.

Rankin moaned. "We have to slow down," he gasped.

"No," she barked. "If you stop now, Rankin, I will smack you."

He pulled back, an arrogant grin on his lips. "You can smack me anytime, anywhere."

She groaned and reached forward to kiss him again.

He pulled back. "No, no, no."

"Rankin," she growled in warning.

He leaned forward, his breath caressing her lips. "Not until you call me by my first name," he whispered.

"Tease," she said. Two could play that game. She reached down between them, found his hard ridge, and caressed it through his jeans.

"Fuck," he gasped.

"I hope so," Molly smiled. She continued to stroke him.

Rankin growled and hoisted her sideways, carrying her further into the room. She yelped as he threw her on the bed.

He made fast work of peeling off his clothes, watching

her intensely as each garment fell to the floor. She let her eyes feast on ripped pecks and hard abs that narrowed down to slim hips, before flaring out into toned, defined quads. She sighed. He was magnificent.

Rankin grinned. "Your turn." Molly reached over to the nightstand to switch out the lights, but Rankin grabbed her wrist. "I want to see you. Don't deny me that pleasure."

She hesitated, but then slowly unbuttoned her blouse and pulled the two sides apart.

Rankin's eyes smoldered as they followed her hands' actions.

She unsnapped her bra and then dragged the straps down, releasing breasts.

"You're so beautiful," Rankin whispered. He stepped closer, and the bed dipped down to accommodate his weight as he crawled toward her.

Holding his gaze, she cupped herself with both hands.

A hoarse growl escaped his lips. He reached forward, grabbing the waistband of her pants. He tore the button and the zipper open, and then ripped the pants and her underwear off her legs in one swoop. His lips left red hot paths as he traced kisses up her thigh, over her hip bone, and then higher.

She gasped as he nuzzled her nipples.

He mumbled something she couldn't quite hear. Something about stars. His teeth grazed her nipples, and then his tongue soothed the delicious ache. Heat radiated through her body. She couldn't breathe.

Rankin caressed her belly, guiding his hands down lower.

She whimpered.

He leaned over and kissed her lips while grabbing her ass. "I can't wait. You feel so damn good."

Molly laced her hands behind his neck, nibbling his ear,

and smiled when he hissed. "Don't wait. I want you inside me."

"Hold that thought." He reached for his jeans and retrieved a foil package from the back pocket. Leaning over her, he deftly covered himself with the condom and then pushed into the wetness between her legs.

She gasped, and he stilled, waiting for her to adjust around him.

Molly grabbed his butt. "More," she growled, a sound she's never heard herself make.

Rankin tumbled forward, bracing himself on either side of her. "There's no rush, we have all night."

"Inside me. Right now. I want all of you inside," she demanded between gasps of breath. She widened her legs to accommodate him.

Rankin thrust his hips forward.

Hard. Deep. Delicious.

She cried out.

He captured her mouth again. "I want you to say my name," he whispered, hot breath against her cheek.

"Rankin," she gasped.

He stopped, holding his body suspended above hers.

She opened her eyes, glaring at him.

"My first name," he demanded, moisture beading on his forehead.

She bit her lip. "Des," she whispered and arched her hips, trying to force him deeper inside her.

He hissed in a breath and slowly pushed himself in, down to the hilt.

Molly whimpered as the head of his shaft bumped against the entry to her womb. She clenched around him.

With a roar, he fell forward, pumping his hips faster and faster.

Heels braced against the sheets, she matched his speed.

"Des," she yelled before white light exploded behind her eyelids, and she forgot her own name.

* * *

MOLLY BREATHED DEEPLY beside him as Des watched her sleep. Curled on her side, she snorted softly.

He smiled and stroked a few curls off her forehead. He thought it was the guy that was supposed to pass out right after sex, but Molly had beat him to slumber as soon as they'd finished.

And what a finish it had been. His cock twitched just thinking about how amazing she'd felt convulsing around him. Pumping him dry.

What they had just shared went beyond sex. The smile drained from his face as a cold sweat broke out all over his body. He sucked at relationships. She deserved someone better than him, but anger and jealousy burned like acid in his chest at the thought of Molly with someone else. She belonged with him.

Resigned, he turned off the lights and pulled her into his arms.

She muttered something in her sleep. It sounded like "Des" and "cold hands."

He grinned.

She had finally used his first name.

CHAPTER 19

*M*olly woke up hearing water running. It took her a few seconds to remember she was still at the hotel. Images of the night before flashed through her mind. Rankin...Des, she blushed when she thought of how he'd demanded that she'd say his name as she came. The sound of running water must be him in the shower. Thinking of him naked in the steam-filled bathroom made her heart race a little faster, all those defined ridges and valleys that made up his muscular body glistening with water droplets. She bit her lip and worried about what it would be like to see him again after their passionate night. Would he be awkward?

The water turned off, and a moment later, Des stepped out of the bathroom, a white towel hung low on his hips. He ran a hand through his wet hair and grinned when he caught her gaze. "Hey, Sleepy." Okay, so not awkward then. Sweet and still sexy as hell.

She smiled back, and her breath caught as he sauntered closer toward the bed. Des sat down next to her. He leaned over slowly and whispered against her lips, "Anyone ever told you how hot you look when you're just waking up?" Before she had a chance to answer, he claimed her mouth with his. The kiss was slow and deep. Heat built in her core, radiating through her body. She arched against him, wanting more of him.

He groaned and pulled away. "You have no idea how much I'd like to continue this."

Molly traced the edge of the towel with her fingers. "Then why don't you?" She threw him what she hoped was a coy glance. Rankin's groan declared it effective.

He caught her hand with hers. "Because Zedler wants me in the office right away. Something's going down."

Molly stopped trying to undo the towel. "Is there a lead?"

Des sat up and caught both her hands in his. "He just sent me a short text. I don't know the details."

Molly nodded. "Sure, I understand. You can't tell me. I'm still a person of interest." She glanced away. Even if things weren't awkward between them now, it would be as the case continued.

He nudged her chin with the edge of his knuckles, making her look him in the eyes. "Hey, I'd tell you if I knew anything."

She shrugged. They may have shared something extraordinary in bed last night, but now in the light of day, things were different. She may have a serial killer targeting her. And Des would have to act as a cop first, and...well, lover second.

He gave her a quick kiss and rested his forehead against hers. "I promise I'll let you know whatever I find out." Leaning back, his eyes searched her face. "Do you believe me?"

She nodded. "I do." Even if she still had her doubts, he

sounded sincere. "I'm just spooked about this whole thing. I'm not sure how to handle the idea that I might be working with a killer. Even worse, I may have been working with them for a while now."

Des grabbed her hand and squeezed it. "You are not alone in this. Zedler and I are officially off the case, but we'll do everything we can to catch this sicko. And the rest of the guys at the station are watching out for you too."

Molly felt honored and humbled by how much support she had. She sat up. "I want to help."

Des frowned. "You may be a target. The best thing you can do is make sure you stay safe."

"How exactly do I do that?"

Des stood and started gathering his clothes, pulling them on. "Stay here and don't leave unless Zedler or I go with you."

"I can't be cooped up here all day. I have to work." No way was she going to let this sick bastard make her a prisoner. She couldn't let fear define her. Not anymore. She refused to live her life that way. The way she'd been forced to when she was a kid and in danger of a beating at any provocation because of the evil that supposedly lived inside her.

Des phone dinged, and he checked the display. "That's Zedler wondering where I am." He shrugged into his jacket. "Can't you work from here?"

"I don't want this asshole to win. I don't want anyone to define what I can and cannot do."

"Honey," Des sat down again. "This not defining you or your life. This is just a short term solution." He kissed her again. A quick but heartfelt meeting of their lips. "I'm not going to let him win. And I'm not going to let him define your life."

Molly thought about it for a moment. "I guess I could. I'd

have to go get some files and supplies from the office, though. I hadn't planned on working remotely."

"I'd prefer it if you could stay away from the office. Or, not go unless I'm with you." He rubbed his eyebrow.

She bristled. "Don't coddle me. I'm not some helpless woman you have to save."

He watched her for a moment. "I don't think of you that way."

Liar, he was as alpha as a guy could get. And in this case, it was not a good thing. "It won't take me but a minute to get the stuff I need. I'll be in and out of the office in no time. Plus, it will be full of people."

Des nodded. "Fine, but text me as soon as you're done there."

Molly promised him she would, and he gave her another hot lingering kiss before leaving. As he closed the door, she realized they hadn't discussed whether he would come back to the hotel room, or for how long she would have to stay there. What exactly had last night meant to him? What exactly had it meant to her?

An hour later, she stepped out of the elevator at Berker Studios and was no closer to getting an answer to those questions. Samantha was on the phone and greeted her with a distracted smile. Molly only gave her a small wave before heading down the hallway to her office.

She logged on to her computer and accessed the HR portal. After marking this and the next few days as sick leave, she scanned her emails. There wasn't anything urgent that she couldn't take care of from her laptop. It would suck to work on such a small screen, but she could manage. Especially if she took a large sketchpad and some charcoal chalk with her back to the hotel.

The Marvelous Melon designs were pretty much

wrapped up. She was in the brainstorming phase of her next project and preferred to draw up initial ideas by hand anyway. She sorted through the drawing pads in one of her cabinets and selected two of the right size. The client file folder she needed fit in her computer bag and she was stuffing that in while reaching for her box of drawing pens when her phone chirped that it had a text message.

Des wanted to know where she was.

Rolling her eyes, she tapped out a message telling him she was heading back to the hotel in a few minutes.

His response was short. "Don't dawdle."

If this thing they had was a relationship, they would soon have an enlightened discussion about bossing people around.

She reached for the box of pencils again and frowned when it rattled too much. When she opened it, she found out why. All the pens had been broken into tiny pieces. Obviously, Fred wasn't done with his petty office pranks. She checked her charcoals and found them obliterated into fine dust in their box. At least she'd discovered the damage before she got back to the hotel. Now, she'd just get some new drawing tools from the supply room on her way out.

She gathered her computer bag and the two sketchpads and locked up her office. It wouldn't be hard for someone to retrieve the master key and gain access, but she didn't want to make it easy for sleazy Fred to arrange another childish surprise. The supply room was at the end of a hallway, right next to the emergency stairs of the building.

Molly searched the shelves until she found both pencils and charcoal. She put them in her bag and then heard the door open behind her. Before she could see who'd entered, the light went out, and the windowless room turned pitch black.

She turned toward where she thought the door and the new visitor were. "Hey, turn the light back on."

The only answer she got was steps moving closer, quickly.

What the hell?

She heard someone's fast breathing before she felt the heat of it on her skin. And then a pinprick like a bee sting hurt her neck, and she lost consciousness.

* * *

DES LEANED back in his office chair and studied Zedler sitting across from him on the other side of the desk. "You couldn't take that meeting with the LT by yourself? You had to drag me into it?" The urgent text from Zedler about something "going down," was Lieutenant Lewis explaining why Zedler's and Des' names were not to appear on any case paperwork from now on. It had been twenty intense minutes of Lewis talking and Zedler and Des listening quietly. Her phrasing had been colorful and involved words like "kicking your sorry ass" and "stomping your ego to the ground" if she'd find they'd disobeyed her.

Zedler grinned sheepishly. "She insisted you be there too."

"She makes me feel like I'm sixteen years old, and she just caught me smoking pot." Des was exhausted after the meeting. It'd still been productive though, even if he wished it lasted a much shorter time. The LT had actually done them a favor. She'd fulfilled her duty by giving them an official dress-down and handing off the case to other detectives since Zedler and Des had personal connections with Molly, who was still technically a person of interest. But she also hadn't said they couldn't work the case. Just that they couldn't sign any reports.

"What's next, then?" Des asked.

Zedler sighed. "Faurk is supposed to let me know as soon as he finds out anything about the fingerprints."

The office door flew open, and Detective Faurk rushed into the room.

"Speak of the prodigal detective, and he shall appear," Zedler muttered.

Faurk threw him a puzzled glance but was too excited to ask for details. His body almost vibrated when he turned to Des. "We got him." His eyes sparkled. "The sucker applied for a concealed weapons license five years ago." He waved a sheet of paper. "I found his fingerprints in a civilian noncriminal database."

Des' heart rate sped up as adrenaline flooded his body. Finally, something to do rather than just sitting around waiting. "Who is it?"

"Fred Mueller."

"Fuck me." Des slammed a hand on the desk. That little weasel had made Molly's life hell. Even if she hadn't shared more than a few of the details of how he tried to sabotage her presentation, Des knew she'd been troubled by the guy's animosity. And no one messed with Molly. Not on his watch.

Faurk's phone rang, and he barked out a hello before listening intently. After only a few seconds, he hung up. "I sent uniformed units to his house and Berker Studios, he's not at either place."

Des felt like kicking something but settled for glaring at Faurk. "Where the fuck is he?"

The lousy fucker smirked back. "I also put out an APB on his car." He paused, and Des wanted to punch his smug face. Something must have alerted the detective to Des' thoughts because he swallowed quickly, and the smirk disappeared. "Mueller drives a green Honda Civic, which a patrol unit just located behind an abandoned warehouse off Sprague

Avenue." He waved his phone. "That was them, they're texting me the exact address."

Des slipped his shoulder holster on and reached for his jacket. "I'm coming with."

Faurk nodded. "I didn't expect anything less."

Zedler pulled out his phone. "I'll call Molly to make sure she's somewhere secure."

"She's at the hotel," Des said before he could think and then shrugged when two pairs of eyes narrowed as they glared at him. "She texted me from her office this morning and said she picked up a few things before heading back to the hotel. She's working from there today."

The other detectives relaxed, and Des silently congratulated himself for the small save. There was no reason to advertise his relationship with Molly. At least not yet. It would become complicated soon enough, especially if they worked more cases together.

He paused briefly when he realized that in his mind, he took for granted that the two of them now belonged together. He may have to spend some more time clearing all that out later, but fuck, it wasn't like he could go back now. Molly belonged with him.

"It's going to voicemail," Zedler said, hanging up his phone.

A tinge of unease fluttered in Des stomach. "Call the hotel." Molly should be there by now.

Zedler dialed again and asked whoever answered for Molly's room's extension.

Faurk and Des watched the older detective intently, all three of them listening as ring after ring went through on the other end of the line. The hotel's generic voicemail picked up.

Zedler hung up and dialed again, almost shouting Molly's

name when the hotel reception picked up. They listened to the signals go through again.

Still nothing but voicemail.

Hot white worry slammed into Des. Molly couldn't be reached, and potential serial killer Muller was in the wind. Not only that, he was a possible serial killer with a concealed weapons permit.

CHAPTER 20

*M*olly's head ached so fiercely she thought she'd lose her breakfast. She shook her head to get rid of the fog that had invaded her mind. Bad idea. It just made the nausea worse. She swallowed the bile rising in the back of her throat and opened her eyes slowly.

Her hands hurt like crazy and were stretched above her head. The pain came from the ropes binding her to a hook on a chain suspended from the ceiling. She looked down and discovered that her toes barely touched the ground. She tried to shake her arms to get free, but without the leverage of the floor, she couldn't get any traction and lift them off the hook. She looked around for a clue of her location.

Dark, damp walls loomed to the right. Weak afternoon light filtered through dusty and broken window panes in front of her. The sound of water dripping echoed from somewhere near. Where in the hell was she? Some kind of warehouse?

Out of the corner of her eye, she saw something, someone moving. She turned her head.

Fred dangled ten feet to the side and slightly behind her.

But he was suspended from a rope around his neck, his hands tied behind his back. His eyes stared vacantly back at her, and his blue lips were pulled back in a horrific grin.

Molly screamed.

Footsteps echoed in the empty space as someone approached. Someone wearing high-heels. The same steps she'd heard in the supply room.

"Look who finally woke up," Samantha said, flicking her hair as she stepped into view. Her amber eyes glittered manically.

"Please help me." Molly croaked from her dry and raw throat.

"Why would I do that?" Something glittered in Samantha's hand when the weak sunlight from the window hit it. "I've gone to a lot of trouble to get you here. All lovely and strung up." The smile on her lips was terrifying.

Molly tried to process the situation, but it was so surreal. "Just let me down. Let's talk about this."

The blonde just widened that manic smile. "Are you ready to have some fun?" She held up the thing in her hand, which turned out to be a curved blade with some writing engraved. The menace of the weapon and her cheery tone were eerily mismatched.

Molly swallowed the lump of panic in her throat. "Please, Samantha, you don't want to do this. We should talk."

"I don't think so." Samantha smiled wickedly. "We're done talking." She took a step closer and slashed the front of Molly's shirt.

Molly screamed again.

Samantha cocked her head. "Oh, you're a screamer." She grabbed the front of Molly's shirt and ripped it apart. "I like that. We're just getting started, so I expect to hear a lot of your loud voice."

"What the fuck, Samantha?" Molly shouted as she swung

back and forth, her hands almost numb from pain. "Let me down." She was absolutely terrified, but also furious at how weak and powerless she felt.

The other woman stood back and slowly shook her head. "And here's the reason for you always wearing long sleeves." She executed another perfect hair toss. "You're practically deformed." She stepped closer and traced the blade down Molly's shoulder and arm.

Ice-cold fear unfurled in Molly's stomach and spread through her body. Sweat trickled down her brow. She needed to distract this new crazy Samantha. "What happened to Fred?"

The other woman turned toward the body next to them. She tilted her head as if studying the body swinging slowly to and fro. "Poor Fred, so deluded. He actually thought I would sleep with him. The only thing he was good for was playing pranks on you and hiding evidence in your office." She started giggling and then threw her head back in a full laugh.

Now I know what insane sounds like. Molly tried to keep her tone even, as if hanging trussed up like a cow on the way to slaughter happened every day. "Why did you have to kill him?"

Samantha took a step closer. She grazed the tip of the metal blade over Molly's cheek, down her chin, and over her lips. "Why not?" she whispered. "Why keep him alive?" She leaned forward as if to kiss Molly, tracing the knife down her neck toward the collar bone. "He never learned to do as he was told. I was so angry when he told me he'd killed that homeless man."

Bile rose in Molly's throat again. She swallowed and turned her head.

Sharp pain in her shoulder told her Samantha had stopped teasing and now meant business.

"Look at me," the blonde hissed. "You think you're so special, but you are nothing."

Molly turned her head. The pain in her shoulder made her eyes tear up. She blinked to clear them.

Samantha took a step closer and twisted the blade. "Fred had to learn his lesson. He didn't understand the ritual. He degraded the traditions."

Molly tried to repress it, but couldn't help the scream that ripped out of her throat. Fuck that hurt.

"That's better." The blonde smiled. "You sound just like Carol. She was a screamer too." She smiled.

"You killed Carol? Why?" Molly managed to squeeze out.

"I needed her blood. Just like I needed the blood from the others." Her fingertip traced down Molly's collarbone and traced the edge of her bra. "I'm going to like bleeding you dry."

The other woman's touch repulsed Molly. She shuddered. "You're insane."

"I'm insane?" Samantha looked up and grinned. "Wymer thought he could put his hands on me and not face the reper-cussions. Always patting my butt and drooling over my chest. There's nothing insane about what I'm doing. It's a reckoning."

Molly nodded as if she completely understood why someone had to die for groping the office assistant. "But why Carol? What did she ever do to you?" She needed more time. She needed to keep Samantha talking.

The blonde pulled the blade out of Molly's shoulder slowly, as if she was enjoying it. It hurt even worse than when going in, and Molly hissed in pain.

"That bitch thought she could sleep with Anthony and not get punished." Samantha glared at Molly. "Just like you."

"I've never been interested in Anthony," Molly protested. Her hands felt utterly numb now, and the steady trickle of blood out of her shoulder worried her. Too much blood loss and she'd pass out.

"Of course you are. All you sluts are."

"No, no. He's my boss, that's all. I swear there's never been anything between us. Anthony has always been faithful to you."

The blonde smiled. Her glassy eyes got a dreamy look in them. "Of course he is. We're soul mates."

"So why kill Carol if she wasn't a threat."

Samantha snapped to. Her eyes cleared. "I told you. I needed blood." She leaned forward and grabbed Molly's hair. "And now I need yours."

"Why?" Molly shouted. "If you're going to kill me, I at least deserve to know why." To her relief, Samantha released her hair.

The blood-flow out of the wound on her shoulder increased. Her arms felt like they were being pulled out of their sockets in an inferno of agony. Molly bit her lip to keep from losing consciousness and lifted her head to keep track of where Samantha had gone.

The blonde stood a few feet in front of her. Another crazy smile adorned her lips. "I need it to be with my soulmate forever."

Molly blinked. "I don't understand."

Samantha threw back her head and raised her hands in the air, one of them still holding the curved blade, the tip now covered in blood. Molly's blood. "From eternal pain comes eternal blood becomes eternal life." She whispered feverishly and lifted her arms over her head while kicking off her shoes.

Samantha's skin rippled like water. Her bones cracked and popped. The curved knife fell to the floor as her hands elongated, nails popping out her fingers and forming claws. She shook her head, and her blond hair rippled into a frenzy, then shortened before fur sprung out all over her body. A deep growl erupted from her throat. She flung her head back and sat down on her haunches. Her clothes ripping to make room for broader muscles and falling to the floor.

Molly watched in horror as the woman's jaws shot out of her face to form a snout. Her whole body shaking as bones broke and then snapped in their new shape. In the place where Samantha had stood only moments ago, a big tawny wolf sat instead. It cocked its head to the side and watched Molly with amber eyes. Samantha's eyes.

It was the same animal that had confronted Molly in the parking lot. It grinned, tongue lolling out of its jaws. Then it lunged right at Molly, snapping its jaws a hair-breath from her throat.

Molly cried out in terror.

The wolf landed on its feet, hunkered down, and shook its coat. Its skin rippled, and then the fur was sucked into its pores while the hair on its head grew longer. In a short moment, a naked Samantha stood in its place.

"See, you're not the only one who's special."

Molly was hoarse from screaming and exhausted from hanging on the hook. Her shoulder and arms ached. She felt feverish. Her skin felt clammy and too hot. She wondered if she was about to pass out.

Samantha laughed. "Poor Molly. You have no idea what's going on around you, do you?"

Molly shook her head.

"I need the blood to transform into wolf shape, but you are going to change that. Your blood is going to make me powerful. With your blood inside me, I can change whenever I want, just like Anthony."

Sweat poured down Molly's forehead and stung her eyes. She blinked to clear the blurry picture of Samantha. She tried to make sense of what the blonde had just told her. Anthony was a wolf. An honest-to-god real wolfman, as in her designs. If she hadn't seen Samantha's transformation, she wouldn't believe it. It was getting hard to think. Her skin was on fire now as the fever raged through her body. Her teeth rattled.

Samantha picked up the curved blade and grabbed Molly's hair again. She jerked Molly's head back. "You're nothing special. You think you are because you can draw pretty pictures and work for the police, but I know better." She scratched the sharp instrument along Molly's throat. "I know all about you, Molly. I know about your lightning accident and your family throwing you out. You're a freak, that's what you are. A pathetic little freak who tries to solve crimes."

Molly jerked her head to free it from Samantha's grip.

The blonde laughed and tightened her hold. "Where are your police friends now? Did you think they cared about you? Did you think your detective Rankin loved you? He doesn't. Nobody can love a freak like you." She pulled Molly's head further back.

Molly's scalp burned from the pull, and she whimpered.

"What the hell are you doing?" someone shouted from the doorway. Anthony strode up to Samantha and grabbed the blade. "I told you to wait."

The blonde released Molly's hair, cocked out a hip, and pouted. "I don't want to wait. I want to become a full wolf now." The fact that Samantha was naked didn't seem to faze her.

Anthony leaned in and grabbed Sam's jaw. "Listen to me. You are not ready," he hissed in her face.

"You keep on saying that, but I think you only want me to change temporarily because you want to control me."

Molly watched her boss shake his head and tighten his grip. If she wasn't so worried about her own predicament.

And if the bitch hadn't cut ribbons out of Molly's skin, she might have been concerned about Samantha's situation. As it was, she frantically pulled on the ropes binding her wrists. As long as these two were distracted by each other, she might be able to escape. The burning had intensified in her arm and shoulder. She worried how much blood she'd lost. If the pain kept on radiating like it was, she might not be able to stay conscious. She tugged on the rope again.

Anthony was shaking Samantha by his grip on her jaw. "Listen to me, you arrogant bitch. I'm your alpha, and I tell you when you're ready for the initiation ceremony. Now is not it."

Samantha started to cry. Big drops fell from her eyes. "When will I be ready then," she whined.

The tears must have worked because Anthony let go of her jaw. He stroked her hair. "Soon, baby. I just want what's best for you. My initiation ceremony was a disaster because we couldn't find a sacrifice with enough abilities. I had to make do with someone who had strong intuition."

Samantha curled into him like a kitten. "I know baby. I'm sorry things were hard for you. And I'm sorry you lost your wife, your lupa. At least now you get your revenge."

Molly stopped tugging on the rope when the two of them turned toward her.

Anthony's eyes glowed an eerie green. "That's right," he said, letting go of Samantha and walking up to Molly. "Detective Rankin is quite fond of little Molly." He gripped Molly's jaw and leaned in close.

Molly could see Samantha frown behind Anthony's back. His breath was hot on her face. She closed her eyes.

"Mm," Anthony said as he breathed in deeply. "The smell of terror is such an aphrodisiac."

Molly kept herself very still. She scarcely breathed for fear of what Anthony would do.

"Open your eyes."

She did as he commanded.

His eyes bore into hers. A cruel smile on his lips. "Did you know your lover killed the love of my life?"

Molly shook her head, afraid to look away from his eyes.

"Did he not tell you how his partner was killed? How my sweetie held the mighty Detective Rankin down while I tore out his partner's throat. He wasn't so brave then. Whimpering like a little child, begging us to release him."

Molly stayed as still as she could.

Anthony moved his hand down her jaw and neck. His fingers grazed her collar bone before traveling further. He squeezed her breast.

Molly hissed in pain.

"Maybe I should have some fun with you and send the pictures to your detective." He moved his lips close to hers.

She felt his breath on her mouth and swallowed so she wouldn't gag.

"No," Samantha shouted. "You promised me we would only kill her."

Anthony released Molly and backhanded the other woman. "Shut up, bitch."

Samantha fell down, hand held to her cheek. She glared at Molly as if it was her fault she'd gotten hit.

Anthony shook his fist. "It's your fault we're in this situation in the first place. If you hadn't rushed things, we could have kept tabs on Molly until we were ready. Maybe she'd even develop her abilities and strengthen her blood to where we could both have benefitted from the kill."

Molly's skin was burning up. She couldn't think straight because of the pain radiating from her shoulder and down her arm. She glanced up toward the hook from which she was hanging. Her mind played tricks on her. It looked like her scars were glowing as blood pulsed out of her shoulder wound.

Samantha sobbing. "I only wanted to be a wolf for you." Crocodile tears gathered in her eyes and slid down her cheeks.

"I know, baby," Anthony said and stroked her hair. "But we have to wait until you're fully ready. You've only been a wolf for eight months. It takes at least a year before you can go through the ceremony."

"What are we going to do," the blonde whined.

Molly's boss sighed. "I don't know. I guess we'll have to keep the offering hidden until we can use her. She knows too much."

Molly didn't appreciate being referred to as "offering," but decided to let it go and instead concentrate on getting free. The scraps of clothing around her left arm were smoldering. Flashes of fire leaped from her skin to the rope and burnt her wrists. She closed her eyes and tried to fuel whatever was going on with her scars. This had never happened before, but she didn't have time to figure out what was happening. If she could get lose while Samantha and Anthony were distracted by each other, maybe she had a chance to escape.

Real flame licked her wrists as the rope burnt. It hurt, but she didn't care. An arc of blue light shot out from her arm and landed on a pile of rags on the floor. They must have been soaked in some sort of solvent. High yellow flames immediately leaped up and hungrily consumed the cloth and some wood stored beside it.

Anthony turned around just as Molly's bindings broke.

She fell to the floor in a heap. Hearing Anthony rushing toward her, she flung her left hand out. Wishing with all her might that he'd stop. Blue light shot out again, and Anthony yelped in pain. A burning hole appeared in his suit.

Molly could feel the flames behind her grow. Heat built

inside her, and she tried to calm down. Her hair crackled with static electricity. She turned to run from the couple, but a big wall of fire stopped her in her tracks. Flames were licking the walls and the ceiling. The dampness from before was dried, and the fire ate up the loose debris on the floor.

She turned around to confront the couple, but Anthony was no longer there. She caught only a glimpse of him as he bolted out a door on the other side of the room. Closing it behind him.

Samantha stared after him. "Bastard," she shrieked. She turned around and faced Molly. "It's your fault. You ruined everything."

Molly thought about telling the woman what an idiot she was, but decided to make a run for it instead. She feigned left, and as Samantha swept the curved knife in that direction, Molly instead jerked right and ran.

She was almost at the door when Samantha grabbed her hair and pulled her back. "You're not going anywhere, bitch. We're not finished. I'm going to be a full-fledged wolf, and you're going to make me one."

Molly kicked back and felt her heel connect with the other woman's shin. Samantha went down, grunting as she hit the floor. Metal clanging signaled she'd lost her grip on the blade.

Molly turned around, trying to see where the instrument had landed, but there was too much smoke. She could barely see Samantha. She felt her, though. The other woman grabbed Molly's legs and pulled her down on the floor. Her head hit the concrete and stunned her motionless for a few seconds. That's all it took for Samantha to push her down. Straddle her chest and shake the curved blade in her face.

"You're going to pay for this."

Molly's arms were trapped by Samantha's knees. She twisted, trying to dislodge the taller woman. She managed to free her right hand and grabbed the blonde's wrist just as she swooped down with the knife.

The blonde was so strong, and Molly felt her grip slipping as they struggled. She closed her eyes and reached inward with her mind, trying to reproduce the flames that had zinged Anthony. One weak zap leaped from her arm, but it was enough to startle Samantha. The blonde loosened her knee vice around Molly's body and fell back.

Molly couldn't stop her hand as inertia completed the arch of her arm, forcing Samantha's arm to follow back. The blonde's eyes widen as Molly's hand forced Samantha to bury the blade in her own chest. She slowly crumpled to the ground as Molly scampered away.

She couldn't see anything in the haze of the fire. She'd lost her bearings during the fight and couldn't tell which way the door Anthony had disappeared through was. Desperately she turned around over and over, trying to see where the windows were.

Smoke crept into Molly's lungs, making it impossible to breathe. She needed to find Samantha and get both of them out of the building. She tried to turn back to the spot she'd seen Samantha's body fall.

The fire spread. Voracious flames devoured every scrap of material it could find in the empty room. There were flames and walls of heat everywhere.

Coughing, she crept along the concrete floor, crying out in pain when burning debris fell on her hand, scorching her skin.

Over the roar of the fire, she thought she heard someone calling her name. I'm here, she wanted to scream back, but her cracked, dry lips couldn't shape the sounds.

The flames moved in closer. She thought it ironic to survive a lightning strike, only to die of smoke inhalation and be burnt to a crisp. She wished she could have told Des about it, he would have found it funny too. She wished she could have told him so many things, most importantly, how much he had come to mean to her and how much she loved him. Fuck, to use his favorite phrase, she was going to tell him. If nothing else, he needed to know about Anthony killing Mitchell.

She continued crawling. One inch at a time. She had no idea if she was getting closer to the door, but the air along the floor seemed to be easier to breather. Hopefully, she was heading in the right direction.

Someone called her name again. A rain of embers fell, and she shielded her eyes with her arm. When she opened them again, she saw a big hole in the wall. Through the amber flames, she glimpsed the outside. One last huge heroic effort and she could draw in a lungful of fresh air. Her burnt hand throbbed. She could feel more burning debris falling on her back.

Hands grabbed her and dragged the rest of her body out of the building. There were voices.

"Molly. Oh sweet. Hang in there. I got you."

Des?

"Over here. I need the fucking paramedics over here, right fucking now.

Definitely Des. Blissful blackness claimed her.

CHAPTER 21

*M*olly woke up in a hospital room under crisp white cotton sheets. Her shoulders and arms were covered in gauze, and she felt like she could drink the entire Prairie Falls Lake. She turned to look for a glass of water.

Des sat in a chair by the window next to her bed.

His chin touched his chest as he slept in the most uncomfortable position possible to achieve in a chair. The stubble on his chin was several days thick.

Molly tried to say his name but managed only a croak.

Des bounded out of the chair and came to her side. "Fuck Molly, don't ever scare me like that again." He grabbed her hand.

"Thirsty," she managed to whisper.

Des handed her a giant plastic cup with a straw and then held it for her when she couldn't get her arms and hands to cooperate. With his free hand, he stroked her forehead and hair.

"I thought I'd lost you. You've been out for four days. When I saw you covered in blood—" He shook his head.

"The others?"

Des looked at her for a long time, as if he wanted to memorize her features. "We found Samantha and Fred. They're both dead."

A stab of guilt hit Molly, but she pushed it away. If she hadn't fought back, Samantha would have killed her. "What about Anthony?" Molly said and then coughed. She resumed sipping the water.

"That fucking bastard got away," he said with a clenched jaw. "It was Fred Mueller's fingerprints on Wymer's glove. He planted it, but Berker probably put him up to it."

Molly shook her head. "Samantha," she croaked.

Des nodded. "That also makes sense. A guy like Mueller would be easy for her to manipulate. Anthony Berker is completely in the wind. His bank account is empty, as is his house." Des stroked her cheek.

"How did you know he was involved?"

"Our accountants finally cracked the financial code and traced Sinful Soul ownership to him."

"He killed Mitchell," Molly whispered.

Des jerked. "What are you talking about?"

"Anthony. Wolf. Killed Mitchell. Old girlfriend helped." Dang her throat hurt.

"Are you saying Berker can turn into a wolf? A wolf that killed Mitchell?"

Molly nodded, grateful that he understood.

Des reached for her and held her tight, loosening his grip when she squirmed a little. "I don't remember seeing Mitchell die," he whispered against her hair. "Just the sensation of being held down. Helpless."

Molly watched him, her heart hurting with the anguish she saw on his face. "I'm so sorry." She struggled to sit up.

He stroked her hair and gently gathered her in his arms. "Thank you for telling me." Des sat silent for a long, just holding her, before saying, "It doesn't matter anymore. As long as you're okay, it doesn't matter."

Molly smiled. She didn't believe a word of it.

She studied his face. She loved his angular features and his hazel eyes. The sunshine angling in from the window made them bright green with golden specks.

Des caressed her cheek and hooked a strand of hair behind her ear. "I will have to hunt him down, though. He has to answer for the murders he's responsible for and for hurting you."

She nodded. If that's what he needed to tell himself, she'd let him pretend for a little longer.

"Move in with me," he said suddenly.

Molly choked on the water she'd just reached for.

"Just think about it," Des said hurriedly. "You need someone to take care of you while you're injured, and as long as Berker is out there, you'll be safer with me."

"Fuck no," Molly managed to rasp out.

Des arched an eyebrow. "I beg your pardon." A smile played at the edges of his mouth.

She loved that mouth.

"I got myself free after being hung on a hook like a dead cow. And then I stabbed a murdering bitch. I don't need you to take care—" she ran out of breath and had to cough.

Des held the cup of water out of the way until she was done and then moved it closer so she could take another sip.

She glared at him.

"Maybe I need you to take care of me." He squeezed her hand. "Move in with me."

"I'll think about it," Molly whispered.

Des grinned.

Damn that man for already knowing that she'd say yes as soon as she could stand on her own. She looked into his face again.

She could get used to waking up next to his chiseled chin with the sexy cleft every morning. Her gaze traveled down his torso to where his shirt tucked into his pants, and then lower. And the other body parts that came with the face.

She could get used to spending time in bed with those too.

* * *

THANK YOU for reading this book! If you would like to know how Molly & Des's story continues, read the second book in the Powers of Lighting series, *Flash of Fate*.

If you liked this story, subscribe to my newsletter at: www.AsaMariaBradley.com/newsletter to stay up to date on all book news, qualify for exclusive giveaways, and have access to free reads.

If you are a fan of paranormal romance and/or romantic suspense, join the Midnight in the Garden Readers Group on Facebook. It's a multi-author readers group and I hang out there several times per month and most weekends. I'd love to see you there!

ACKNOWLEDGMENTS

Writing a book often feels like a solitary activity, but the truth is that there's a whole team behind every novel. For this book, my first full-length independently published novel, I leaned on a lot of fabulous and generous people.

My amazing book production team include editor Thalon Riordan of Seed Editing, proof reader, Cassie Hess-Dean, and cover designer Olivia of Olivia ProDesign.

A slew of friends propped me up and cheered me on as I ventured on this journey.

For fun chats, support, rant-listening, and needed kicks in the butt, I owe thanks to authors Piper J. Drake, Katee Robert, Tamara Berry, and my Arctic Thunder sisters: Rebecca Zanetti and Boone Brux.

My Dreamweaver Sisters—the 2014 Golden Heart Finalists class—were there to answer every major and minor question I had about how to deliver my first indie novel. I can't imagine what my writing career would look like without them by my side. Also big thanks to everyone at the Smoky and Drake writing retreats. All of you, when I said I was thinking about an indie project, firmly said, "Do it! Do it now!"

My life would be very bleak if I didn't have my husband by my side. He is my biggest supporter, and my most constructive critic, depending on what I need most in that moment. This year we celebrate our 20th anniversary and I can't wait to see what adventures the coming decades bring.

Also a HUGE thank you to my friends and family, your support of and faith in me means the world. Special shout-out to my bestie Jere', who's always there, whether I need to celebrate or rant.

And finally, the biggest THANK YOU goes to the readers. Without you, there would be no immortal Vikings, no shifter mermaids, and no Molly and Des. <3

ABOUT ASA MARIA BRADLEY

Asa Maria Bradley grew up in Sweden surrounded by archaeology and history steeped in Norse mythology, which inspired her sexy modern-day Viking Warriors paranormal romance series. She also writes urban fantasy about empowered heroines who kick ass while saving the world.

Booklist attributes her writing with "nonstop action, satisfying romantic encounters, and intriguing world building" and *Entertainment Weekly* says "when it comes to paranormal romance with explosive action scenes, Bradley has that nailed." Her work has received the honors of a double nomination for the Romance Writers of America's RITA contest, a Reviewers' Choice Award nomination, a Holt Medallion win, and a Booksellers' Best Award win.

Asa came to the United States as a high school exchange student and quickly fell in love with ranch dressing and crime TV dramas of all flavors, two addictions she unfortunately still struggles with. Currently, she lives on a lake deep in the forest of the Pacific Northwest with a British husband and a rescue dog of indeterminate breed. Sadly, neither of them obeys any of her commands.

Connect with Asa on her website: www.AsaMariaBradley.com. To stay up to date on new releases, receive exclusive content, have access to fabulous giveaways, and receive access to Asa's free reads, sign up for her newsletter at: www.asamariabradley.com/newsletter.

Printed in Great Britain
by Amazon